"Come, another d̶̶̶̶̶̶̶̶̶̶̶̶̶ ̶̶̶̶̶̶̶̶̶̶̶̶̶ ̶̶̶̶̶̶̶̶̶̶̶̶̶cannot harm you! I insist!"

There was nothing for it but to resign herself to a second dance with the irritating man.

"Not so fast, sir. The dance is promised to me." The voice was unmistakable. The highwayman was wearing a dark domino encrusted with jewels and lined in red satin. "Is it not, my dear?"

"Indeed it is, sir, and I must scold you for being so tardy!" She could see the smile flit over his generous mouth in appreciation of her quickness. The officer uttered a brief objection. He was quelled by a single look, and found he had urgent business elsewhere. Clementine was never so pleased in her life.

"Just what I needed!"

"And I!" His eyes were upon her and Clementine could almost feel them burning into her own. She swallowed. It would be hard to maintain an easy banter when her heart fluttered so. She wondered briefly how he had gained entrance to such a society event. Then she realized that the cover of the masquerade must have made entrée easier. She was grateful that he had thought to go to so much trouble on her account. On her account? She harbored a momentary doubt.

No, with the way he was looking at her, bold and warm and as shockingly sensuous as even she could wish, there could be no doubt. It *had* been on her account. She was glad. The smooth image of the Viscount of Trent flitted for an instant into her mind. Only he had the same powers of attraction as this man.

His hands brushed hers as they moved up to her face. The moment was electric. "You have no notion how I have longed for this!"

Clementine found herself engulfed in his embrace . . . .

BOOK YOUR PLACE ON OUR WEBSITE AND MAKE THE READING CONNECTION!

We've created a customized website just for our very special readers, where you can get the inside scoop on everything that's going on with Zebra, Pinnacle and Kensington books.

When you come online, you'll have the exciting opportunity to:

- View covers of upcoming books
- Read sample chapters
- Learn about our future publishing schedule (listed by publication month *and author*)
- Find out when your favorite authors will be visiting a city near you
- Search for and order backlist books from our online catalog
- Check out author bios and background information
- Send e-mail to your favorite authors
- Meet the Kensington staff online
- Join us in weekly chats with authors, readers and other guests
- Get writing guidelines
- AND MUCH MORE!

**Visit our website at
http://www.zebrabooks.com**

VISCOUNT VICTORIOUS

Hayley Ann Solomon

Zebra Books
Kensington Publishing Corp.

http://www.zebrabooks.com

ZEBRA BOOKS are published by

Kensington Publishing Corp.
850 Third Avenue
New York, NY 10022

Zebra and the Z logo Reg. U.S. Pat. & TM Off.

First Printing: November, 1998
10 9 8 7 6 5 4 3 2 1

Printed in the United States of America

Chapter One

"Lord Trent! I *beg* you pay attention when I speak!" The dark-haired young minx who dimpled at him every time he caught her eye cast the seventh Viscount Trent a clever little pout. Too bad for her he was immune to the tricks of the *ton*. He was not going to be caught by some rackety society miss, that was certain.

The viscount bowed politely and paid the obligatory compliment. His heart was not in it, though, and the pout became a little more marked. Randolph Lord Trent did not even afford her the felicity of noticing. Neither did he remark upon the delicate female who swooned enticingly at his feet as he made good his escape. It was left to the manservants to pick up her languishing body and remove her to the nearby sofa. His blatant lack of chivalry did not go unremarked. Miss Anderson, feebly waving away the smelling salts, was mortified. Happily, the viscount remained oblivious.

When the orchestra struck up the first waltz of the evening, all eyes flickered in his direction. Gentlemen of his breeding, fortune and outrageous good looks could not that easily be ignored. True, there was a cloud that hung over him, but that was all in the past. It was no longer necessary to give him the cut direct now he was as rich as a nabob and still, miraculously, single.

If people still spread the old rumours, it was more out of spite than anything else. No one cared for stale gossip, and the tale of Randolph's misdemeanours was now certainly of little interest. To the despair of less well-endowed bachelors, the ladies persisted in their pursuit. The more he disdained, the more they dangled.

My lord bit his tongue. He would have none of it. Not when the Inglewood estate was a deplorable mess and the tenants groaning under the unfair burdens laid down by his brother. Randolph's lips twitched in a silent sneer. If only his father could have been brought to believe it was Oscar, not he, who had forged his name and thieved from the farming accounts. He could forgive the beating, even the banishment, but not the disbelief he had seen in the old earl's eye. Well, it was done now. Bygones were bygones, still, it rankled.

Worse by far, now that he'd seen the estates close up, the misery of the tenants was a disgrace to his name. He'd do something about it. He set down his glass with decision. By Jupiter he would do something, or he was not a De Lacey born and bred. The question simply was what?

The young lady with quivering lashes batted them one more time in his direction. His bow was so distant that she sighed and clipped her fan tightly shut. She could see there was little chance of being invited for the supper dance now. She turned toward Lord Bradley on her right and smiled.

In another part of town entirely, a pair of exquisite red lips trembled. Not consciously, or with any degree of impropriety, but to the discerning viewer, a slight tremor could definitely be detected.

With a superlative effort, Miss Clementine Deveraux fixed her eyes on the middle distance and endeavoured not to sniff. The effort cost her much and was to no avail. The glimmering tears that sparkled behind her intelligent sea green eyes were as plain as a pikestaff to anyone with a wit of sense.

Mr. Buckley had that and more. He was well used to dealing with any number of gentry folk fallen on hard times. What he was not used to was the strange stirring of compassion he now experienced. Perhaps it was her beauty, perhaps her stillness, perhaps the limpid appeal in her magnificent eyes. Whatever it was, he did not like it. Such sentiments were unsettling to a man of his profession. He replaced his monocle and returned to the calculations.

The lady brushed aside a wisp of her long, curling, impossibly tangled hair. The golden strand rebelliously peeped from her bonnet, threatening to once again tumble to her shoulders and almost down to her waist. She sighed and turned her attentions to the more serious matter at hand.

"Surely *not,* Mr. Buckley!"

"I am afraid so, Miss Deveraux. Whichever way you look at it, a higher figure simply cannot be offered."

The lady, clad in her very best polonese robe of rose jaconet and ermine trim looked, for all the world, as though she had just lost her last farthing. Since this calamity was not so very far from the truth, she was perhaps justified in feeling panic rising in her throat. She swallowed.

"Very well, sir. But I ask you to consider the silver plate yet again. The tea service is from the court of Russia, I believe."

Mr. Buckley sighed and nodded. He was not worried about the tea service's authenticity. That he was dealing with a lady of impeccable standing and excellent lineage was not in contention. In fact, the only thing that was in contention was the value he had set on her few remaining trinkets. True, the silver was excellent plate and by the looks of it seldom used, but the brooches! Quite in the Gothic way. They would fetch little beyond the value of the stones. Now the chess set . . . He took up his glass yet again.

The figures were exquisitely worked in silver and ivory, the design a delight to behold. He weighed each piece carefully and felt the lead to be accurate and well balanced. The sapphires inlaid in the eyes of the bishops, queens and kings were of tolerable quality but more remarkable for their rarity in setting. This might fetch a price, given its antique nature, but the market would necessarily be small, the risk too high.

He sighed and shook his head. The flash of green took him by surprise. His fingers hovered over the set, then descended on the small, delicately wrought silver queen. The eyes were inlaid with emeralds. He put the piece down with decision

"Not a guinea more, Miss Deveraux! I'm afraid the emeralds in this set devalue the piece immeasurably."

Clementine's fingers trembled and she willed them to be still.

"How so, sir? I have always wondered at them and felt them to be so very beautiful!"

The jeweller cleared his throat deprecatingly. Women always had such strange notions about these things!

"Beautiful is as beautiful does, Miss Deveraux." He nodded at her patronisingly. "The gentleman that purchases a set like this would expect to find it in immaculate condition. New stones inlaid in antique, believe me, it is *not* to be credited." He shuddered a little at the thought.

Clementine fingered her reticule. The letter of introduction from the Reverend Barnabus Hill was tucked safely in the satin. It seemed she had no option now but to use it. She only hoped that the Earl of Inglewood's daughter was not as much of a handful as she had heard rumoured. She hoped, too, that she could look upon life as governess with equanimity. She made her decision in that instant and looked up at the aging Mr. Buckley with regained poise.

"I'll let you have the brooches and the tea service, sir! The chess set I will keep, if it is all the same to you! It has sentimental value, and if it fetches as little as you say, it is simply not worth the sale."

The jeweller raised his brows in surprise and bowed. For an instant he thought of offering her more, then shook his head. By his reckoning, the wench had made the right choice. He counted out the sovereigns carefully, then wrapped the chess set in dull blue tissue before returning it to her with a small smile.

So sad what happened to the best of families. So sad! With this fleeting thought, he turned his most ingratiating smile on Mr. Peter Rivers who had just entered his establishment. Miss Deveraux and her paltry matters were soon forgotten.

"Mistress Clementine!" Agatha's bosom heaved as she turned her attention to her young employer. Every inch of her oozed disapproval, from the tip of her well-starched cap to the soles of her stout black walking boots. She had nursed her mistress since Miss Clementine was a baby and so took leave to voice her opinions when the occasion arose. It arose now.

"You cannot be thinking of setting off without a maid!" Her voice rose to a wail. "And the stage! The common stage! You must have lost your wits, ma'am, that's what I be thinking! As if all the world doesn't know you were quality born!"

Her voice held a hint of scorn. When her beloved Clemmy did not vouchsafe a reply, she pressed home her advantage. "What would your aunt Augusta be thinking, now? She bein' a baroness and all?"

Clementine allowed herself a small chuckle. "That old bag of bones? I wouldn't pin my hopes on Aunt Gussie, Agatha dearest! She'd most likely ogle along with all the rest and give me the cut direct!" Since the aunt, when applied to, had *not* been particularly forthcoming, Agatha had to acknowledge the truth of this. With a disparaging sniff, she offered her pronouncement on old ladies who had nothing better to do with their time than stitch samplers and gossip maliciously with bosom bows.

Miss Deveraux set down the gown she was altering and blew a kiss in the servant's direction.

"Dear Aggie! It won't be so bad, I promise. I daresay I will be quite comfortably accommodated at Inglewood Manor. You know how I enjoy the country. London is so stifling these days, and I find I don't care to meet my former acquaintances."

When Clementine's voice trembled precariously, Agatha could have kicked herself for making her dear little chicken look so sad. She wished again that Miss Deveraux might have been induced to look favourably upon the many suitors she'd had for her hand. It was only last season, after all, that Mr. Charlbury, Mr. Edgemont, even Viscount Brimley had been smitten. Agatha suspected, too, that if the Reverend Barnabus Hill had not already been attached ... But no! Useless to ponder on this well-worn theme. Miss Clementine could be right stubborn when she wished, and on this topic she was like a rock.

Heaving a huge and conspicuous sigh, Agatha hurried off for a hot posset. In her heart of hearts she knew that, like her charge, she would have to resign herself to the inevitable.

Well, if her little Clementine was forced into service, no one, at least, would be able to find fault with her attire. She would arrive with her gowns well pressed and her underwear exquisitely stitched. Too bad Miss Clem had forsworn all her bright colours. There was no need, after all, to look *ancient!* Still, if she took the russet merino and the tourmaline satin, perhaps some ribbons of velvet and the odd smidgen of lace ... Lost in thought, she forgot, to Clem's relief, to scold any further.

The corn was ripe for harvesting, but few men could be spared for the task. The Earl of Inglewood's vinery needed planting, and his landscaper was known to be impatient. The earl had been deaf to the entreaties of his tenants. Rather, he had taken the opportunity to upbraid them on their idle, selfish ways and had increased the rents twofold.

The money would come in handy at Watier's, where the bank was a cool ten thousand pounds. The lure of hazard and macao put all thoughts of husbandry right out of the peer's shallow head. His little barques of frailty were costing him a prime fortune, and what with Drury Lane and Mr. Kemble's Covent Garden charges, the cost of living was prohibitive. He felt a tiny twinge of conscience, then called Clayton to put the finishing touches to his cravat. When the landau was summoned some time later, the twinge had passed.

The sight of tiny children, barefoot in a chill night moved him not at all. He was a member of the old school, who believed quite firmly that the lower classes did not have the same sensibilities as he himself. Not for him were the agricultural innovations of Coke, or the socialist ideals of that upstart poet Shelley. No. To him, the universe had an order, and that order was subordinate, always, to his own comfort.

For an instant the image of his brother—young, tousle headed and laughing—disturbed his view. Randolph had always appealed to his better half. A most unendearing quality, that! The earl had heard tell he was back in town. Well, he'd do well to keep his mouth shut. The earl was inclined to think Randolph would.

Who, after all, would wish to remind the *ton* of the black mark set against his name? The earl gritted his teeth as the memories came flooding back. No! That was in the past, and past was past. He tapped on the carriage door with his cane. As the horses drew up, he saw fit to berate his groom, who was not driving fast enough. "Spring them!" was all he said.

"Care for a lark?" Grantham Davies downed his third glass of brandy and sniffed appreciatively. "Where've you been hiding this, Randy? Jolly good stuff!" Without waiting for a response, he pulled out a cigar from his bosom friend's case and grinned at him.

Lord Randolph De Lacey shook his head forbiddingly, but his eyes twinkled. Grantham, at least, had changed not a jot since he last had the pleasure of his acquaintance. Quite some years now.

"Whippersnapper! I'll wager my last groat you've got a sizeable cellar of your own to drink your way through. And as for my Havanas—"

"Touché, my friend! But as I said, how about a lark? I find

the season tiresome and cannot believe you don't feel the same way yourself.''

His lordship's eyes veiled, and for an instant the hint of derision that Grantham had noted so frequently of late reappeared across the lines of his compelling, wide lips.

''Tiresome? I can vouch for that! A lot of silly chits with nothing better to do than lay traps and snares of their own making. If they think I'm easy game, they're mistaken. My memory is longer than most, you know. . . . When I was the penniless younger son disgraced by scandal, no one would give me the time of day. Several, in fact, gave me the cut direct. Now that I have a tolerable fortune in hand, I find I am suddenly acceptable.'' His eyes darkened. ''Oh, not in the best circles of course . . .''—the bitterness could not be kept from his tone—''but I'm now sufficiently passable I find. The duplicity of it! As for my dear brother . . . But I'll say no more.'' He folded his arms resolutely, but his eyes looked bleak.

Grantham coughed in quiet understanding. He could have killed Oscar for the pain he detected in Randolph's eyes.

''I don't know how you put up with me, Grantham! Self-pity can be so dreary, can it not?'' His lordship's voice was suddenly self-deprecating. Davies seized his moment.

''Exactly my point, Randolph! We need something to occupy our attentions!''

''Like what?''

''I don't know. . . . A challenge of sorts!''

His lordship maintained a bored disinterest. ''A wager you mean? Curricle race, something of that nature?'' He hid a slight yawn. His childhood friend remained undeterred. ''No . . . that is too commonplace by far, Randolph!''

The viscount's eyes quickened with interest at last. ''What then?''

Mr. Grantham Davies leaned towards the viscount and whispered something almost inaudible. The light of mischief danced in his tiger brown eyes. Astonishment darkened my lord's, then amused comprehension flashed for an instant and was gone.

"I take it you have quite taken leave of your senses, my good man?"

Grantham grinned in malicious satisfaction.

"There you are off your mark, Randolph Sebastian De Lacey! I think it is just the thing to keep us amused this season. Besides, it will have the added novelty of seeing that justice is done. If you cannot think of yourself, think, at least, of your tenants!"

"Not *my* tenants, Grantham!" Randolph inspected the impeccable shine of his top boots. His voice was strangely sober.

Davies shrugged at the quibble. "Maybe not technically, Randolph, but surely you will own to a little moral responsibility? Think of old Mrs. Owens and Peter Ridgely and even Vicar Oldfield! They're all suffering as a result of your brother's foolish selfishness!"

Randolph sighed. "Do you think I am not horribly aware of all that, Grantham? My mind has this last month been bent on how to ease the problem without inadvertently fattening up my brother's purse still further. I would gladly part with my blunt to ease their problems, but frankly, sir, it is none of my business!"

"No, strictly speaking, it is not! That is the beauty of my plan, Randolph! No one need ever know the source of the revenue, and we could have fun playing may games with your stiff-starched, toad-eating, rump-necked, son-of-a-bacon-brain brother!" His tone grew quite animated. "Admit it has some appeal, Randolph! I insist!"

His lordship set down his glass and shook his head. "You forget one small trifle, my friend."

Davies afforded him a veritable chuckle of amusement. "I warrant I do, Randolph. You, of all people, know I've never been one for details. However, there is nothing, I am perfectly certain, that cannot be overcome if one simply applies oneself."

His lordship was silent as he took up a quill and began a quick but graphic sketch.

"How does one overcome *that,* my friend?" Randolph thrust the paper across the table.

His old friend squinted at the sheet, then afforded him an elegant shrug. ''With cunning, my dear Randolph! Cunning and resourcefulness! Qualities I realise you have an abundance of.''

Before his lordship could think of a retort, Davies gulped his fourth brandy with aplomb and left as quickly as he had entered.

My lord was still for a long time. Then he stood up with resolution and reached over for the paper Grantham had just dismissed. A good likeness, if somewhat sinister. He crumpled it and threw it in the warm embers.

In the morning, the second housemaid was intrigued to find, while clearing the grate, a slightly charred image of the hangman's noose.

The passage of Miss Clementine Deveraux had, up till now, been smooth. To be sure, there had been some degree of argument when her trusted servant Agatha had tried to press three bandboxes, two well-wrapped parcels and a portmanteau upon her, but the issue had soon—and firmly—been resolved.

The final result of the heated discussions had been that Miss Deveraux now sat perched inside the accommodation coach with one portmanteau tightly strapped behind and one bulging reticule containing a handkerchief, a letter of introduction, a necklet of seed pearls, two miniatures of her parents, a chess set, a purse of several guineas and sundry small items like tooth powder. Agatha's sugar candy had long since been eaten, the last remnants still sticking slightly to her soft, grey travelling dress.

Several phaetons and one particularly foolhardy curricle had threatened to overset the coach, but fortunately nothing as calamitous as this had actually occurred. The hours had been dreary, however, as the damp, cold weather afforded no great view of the countryside. Miss Devereaux felt herself quite cramped within. Almost, now, she regretted not taking up a position outside of the coach. A breath of fresh air seemed an inviting thought to one slightly queasy from the endless rumbling of wheels and chatter of nameless strangers. Still, she was warm and inside which was more than could be said for the postilion passengers, who hunched up closely against the biting wind.

When the carriage came to a jerky halt outside the White Hart's tavern, she waited impatiently while the other passengers pushed their ways out, each in search of the tankard of ale and slices of cold beef, turbot and marrow pudding that awaited within. The last person out, she flushed under the annoyed gaze of the ostler, who was impatient to change the horses and have done. Clementine wanted to stretch and breathe deeply of the chill but fresh afternoon air. Instead, the groom's eyes upon her, she maintained her quiet dignity and entered the taproom of the old English inn. The idea of ordering her meal and paying her shot was a novel experience. She wondered briefly whether she could really afford to part with the two shillings required for her repast, then decided, with the certainty of the really hungry, that she could.

She took up her place next to an old woman wearing a melton cap of uncertain quality. She was tolerably pleased with this arrangement for it afforded a view of the activity outside and shielded her from the brazen eyes of a man she judged to be a linkboy at the next-door table. She had steadfastly refused to acknowledge the low whistle he had emitted when she first made her entrance. Unabashed, he was evidently trying to catch her eye once more. Miss Deveraux was made of stern stuff. She pointedly ignored him and set to with uncustomary zest.

"I'll do it, by all saints holy!" Lord Randolph De Lacey had spent an uncomfortable night in spite of his feathered quilts and the extravagant spaciousness of his tent bed. Now he pulled aside the crimson silk curtains and eyed the breakfast tray with satisfaction. Eggs and ham and lashings of butter on fresh baked bread. He smiled. He would need all the sustenance he could get if he was to think the plan through properly. He knew for a certainty that his new mount, begat of Eudora and sired by Flinders, would serve his purpose well. The stallion was bred for speed and as dark as midnight in a moonless sky.

He wondered idly what Grantham had in mind when he had laid his challenge. The rascal had always been tumbling from one scrape to the next, but this, surely, was the outside of enough! Randolph's eyes gleamed in appreciative amusement. Modern-day Robin Hoods. Well, of all the chuckle-headed notions he had heard to date, this took the trophy! Still, the idea had the merit of lifting his spirits and that was to good account.

They were both to divest the current Earl of Inglewood of a small fortune and report back on a mutually agreed-upon date. Intriguing. For an instant, Randolph wondered whether his friend planned on turning house burglar. He grinned at the thought, then sank his teeth into some of the ham before picking up a crisp copy of the *Morning Post.*

Some several miles away at Inglewood, the Honourable Lady Henrietta Stenning was in a vile mood. Far from the hours of freedom she had envisioned when she'd so cleverly rid herself of her last governess, she found she was now obliged to fill her time entertaining the odious Sir Andrew Cunningham.

Equally irksome was his mother, the Dowager Baroness Fawnstone. What her guardian was thinking of when he'd invited them down to Inglewood, she could not imagine. The man had a horrible leer and quite made her flesh creep. She had a mind to be insufferably rude, but then quelled it.

The last interview with her guardian had not been pleasant. His tone had been mild, as always, but she had seen the telltale signs of anger that had played at his mouth. Though she was seventeen, and far too old, in her opinion, for the punishments she'd been accustomed to of yore, she didn't quite like to try her luck. Lord Oscar's riding whip lay across his desk, and while it did, she resolved to hold her peace.

Thus it was that instead of the lazy days of sunshine she had envisaged, she found herself compelled to listen meekly to the pronouncements of the snappish baroness. She could stand this, but the sibilant innuendoes of Sir Andrew were becoming intolerable. Almost she found herself wishing for the arrival of her new governess. Another wizened old spinster, no doubt, but at least a welcome excuse to retreat to the schoolroom.

"Hammer them, girl! Hammer them!"

"I beg your pardon?"

"You've got ears, miss, haven't you? I said hammer them!"

"Hammer what, Baroness?"

The old lady looked at her in exasperation. She poked a bony finger in Henrietta's face and pointed to the flowers. "The peonies, you idle creature! Have you not been shown to hammer the stems?"

Henrietta, for once, was without words. The baroness twitched her finger, and a footman bowed attendance.

"Get me a mallet!" she demanded. Ignoring the bemused features of the minion, she turned her attentions to Henrietta.

"I see I will have to show you how I expect things done about a place. Sloppy work, sloppy mind, that is what I always say! My dear Sir Andrew will have to take you in hand." She paused to take breath then continued the train of her thoughts.

"*Give* me those, girl!" Henrietta dutifully handed over the cut flowers Adams had acquired from the hothouse only that morning. Her mind was only half on Lady Fawnstone's scolding. In truth, she had become almost immured to the sound of the raspy voice and its incessant tones of nagging.

At the back of her mind, she wondered again why Lady Fawnstone should think she cared for her twopenny ha'penny opinion. As for Sir Andrew taking her in hand, well she may not yet be out, but she knew that to be beyond the bounds!

Footsteps again, and Sir Andrew's unless she missed her guess. She sighed and braced herself. She was glad, of a sudden, that the gown she had chosen for the day had not been of the first stare. She had nearly given it to Millet, then had thought better of it as the sickly hue lent itself to an idea.

Her dresser had nearly called for the smelling salts when

she'd waved aside the curling tongs and chosen, instead, a style that was as dowdy as it was plain. Two braids hung now from either side of her head. They looked somewhat oversized beneath her small cottage bonnet of salmon cambric, but that was all to the purpose.

Sir Andrew's strides halted as he took in the vision. His brows crossed slightly, then were stilled as he took the few steps required to reach her. Her hands hovered over the flowers before fluttering to her sides. Her throat constricted with loathing, but she maintained an admirable outer calm. The baronet's eyes seemed to bore into her own. As if reading her thoughts, he laughed unpleasantly and bade her good day.

Henrietta just managed a small curtsy. When the lackey returned with the mallet, she found herself hammering the stems with a gusto that displeased even the Lady Fawnstone.

"Stop that, girl! And fetch my paisley shawl, if you please! I find the interior of this establishment strangely cool. I cannot conceive why the earl is such a nip farthing when it comes to accommodating his guests!"

Coming from the dowager baroness, a notorious miser in her own right, this remark struck Henrietta as a bit rich. She bit her tongue, however, in an uncharacteristic display of restraint as the old lady warmed to her theme.

"One would expect that at this time of year a warm fire would not run amiss, but there you have it! No respect for my generation. No respect, I say!"

Sir Andrew soothed her jangled nerves, then suggested she remove herself to the lilac salon.

My lady took this remiss and demanded to know why she was being shuttled off to some little-used quarters of the manse. Besides, she quibbled, she could not well leave Henrietta alone with him, unattended. She shot him a sharp look from under her hoary lids. For once, Henrietta was in full agreement.

Sir Andrew seemed simultaneously amused, irritated and smug.

"Oh, but my dear mama, I have something very *particular* to say to Inglewood's ward!"

His mother, evidently perceiving some nuance that entirely eluded Lady Henrietta, nodded in grudging comprehension. She allowed herself to be steered in the direction of the afore-mentioned salon, stopping only to admonish her son to be brief. He watched while she pattered off, grumbling, across the padded corridor.

Then he returned and shut the door.

Chapter Two

It was some time later that Clementine found herself pacing up and down the footpath of the White Hart Inn. What had started off as a simple stop had turned into a lengthy delay as one of the wheels was found, on inspection, to be loose. Compounding the problem was a flighty chestnut mare that had chosen this particular moment to lose a shoe.

While the blacksmith and wheelwright were called in, the passengers were left with little other choice than to return for a few more pints of freshly brewed ale or to remain outside, grumbling at the perversity of their luck.

Clementine began to worry that she might not make Inglewood by nightfall. Apart from the inconvenience, she was loath to spend the evening alone. While she may have fallen on hard times, she was nevertheless a gently bred young lady and the idea stuck in her gullet.

If only she had listened and let Agatha travel part of the way! Still, if she were wise she would go inside and secure a place before the notion struck her fellow passengers too forcibly. The idea of sharing did not appeal, but the thought of a small fire in a private chamber was gradually growing more attractive.

She moved aside and rang the bell. It was quite a wait before anyone appeared to take notice of her. She was thankful that the linkboy seemed to have vanished from view. The last thing she needed at this wretched moment was an unwanted admirer. She pulled her bonnet on tightly and smoothed down the folds of her serviceable merino carriage dress.

It was as well for her peace of mind that she had no notion how attractive she looked, with her utterly creamy complexion and the large, doe-shaped eyes that stared out from under a fringe of tumbling bright hair. She had pulled the remainder back severely, brushing the locks right down to her waist then upbraiding them in a coil that fitted snugly under her charcoal travelling bonnet.

Her long black lashes, however, could not be hidden and they framed her eyes, emphasising her high cheekbones and wide, sensuous lips. Although she had taken pains to dress modestly as befitted her new station, her posture and impeccable carriage cried out that she was a lady born.

It was not surprising, then, that quite a few curious glances were cast her way. The linkboy was long gone, but she still had to endure the curiosity of several farmhands, an impertinent and slightly intoxicated gentleman of uncertain years and the quizzical glance of a gentleman of unquestionable amiability and breeding.

In fact, Clementine thought she handled herself excessively well under the circumstances, until she fell under the influence of this Corinthian's impenetrable gaze. She was astonished at how her poise evaporated under his quiet, good-humoured scrutiny and how a faint blush mounted her cheeks as their eyes met for an instant. She did not know whether to be pleased or sorry when he set down his glass, made her a swift, self-mocking bow, rang the bell yet again on her behalf and left the premises.

His efforts were at least rewarded with the appearance of the landlady. Unfortunately, she looked distracted beyond measure and not entirely pleased to have been disturbed. On being applied to for a room, her eyes had taken in Clementine's outmoded carriage dress and singular lack of attendants. Divining rightly that she was dealing with a mere governess or travelling companion, she inquired as to her name and consigned her to one of the free attics she kept available for just such a purpose.

Clementine was relieved to have the issue settled, but could not help raising slightly imperious eyebrows at the price. The landlady, used to sizing people up in an instant, had noticed that her dress was neither patched nor darned. Rather, it was made of a superior quality velvet and matched perfectly the gloves and slippers of its owner. This circumstance, as she later told her husband Ted, immediately called for the doubling of the cost of lodgings.

A small dispute ensued, in which Clementine steadfastly refused to pay a penny more than what she deemed fair. Her tone was quiet but firm. The landlady teetered on the brink of refusing her the room, but something in Miss Deveraux's bearing gave her pause for thought. While they were engaged in this unedifying wrangle—few could know how Clementine's pulse was racing—they were interrupted by a gentleman of sallow face and slightly distasteful manner, who made his bow in an ingratiating sort of a way and begged a few words with the landlady.

Mistress Mudgeley at once turned on one of the fulsome smiles she reserved exclusively for the gentry and made her curtsy. The said gentleman drew her out of earshot. Miss Deveraux, it must be said, was somewhat annoyed by this out of hand behaviour. She, after all, had first claim upon the landlady's attention. She watched with mounting irritation as the woman simpered over the stranger, then cast a surprised yet knowing glance in her direction. Finally, she managed an almost comical court curtsy to the gentleman before sidling up to Clementine once more.

"We are fully booked, ma'am! You will have to search elsewhere for accommodation. I am most awfully sorry, dear!"

Her tone belied her words, and she sent another sidelong glance to the gentleman now stationed at the entrance to the taproom.

The colour rushed to Clementine's cheeks. The woman was as transparent as they came. Of *course* there was a room for her! Before she could vent her indignation, the lady had presented her back to Clementine and was now fixing lodging for two of the travellers she recognised from the stage.

For the first time, Clementine began to feel truly alarmed. She decided she would have to step out and inquire of the ostlers the likely time of their arrival at Inglewood. She could only hope the journey would be completed by nightfall. Loath as she was to arrive travel stained and late, it was still better than being obliged to spend the night alone without the benefit of a private chamber.

She moved out of the way as a lady's maid bustled in search of hot bricks and a stack of linen. Lost in thought, she'd almost forgotten the unwelcome presence of the stranger who'd clearly cost her her room. Now he came forward and, with a slight bow, cleared his throat and uttered her name.

"Miss Deveraux?"

The young lady appraised him, and he was not altogether sure he liked the feeling. He felt his lips thin, but made no comment as he doffed his hat and offered a small bow.

"I do not believe we are introduced, sir." Clementine's voice was hard as she stood her ground with the stranger. She could not positively accuse him of sabotaging her plans for a room, but all her instincts told her the gentleman in the well-padded box coat of dull serge was not to be trusted. The coldness of her voice was reflected in the well-bred, arctic arch of her brow.

He remained undeterred. In his mind, she became all the more desirable. He'd seen from the first that she was a young woman out of the common way. As a matter of fact, he was notorious—and rather proud of this reputation—for finding little pieces quite out of the ordinary style. Well, if this little filly needed schooling, all the better! How fortunate for him that she'd dropped into his lap like a plum ripe for the picking. If he judged it right, fortune favoured him on this account.

"Forgive me if I am in error, but I believe you to be the governess of her Ladyship Henrietta Stenning, the Earl of Inglewood's ward?"

Clementine gasped. How could the man know such a thing? Not from the landlady, certainly, although she was ready to wager her small supply of sovereigns he had her name from her. He noticed her confusion and smiled thinly. "It is fortunate I happened in on this inn, Miss Deveraux. I hear tell there is a delay with the stage, and I am in a position to offer you my services."

Clementine afforded him a hard stare. "How so, Mr. . . . ?

"Sir!" He saluted her. "Sir Andrew Cunningham at your command."

Clementine did not respond. Sir Andrew's eyes narrowed slightly, then he smiled graciously.

"I am at present travelling in his lordship's chaise. I will be most happy to oblige you with a ride."

Clementine's heart sank. The offer appeared genuine, but she had distinct qualms about the man. Besides, without a maid she would be put beyond the pale.

The man's grey eyes slid to her ankles. They were hidden by her half boots, but nevertheless offered promise. He hooded his thoughts and waited. No doubt the wench would soon see reason. He nodded as he saw her inward struggle. Miss Deveraux was realizing, truly for the first time, what it meant to be a mere upper servant.

She was at the service and convenience of her lord and master. If Sir Andrew reported that she had been offered a ride and refused in favour of arriving late and by stage, she would doubtless be turned off without a character. It was not for a woman in her position to have scruples.

Still, she wavered. "May I ask what relation you are to the Earl of Inglewood, Sir Andrew? I do not think he mentioned your name in my letter of employment."

The baronet's eyes gleamed. "You are very careful, Miss Deveraux."

She looked at him and her sparkling green eyes flashed

triumph. If he had not a bona fide position in the household, the earl could not expect her to accept a ride with him. In fact, she would be discredited if she did.

Her lips opened to refuse his services. The green and gold accommodation coach, top heavy with roof passengers, was preferable to travelling in a closed landau with this man. He swallowed in satisfaction as he caught a glimpse of the soft inner pink of her lips. In that split instant he noticed, too, that her teeth were a delicate pearl white and perfectly even.

She straightened her back.

"Allow me to enlighten you, my dear." A wicked smile played on his mouth. Clementine looked at him with unease. He laughed, enjoying the cat-and-mouse quality of the encounter.

"You have the pleasure of addressing your pupil's future husband."

He was grimly amused by the expression on her lovely face. Lest she doubted, he explained further. "I am, of course, Lady Henrietta's betrothed. I have hopes you will help her acquire a little town polish. Perhaps I should have said."

A flush suffused Clementine's face. Their eyes met at last. He had played his trump card.

She swallowed hard as she entered the antiquated travelling chaise emblazoned with the Earl of Inglewood's crest. She could not quite like the way her escort had summarily dismissed the outriders. Nor could she be thankful that he had extracted, at some small expense, her portmanteau from the stage.

She disliked being beholden to this man, more particularly as he was leering at her with a stare that was as unpleasant as it was disconcerting. With nothing but a groom—occupied totally with the dappled team he was driving—there was precious little to separate Miss Deveraux from the lechery she feared. She held her breath and prayed she'd woefully misjudged Sir Andrew.

Of course, to her chagrin, she had not. The bright bustle of the way station receded in Clementine's ears, giving way to the steady sound of hooves along the beaten path. All seemed suddenly eerily still, and Miss Deveraux found herself uncomfortably aware of the grey eyes, speckled with gold, that bored into her forehead. She looked up and a wry smile of satisfaction crossed the gentleman's face.

"Much better, my dear! This journey is far too tedious as it is without having to look, the whole length of it, at the top of that deplorable black bonnet!"

Clementine, in other circumstances, would immediately have pointed out that charcoal was very different from black, but in this particular moment she desisted. Instead, she pondered with slight unease the gist of the man's words.

"Journey, sir? I had not thought the road to Inglewood Manor could really be described as such!"

The man removed his gloves and leaned back languidly. Although he yawned, slightly, his eyes remained sharp as flint. Clementine was not deceived. The smug smile that illuminated his face for an instant was not altogether pleasant.

"Sir!"

"Ah, yes, Miss Deveraux! I find I must disabuse you of the irksome notion that we are travelling east to Inglewood! My dear, I have just spent a fortnight there, and you may rest assured it is entirely without pleasures!"

Clementine was stunned. She knew, now, quite fully, how dangerous her predicament was. Her senses reeled, but she schooled them to silence. She would need a clear head about her if she was to emerge from this coil unscathed. While she scanned the chaise for a possible weapon, her quick wits reviewed her options. At all costs, she must keep the man talking. Already, his hand was creeping to her skirts. It was all she could do to remain calm and quell the panic that threatened to rise and engulf her.

"Without pleasure, Sir Andrew? I believe you were visiting your betrothed!" Perhaps that reminder would dampen his ardour. Clementine did not hold out much hope, but stalling him was worth the effort.

The baronet gave a moue of dismissal. "Henrietta? If it weren't for her fortune I doubt I'd give her the time of day!"

Clementine took a moment to digest this snippet. "I'm sure the earl would be interested to hear those views!"

Sir Andrew relaxed his grip on the cravat he was slowly loosening. His lips quivered in the silent triumph of self-congratulation. To Clementine, what crossed his features looked unpleasantly like a smirk.

"Oh, he knows, my dear! He knows! I hold an interesting little proof that will ensure my marriage to his ward *quite* without doubt! It is amazing how profitable a youthful indiscretion can be in the hands of one such as I."

His tone changed. "It is as well we understand each other before beginning our delightful association, is it not?" He reached out his hands and gently touched Clementine's chin. She recoiled as if struck by a viper. Her reaction did not deter him. In fact, he was rather titillated by the response.

"Shall I have to tame you, dear one?"

"You'll not find that easy!" Clementine's hand crept to the panelling behind her back. Slim chance, but there were many who hid pistols as protection against highwaymen along the road. If the earl had adopted the same custom. . . .

Her tormentor's eyes dropped to the outline of her bosom, the material straining slightly at these hidden efforts. He licked his lips. "Not easy? How very fortunate indeed! I shall enjoy gaining the mastery of you, my dear."

"You shall not!" Clementine was provoked into this outburst. He leaned forward and wickedly played with the top lace of her sober gown.

"Shall not what? Shall not gain mastery, or shall not enjoy it?"

Miss Deveraux grew hot with anger and frustration. The man was vile! She pushed his fingers away in rising horror. He chuckled and lay back against the squabs.

"How right you are, my dear! Delayed pleasure is always so much sweeter for the wait." He looked at her closely, and the gold flecks in his eyes seemed to strip her naked. Clementine shivered in spite of the hot bricks that had been provided for the baronet's travelling comfort. She determined not to provoke

Sir Andrew any further. What was the use? It only seemed to
please him the more.

She was rewarded for her silence when Cunningham closed
his eyes and bade her do the same. ''After all''—she caught
his whisper—''it would be well if we were both refreshed
before our journey's end.''

Clementine acquiesced at once, eager to continue her explora-
tion of the carriage's satin-lined panelling. Sir Andrew's breathing had deepened almost to a snore and her hopes of finding
a weapon—a gun or even a stick of some kind—were steadily
rising.

Her fingers feverishly fingered the oak and satin in the hopes
of a catch. The awful thought dawned on her that if there was
a secret enclosure, Sir Andrew was probably lying on it. She
put the defeatist notion from her mind and continued with
caution.

Her immediate thought had been to call a halt to the chaise,
but the groom would not hear a whisper and she dared not risk
wakening her tormentor. Besides, the servant was probably no
more to be trusted than his master. Noiselessly, she moved
closer to Sir Andrew's part of the panelling. She was a reasonable shot, and if she could get her hands on a duelling pistol
she would not hesitate to use it.

Her heart beat faster as she drew closer to the sleeping form.
She stretched out her arms. She was close to the panelling. A
little further and she would know for sure if there was a secret
catch. She leant slightly closer, taking care not to dislurb her
tormentor. Her fingers were touching. She felt them clamped
in a vise. The eyes opened and in that instant she knew that
the reclining form of Sir Andrew had never, for one instant,
been sleeping.

''How pleasant, my love! But I thought we had agreed to . . .
ah . . . postpone the delights of our no doubt. . . . *enjoyable*
encounters?'' He licked his lips.

Clementine would have slapped his face if she could. Since
she couldn't, and he was now patting the space beside him

with ill-concealed satisfaction, she was forced to bite her tongue as he released his grip.

Miss Deveraux's knee was the next to suffer the ill effects of this encounter. She felt the baronet's hand run smoothly over her overskirt of thick velvet and thanked the heavens she'd had the sense not to dampen her skirts.

No, Sir Andrew's fingers would have to make do with the velvet frogged pelisse, the thick cambric underskirt, the petticoats of fine stitched muslin, the clocked stockings of silk and finally, her unmentionables of a staid but serviceable linen.

Clementine's eyes flashed dangerously as she wished Sir Andrew to perdition. Her virtue might be safe for the present, but her feminine apparel did not shield her dignity in quite the same way. She determined to kill him if she could. Catching her look, the object of her rancour crossed his arms and smiled. The stopover at the Golden Dove would prove more interesting than he'd first anticipated. He closed his eyes, but the artless Miss Deveraux remained undeceived.

Chapter Three

The highwayman cocked his pistol and pulled the dark kerchief over his mouth. His stallion pawed the ground in high fettle, sensing something of his master's tension. He was gently soothed into a calmer frame of mind, but his fetlocks nevertheless rippled with an energy mirroring that of the man he served. The voice that cajoled was gentle, but the stallion felt the strength behind the dulcet tones and gradually grew quieter.

Despite the chill of the approaching eve, the man did not huddle upon his horse. Rather, he sat with his back perfectly straight, warmed through and through by a dark greatcoat that boasted several rather well-cut capes. His head was rakishly covered by a beaver of the first stare, although he would have been annoyed to realise just how distinctive the headgear was.

The stranger seemed hardly aware of the well-powdered wig that fitted beneath the chapeau-bras as if made for it. That it was, was beyond the point. Though their lustre was dimmed by travel dirt, the boots that rested negligently in the stirrups were undoubtedly produced by Lobb and Lobb of London.

In short, the man's appearance spoke of several of the more exclusive establishments of Conduit Street. Were it not, indeed, for the kerchief, his quarry might have been forgiven for mistaking him for a gentleman of considerable standing. As it was, the kerchief gave him a quixotic air of villainy, besides providing more tangible evidence of his criminal intent. The man was sitting, fully alert now, upon his mount. The sound of a rumbling chaise was unmistakable in the quiet of dusk. Only the priming of the pistol indicated that anything was amiss.

"Easy does it, Santana!"

The horse whinnied for a moment then was silent. The rider held the reins with a lightness of touch that in another time had gained him membership in the famed Four Horse Club. Now his eyes squinted in the dull light. He had to be certain of the crest gilded on the oncoming landau.

Dusk crept in through smoky glass windows as the passengers settled to a ride of self-imposed silence. The onset of nightfall was a bitter reminder to Clementine that her reputation was in ruins. Worse, unless she was excessively quick off the mark, her innocence itself was under severe threat. Notwithstanding these unpleasantly prosaic facts, she was too proud and too stubborn to allow Sir Andrew to bait her any further.

Since nothing was to be gained by reasoning, she would hold her peace until something occurred that she could use to her advantage. Perhaps, when the horses were changed, she could effect an elaborate escape. Until then, she would not give the baronet the satisfaction of a struggle.

Baulked in the chase, Sir Andrew postponed the hunt. He did, after all, need to spare his strength. More to the point, he was perfectly certain his little quarry could get up to precious few tricks in the chaise. So thinking, he allowed himself the luxury of a pleasant reverie as the wooded landscape passed him by.

"What was that?"

The words were no sooner out of Sir Andrew's mouth than Clementine was catapulted onto his lap. The sounds of pistol shots belatedly reached her ears as she became aware of galloping hooves and the tumultuous whinnying of horses.

The dappled coach stallions, true to their natures, were struggling to break free. The groom was far too taken up with the task of controlling them to take up the blunderbuss he had at the ready. Clementine looked into the eyes of her captor and fell back onto her seat. He was alert again, cursing the groom and the lack of outriders.

Miss Deveraux could not help reflecting with a smidgen of enjoyment that it served him right. He'd dismissed the outriders simply to facilitate his abduction of her. Well, he was well served now. She hoped the highwayman would divest him of a fortune.

"Stand and deliver!" The words rang true in the darkening sky. Sir Andrew cursed, then cursed again, hissing a warning to Clementine not to stir. Her eyes flickered in scorn. If she could turn the situation to her advantage she would. Her ears strained to hear the muffled directives the groom was receiving. He had the horses under control now, but Clementine would not vouch for how long this would be the case.

Sir Andrew was cursing under his breath, feverishly removing his fob and hiding it among the squabs. He was just pulling off his signet ring when the rider drew close. "Open the door!" came the command in muffled but nonetheless authoritative tones.

Sir Andrew fiddled with the catch, his hand shaking to such a degree that Clementine pushed his fingers from it and undid the catch herself. She was feeling surprisingly cheerful after the spine prickling tension of the last few hours. The highwayman stepped back in amazement at the vision that met his gaze. Clementine's emerald eyes were flashing with the brilliance of excitement.

Long tendrils of lustrous gold escaped their charcoal prison and framed her perfect form. She looked exquisite. Beyond that, she seemed an angel. The highwayman took a pace back. This was not what he'd intended. Neither the man *nor* the lady were his intended victims.

Still, on reflection, the gentleman would do just fine. Just fine. Momentarily distracted, he relinquished for an instant his cover of the groom. Ballard made a reach for the blunderbuss. Clementine turned her head, and in that instant saw the man take aim.

"Watch out!"

The words were wrenched from her mouth as she saw tragedy but a hairsbreadth away. The man's eyes flickered, then he moved with an electrifying speed. Clementine heard the report of the gun. She saw it smoking in Ballard's hand. The highwayman, however, had baulked the groom of his intended target. Although Clementine detected a small brown patch marring the elegance of his otherwise immaculate greatcoat, the wound was in the shoulder, not through the heart.

She exclaimed and descended from the carriage. The highwayman pushed her roughly out of the way as Ballard reloaded. To her horror, the highwayman's pistol was primed as he turned to take aim. He fired before she could blink and the shot was true. She saw Ballard's blunderbuss lying useless upon the ground and began to shake.

Then she looked up to find the groom still sitting, bemused, upon the carriage perch. She could not believe her eyes! The highwayman winked. It was a familiar sort of a wink, and in a rush she knew where she had seen it before.

"I'm acclaimed a good shot, me lass!" His voice was muffled, but had a slight, lilting ring to it. She laughed as she watched him reload.

"You are at that! May I be the first to present you with my treasures? I have only my portmanteau about me, but I do have my reticule. . . ."

The highwayman's face darkened; then he seemed to remember his role. "Ay, lass! No tricks, mind."

She climbed up into the chaise and looked Sir Andrew directly in the eye. He was pale with anger and hissed a vitriolic warning that only strengthened her resolve. Whatever happened, she would not recommence the journey with this man as her escort. The thought gladdened her heart.

It may have been a case of out of the fire and into the frying pan, but surely nothing could be worse than another instant in Sir Andrew's insinuating company. Besides, what a frying pan! She blushed at this unmaidenly thought. She stifled a childish urge to pull a tongue at Cunningham, but aware of the highwayman's breath upon her back, preserved her dignity.

Sir Andrew's eyes narrowed as she retrieved her reticule. Were it not for the pistol levelled firmly in his direction, Clementine was perfectly certain obscenities would have streamed from his mouth. She smiled and extended her bag.

The highwayman covered Sir Andrew and the now defence-less Ballard. He shook his head.

"I be not in the 'abit of openin' ladies' reticules, me lass!"

Clementine lifted her eyebrows in surprised amusement.

"Are you a novice at this, then?"

The highwayman's eyes twinkled. "Nay, jest me trademark, lass! A fellow 'as to have some standards, mark ye!"

"But surely that is unprofitable, sir?"

The highwayman laughed, the kerchief not sufficient to mask all of his astonished mirth.

"Not so, dear lass! See ye! I'll be bettin' ye *all* yer fine trinkets ye'll be helpin' me rob this man milliner blind! I'll not scruple to take his money bags I tell yer! Up ye go, there's a bonny lass, fetch me 'is purse if ye please!"

She dimpled at him. "*And* his fob and his ruby signet! They're hidden in the squabs, you know!"

He chuckled. "What did I tell yer, ye saucy minx! Up ye go!"

Obligingly, Miss Deveraux relieved her captor of his purse, his watch and his ring. The telltale signs of fury were etched in lines on his face. Clementine beat a hasty retreat and handed the goods over to her unlikely saviour.

He indicated to his saddlebags, and she stowed them away safely. Santana was strangely quiescent at her touch. The high-wayman took inward note and was satisfied. The lass had spunk and character. The midnight stallion was as good a judge as any.

His eyes covered the duo on the chaise. Time was marching on. The stagecoach to Riverton was due shortly, and he did not wish to be caught in a compromising position. He'd led a charmed life and the thought of ending it on the hangman's noose did not appeal.

He kept his pistol carefully levelled, but drank in Clementine's spontaneous and charmingly unusual beauty one more time. The last time. "Lass?" The words were almost whispered.

"Yes?" Clementine's throat was constricted, and she knew not why.

"I will not take yer valuables. Ye'll keep yer portmanteau and yer treasures. I ask one boon and one only."

"What is that?" The prudent Miss Deveraux found her heart beating far faster than it ought. Her hand fluttered to her chest.

The highwayman smiled, and though she could not see his mouth, it was wide and warm and sensuous.

"A memento, me sweet! Something to remind me of ye on a cold winter's night when I'm 'idin' away in me den of iniquity!"

His tone was light and self-mocking, but Clementine trembled nonetheless. The thought of the man holding something of hers was sheer delight. How strange and troublesome was that thought! A common felon to elicit such feeling when all the passion of the Messrs. Charlbury, Edgemont and the Viscount Brimley had never stirred her thus . . .

She covered her face in confusion, but the highwayman did not miss the flush that stained her creamy cheeks. If anything, he loved her—for what he felt were surely the first glimmerings of love—the more. She dropped her hands and determined to be as lighthearted in her manner as he was in his.

"To be sure, my lord the highwayman!" She curtsied at the roadside and opened her reticule. The chess set was the first item that fell to view. The first and most valuable. She held it out, explaining apologetically that its salability was diminished by the emerald queen. For an instant the highwayman did not speak. He had expected a trifle, a lock of hair. Not something as beautiful as that which she, of her own will, had volunteered.

He did not wish to insult her by refusing; yet, by his own standards taking it would have branded him a cad.

"Let me see this queen, then." His voice was quiet. Clementine opened the small, precious set and extracted the piece. He held out his left arm and winced.

"You're bleeding!"

He waved that aside impatiently. "It is no great affair, I assure you!"

She remained concerned.

He shook his head dismissively. "The groom missed his mark by a mile, I swear it!" For an instant he lost his broad, lilting accent. When next he spoke, his voice was heavily muffled and the fleeting resonance of his tone was lost.

"I'll take it, bonny lass! This piece and this alone, mind! My silver queen with emerald eyes." He turned it over in his hand, his eyes darting from the piece to Sir Andrew and Ballard, then back to her.

"A true likeness."

Clementine did not miss his meaning. The piece, with its intricately wrought, fair flowing hair and emerald eyes could well have been a likeness of herself. She was amazed at her audacity in giving him such a treasure. In her heart of hearts, she knew she'd not regret it.

The man sighed, then waved her into the chaise. "Up and on ye go, me lass!" He turned to Sir Andrew, and his eyes hardened visibly. "If aught happens to the little princess, I will hear on it. I will hear and I will find ye. Got that in yer shifty noggin?"

Sir Andrew quivered in impotent cowardice. Clementine was amused to see him nodding slowly, although his eyeballs bulged. The highwayman, aware of the advancing time, bent to help Clementine mount the landau. As his hands touched hers, she shivered slightly. Then she made her final, irrevocable decision. It astounded both Sir Andrew and the highwayman in equal measure. In clear, bell-like tones, she was heard to calmly inquire, *"Must* I, sir?"

"Get in!" Sir Andrew blustered in disbelief. To be divested

of his purse was one thing, to be baulked of his virgin wench quite another. He could scarcely credit the evidence of his ears. Mercifully, he was very sure the highwayman would not agree to such an unlikely encumbrance. The Riverton stage was due shortly, indeed.

After the initial flicker of surprise, the highwayman's reaction was all that Clementine could have wished. He indicated with a jerk of his hand to Ballard that her portmanteau be retrieved. While the man busied himself with this chore, all the time covered by the excellently balanced pistol, the highwayman took it upon himself to address Sir Andrew in scathing terms. It is not necessary here to repeat what he said. Suffice it to say that when the baronet's carriage wheels finally resumed turning, the villain's cheeks burned an angry purple. He would not soon forgot the tongue-lashing he'd received at the hands of a highwayman.

Clementine had no time to regret her choice. The moment the carriage was on its way, and her rescuer had retrieved the blunderbuss that still lay fallen upon the ground, she found herself firmly led in the direction of the trees. The Riverton stage was rumbling close, and the highwayman could only put a finger to his lips to indicate that she be silent.

For a fleeting moment Clementine wondered whether he was preparing to hold up the stage. After all, that must have been the real reason why he was lying in wait in the evening dusk. He could never have been certain of a private chaise upon the road, but the Riverton stage . . .

She noticed he was looking down at her, and a warm glow crept into her cheeks. She should have felt slightly ridiculous, huddled with her reticule and portmanteau in this outlandish position, but she felt nothing but pleasure. She reflected wryly that she was beyond the pale indeed. Agatha would succumb to a fit of scolding, but then, there always had been a slightly unconventional streak in the demure Miss Deveraux!

She wondered for an instant what fate intended for her. Then she pushed this question from her thoughts as she noticed that her rescuer's arm was now soaked and he looked a trifle pale beneath his faintly tanned complexion.

Miss Deveraux was not one to mince her words, nor was she so paltry a miss as to be squeamish at the first sight of blood. She did, however, shock the highwayman out of his silent wonderment when she demanded prosaically whether he meant to hold up the passing accommodation coach.

"For I must assure you, dear sir, that there is not much to steal upon that particular conveyance!"

His brows furrowed with his silent laughter, but Clementine misunderstood him. "I do assure you, sir!" she said earnestly.

"Unless I very much mistake, that is the same coach I took upon my journey from London to Inglewood! I won't bore you with the details, but I can most truthfully say that the travellers were a weary lot, dirty and hardly looking to have a penny piece between them. If it is a few sovereigns you're after, why, there is still my purse for the taking, after all!"

Triumphant at this logic, she smiled at the highwayman, removed her bonnet and sat down. She patted the spot beside her and coaxed him down gently. He made a push to convince her it was not, by any manner of means, his intention to hold up the stage, and his voice held a reasoned indignation that was entirely lost on Clementine, who had vastly more important matters on her mind.

"I hate to seem a nag, dear sir, and I am wholly conscious of what you have already done on my behalf, but really, I must insist on seeing that wound."

The highwayman had not had anyone dare insist on anything since he was a wee one in shortcoats. Now, however, he succumbed to the emerald queen's bullying with remarkable humility and not a little amusement lurking at the unseen corners of his very masculine mouth. He allowed himself a small, token murmur of complaint before giving himself up to her ministrations.

"It is a mere scratch, I assure you!"

Clementine looked up sharply. Again, his tones seemed more those of a gentleman than of a villain of his profession. Then she relaxed. No doubt the man was a by-blow of one of the gentry folk hereabouts. She heard tell that in some circumstances they even educated them with their own sons.

The puzzle thus explained in her mind, she paid no attention whatsoever to his obviously inferior reasoning. Scratch indeed! By dint of great care, she removed the sleeve of his greatcoat.

It was no easy matter separating his impeccably white starched sleeve from the blood oozing from his arm. There were times Clementine faltered, and there were times the gentleman closed his eyes and uttered curses she really ought not to have heard under his breath. Eventually, however, the deed was done, and Miss Deveraux found herself able to patch the wound with tolerable dexterity.

Of course, she had not, in that short time, been able to dislodge the bullet, but the highwayman, knowledgeable in such matters, commented only that this was not necessary as a first measure. He would soon be in a position to consult the village doctor and none the wiser. With this Clementine had to be satisfied.

The accommodation coach rolled by just as she was retrieving what was left of her fine muslin petticoats. She had torn a great strip off them to staunch the blood, but now felt in sore need of what remained of the shreds. The highwayman's eyes were gleaming in a manner that made her pulses quicken quite incomprehensibly, and she experienced a dire need of a few yards of shift between her and his gaze. When she glared at him crossly, he actually chuckled!

Infuriated by his ingratitude, she wriggled into her last remnant, taking care that he did not catch a glimpse of her ankles as she did so. Not care enough! The highwayman took stock of quite the most well-turned pair he'd seen for a while as she wrestled with the shift. A gentlemanly impulse, however, caused him to make no remark. When she was finished, Clementine cocked an inquiring brow, aware for the first time of what an encumbrance she must be. Night was threatening to fall, and though the thought of an evening shared under the stars held a degree of unlooked-for appeal, virtue and practicality had the last word on her strangely delinquent conscience.

"We must get you to a doctor! And your horse. . . ."

He grimaced. "I'm more worried about Santana than I be 'bout meself! And that be fact!" His eyes softened. "If off to a quack I be, then ye'd best be gittin' on yer way, little emerald queen! There is an 'ostelry nearby. I can take ye as far. Any number of mail coaches pass that way. In the mornin', ye may take up yer journey!"

Clementine looked a trifle mournful and shook her head.

"I'll be turned off without a character if I arrive at Inglewood now!"

"Inglewood?" The man's eyes held an arrested expression.

Miss Deveraux nodded. "I'm meant to take up the position of governess, starting today."

The man shrugged. "Tomorrow will do yer fine enough!"

"It shall not!"

"And why not if I may make so bold?"

Clementine permitted herself a small shrug. "That loathsome creature we just sent along the way is my young charge's affianced!"

"Shhh!" Before she could elaborate, he'd pulled her back into the shadows. A curricle and pair passed them at a breakneck rate, almost overturning at the bend.

"Whipster!" The highwayman muttered under his breath. His thoughts then returned to the lady beside him.

"Betrothed is 'e? I could have sworn there'd be not much love lost between . . . Unless . . ." His eyes startled into amusement.

So *blackmail* was the honourable Sir Andrew's game! Well, serve Oscar right to do a little squirming. Andrew Cunningham would have been the only one among his set who could vouch-safe positively that it was Oscar, not Randolph, who had committed those forgeries.

Still, it was all such a long time ago. . . . He brought himself up short. His companion was staring at him, bewilderment etched all over her very lovely face.

"What was that? I couldn't quite catch. . . ."

The highwayman breathed a sigh of relief. That was a near-run thing! He must not again allow his disguise to be so easily forgotten.

When he spoke, his voice sounded more muffled than ever.

"Never fear, lass! Go be a governess if ye will! A fine one ye'll make to be sure! That rascal will not think to report against ye, mark me words 'e won't!"

Though she tried not to look sceptical, the highwayman proceeded to convince her with quiet, undramatic logic.

"To rat on ye, me lovely,'e'd first 'ave to admit to abductin' an innocent with intent to deflower." She blushed scarlet, and he pressed his point home. "And that in 'is betrothed's very own chaise! 'Ardly a creditable tale that, ter be sure!" Clementine looked doubtful.

"Well go on then, lass! Don't ye be stand about gawping! If ye think 'e 'as got more rumbunction than I do, think on it again! It is 'ardly likely, is it, that 'e's goin' to admit bein' given comeuppance by a common sort o' git like meself, is it? Why, 'e'd be the laughin'stock of all the county!"

While this was true, Miss Deveraux still wondered whether Cunningham might be inclined to tell a different, altogether embroidered and completely false account of the day's misadventures. She put this to her partner in crime who considered it carefully before shaking his head.

"Still won't fadge, me dear! 'E 'as a dowry to consider, mark ye! 'E'll not want the gal to go squeamish before the nuptials, I'll warrant! After, maybe—likely—who can tell? I'm willin' to take a wager, though, the man will be silent. Besides . . ."—his voice grew ominously deep—". . . 'e 'as 'ad my warnin'. I say no more, me little queen, but I think the man is not such a fool as ye think. 'E'll not make trouble if 'e knows 'e's bein' watched."

"And will he be?" Miss Deveraux's heart raced shamefully. She glanced up at the highwayman and could see he was amused.

"Is that what ye want, my adorable one?"

Despite the growing chill, Miss Deveraux felt hot.

"No!"

The highwayman chuckled. "What a bouncer, to be sure, me lass! No indeed!"

Clementine hardly knew where to look, for flirting—even with a highwayman—was hitherto wildly beyond her province.

His voice softened. "I'll watch out fer ye, never fear, me bonny lass! If that little toad touches so much as a single strand on yer angel gold 'ead, 'e'll 'ave old Quicksilver John to account for it!"

"Quicksilver John? Is that your name?"

"Near enough, lass! Near enough!"

Miss Deveraux's sense of the ridiculous could not be suppressed as she emitted a mirthful gulp that brought a twinkle to the highwayman's eye.

"What a strange mother you must have to be sure, sir! Fancy calling you Quicksilver. It is no wonder you've chosen the profession you have!"

The highwayman entered into the spirit of things. He nodded solemnly and sadly. "Well, I could 'ardly be a land agent or a tailor, now could I?"

"To be sure not, dear sir! There is no one at hand to introduce us, so I shall do it myself. Clementine Deveraux. Miss."

"Miss?"

She blushed. "Miss." The word was firm.

He took her hand, and his eyes held a warm, appreciative smile. His voice was deep as he took in her tumbled appearance and enticingly well-laced bodice.

"Well met, Miss Deveraux."

The sun dropped suddenly and the shadows of night seemed to creep up on them without warning. He dropped the mocking pose and once more seemed to realise both his danger and hers. The last thing in the world he wanted was for Miss Clementine Deveraux to be taken up and charged with aiding and abetting. He knew the risks he took upon himself, and he accepted them with the quixotic, boyish charm of his nature. He found he could not do the same for this lady, to whom he was rapidly losing his cynical, world-weary heart.

"Come lass! We linger too long! That encroaching man milliner will 'ave taken fright, I can promise yer! Probably 'ave the watch upon us 'afore long!"

Clementine started. Somehow, she was at once frightened and reassured. She could sense the fleeting menace and strength behind the words and could only be thankful it was Sir Andrew, not she, who was the butt of this strange, strong man's displeasure.

The highwayman could read the thought that was etched in her uplifted brows and in the tiny, questioning curvature of her lips. He urged her on in a lighter, nevertheless more urgent, vein.

"See here, me bonny mistress fair, no more argumentation an' you please!" He paused and looked her up and down. "Much as I would like—very much I might add—to continue on in yer company, I'm not that much of an out and outer! Spend the night respectable ye will, and that is my last word on it!"

Clementine pouted but her eyes were dancing. She could hardly believe, brought up as she had been, that she could be so entranced and touched by a man of his station. She wished she could remove the silk kerchief, that she might drink in his face and forever etch it upon her memory. She held out a gloved hand to his chin. Not a moment too soon he divined her intention and stood back.

Lord Randolph Sebastian De Lacey, Viscount Trent and part-time highwayman, had no wish to be revealed as such just yet.

"Oh, no, ye don't, me beauty! Whoever heered of a 'ighway-man unmasked by a little chit of a thing like yerself? I 'ave me reputation to consider, after all, me dear!" His eyes gleamed. "Besides, uncover me mouth and it wild hunger for yours as sure as my name is not Dick Mackleby Turpin!"

She smiled.

"Oh yes, blush, me little queen!" He traced her lips for an instant, then remembered himself.

The tingle that went down Clementine's spine had little to do with the crisp night air. In fact, her body was experiencing a quite novel degree of warmth despite her ripped petticoats. She could not believe how brazenly disappointed she was when the man withdrew his hand and ordered her into the saddle.

"No more roundaboutation, me lady. It is off to a respectable 'ostelry for you an' that's me last word on 't!" He picked up her portmanteau and led Santana by the reins. "I can take ye as far as the north toll gate. From there, I 'ave no doubt, ye will have all the aid ye require. They be right 'ospitable at the Newbrook Lodge. Just tell 'em ye lost a carriage spoke and was obliged to walk part of the way. Ye'll be as right as a trivet I assure ye!"

Clementine sniffed. Her wide eyes glinted suspiciously, causing the highwayman to curse under his breath. If only he could take her in his arms and wipe away the tiny tear that threatened, at any moment, to traitorously wet her creamy cheeks.

Clementine read his thoughts in his dark, gleaming brown eyes. She felt the feather-light touch as it landed on her cheekbone just beneath her left lash. She trembled in anticipation, but was disappointed and greatly relieved when he did nothing more than swing her onto the saddle and click a command under his breath to Santana. Dark had set in by the time they reached the pike.

Chapter Four

"Good morning, Lady Henrietta!" Clementine appeared cool, though her throat was dry. By all accounts her new charge was a trifle high-handed. It was necessary that she set the tone from the start.

Lady Henrietta, smart in a day dress of saffron silk edged with pale lace, hardly looked up from the fashion plates she was perusing. Miss Deveraux felt her colour rise, but quelled the impulse to offer a crushing snub. Instead, she moved over to the chaise longue on which the quite handsome young lady was seated and peered over at the page.

"Madame Fanchette's, I see!"

Her new charge looked up in surprise. Though her face was a trifle pasty, Clementine noted that her cheekbones were high and that surprise animated her countenance greatly. She guessed, rightly, that the girl had been brought up far too strictly. Her rebellious streak stemmed from years of repression rather than natural bellicosity.

Henrietta, for her part, was forced to revise her initial expectations. Her governesses, in the past, had all been of the same mould: spinsterish and with far too refined a notion of what was expected of a young lady. Inwardly, she sighed. If they had had their way it would have been no fishing, no running, no sneaking grapes from the vinery . . . no Grantham! How she missed him, now he'd left Inglewood! He, at least, had been kind. . . .

Her thoughts were forced back to the present. She looked at Clementine with renewed suspicion mingled with vague hope. Miss Deveraux seemed uncritical of her current occupation. This was slightly irritating, as she had chosen it especially to rile. What was more, Henrietta half suspected the poised stranger understood her motives perfectly!

Miss Deveraux appeared to be a new and interesting quantity. Not at all like the stuffy governesses.

They had uniformly raised their hands in horror at her penchant for London plates. Indeed, both Miss Adams and Miss Houghton-Fish had on several occasions felt themselves obliged to apply a stinging ruler across her palm.

"Such unbecoming displays of frivolity," they would say. Henrietta could mimic them to perfection. Hypocritical old cats! The Honourable Lady Stenning knew for a fact they both kept copies of the *Ladies' Gazette* closeted away in their bandboxes. Still, life was generally unfair, as she knew to her cost.

Her scowl now softened slightly as she surveyed her latest instructor. Not modish, yet quietly smart in an unconscious kind of a way.

"You know Madame Fanchette's?" Her voice held a questioning tone that Clementine was quick to use to her advantage. She smiled.

"I do indeed! And Claudette's, Fincham's. . . . Alvaney . . . the Bond Street milliners, the mantua makers Arden and Arden—"

"Stop! You are hoaxing me!"

"Why should I be?" Clementine removed her bonnet and patted out the few curls she'd allowed to escape her severe coiffure.

Henrietta stared at her in amazement. "My other governesses labelled such interests foolish wastes of time."

"Is that why you were so intent on the plates when I walked in?"

"What if it was?" Though the words were insolent, Clementine noted that the defiance seemed strangely fragile.

"I just wondered. You'd not be the first to attempt frightening off a new governess!"

Henrietta folded her arms, slumping into the back of her chair.

"I don't *need* a governess anymore! I should have been out this year if only . . . "

"If only, if only, if only! Not very helpful words I should think." Miss Deveraux silenced her charge firmly.

Henrietta glared at her, her initial animosity returning with a vengeance. Clementine noted how the pout instantly transformed her face from something quite lovely to something rather petulant and sullen. She thought it a pity.

The girl had a natural beauty that ought not to be marred by the ill effects of childish humours. She did not now regret her own decision to be a trifle authoritative. Though she could not help in her heart feeling sorry for the orphan, she had no intention of being ridden over roughshod.

"Don't glare at me!" Henrietta gave a little dismissive shrug, and once more took up her fashion plate. Clementine hid a smile.

"You may be surprised to know this, but I happen to agree with you fully."

Lady Henrietta's focus on the latest creation of fichu gauze lost some of its intensity. The new governess noticed this with satisfaction and was encouraged to continue.

"What you need is a companion more than a governess and, indeed, a companion I shall be!" The speaking glance she received was reward in itself.

"Between the two of us, mind." She held up her hand as Henrietta began an excited exclamation. The scowl was replaced by a tremulous smile, wholly becoming if quite unusual upon her pretty countenance.

"You'd better at least put up a pretence of doing some lessons, otherwise the game will be up for us!"

Henrietta looked at her sideways.

"That is easy. There is a secret stair leading from the old nursery wing. I always take it when I need to escape. . . ."

"Which I hope will not be often . . ." Clementine interjected.

"Oh!" Henrietta put a hand to her mouth in annoyance, then grinned sheepishly.

"I can't think how I came to tell you of it! I suppose it is because you are not like a governess at all!"

Clementine supposed this to be a compliment of sorts. She opened the pianoforte and ran her hands full across the keys. The tone was pleasing.

"Thank you very much! What did you expect? Pince-nez and a pointer?"

"Pretty much! You can have no notion of the tedious old bores I've been sent in the past!"

Clementine struck a deep bass chord in D minor. She struck it again, then again, then again. Henrietta started to laugh.

"Quite so! I *can* imagine, my dear! I've had my fill of them in my day too." The ice broken, the two ladies settled down to a comfortable coze. Clementine would hardly have dreamed this possible on her arrival.

Her reception by Lord Oscar had been distant but frostily polite. He had little time to spare ministering to the comfort of an upper servant, but had discoursed briefly on the terms of her employment and had offered her the use of a hack for the duration of her stay. He'd added a brief rider to the effect that Lady Henrietta was strong willed and that he relied upon Clementine's good sense to see she was suitably schooled. Miss Deveraux's eyes had flashed at that, but the earl was too caught up in his own pressing affairs to pay much note. With a brief nod, she'd been dismissed.

Clementine had made her curtsy with deep misgiving. The

earl was not a likeable man, but he was not, at least, the cad she'd feared he might be after having made Cunningham's acquaintance.

Sir Andrew, as her highwayman predicted, had evidently said little to Lord Oscar that cast aspersion on her good character. And thank heaven for that! Clementine was certain his lordship would have no compunction in removing her from his employ should she be found wanting in any of the virtues. It was with some relief that she was ushered from the morning salon.

The butler had pointed her in the direction of cook, who'd set a small piece of jointed mutton and game pie aside against her arrival. These, while tasty, were now cold. Miss Deveraux reflected with a glint of self-deprecating humour that the Inglewood staff seemed to have arrived at their own unflattering conclusions with regard to her tardiness. She resolved there and then to take her meals in the schoolroom. Hardly the sort of welcome she could have wished, and certainly not one of which she could write to dear old, anxious Agatha.

Still, events had been interesting. . . . Her mind flicked back to a gentleman in dark superfine and pristine white ruffles. She could almost smell his strong, pervasive scent as he leant towards her, one black patch almost visible through the dark of the kerchief. Strange that he still used wig and powder. The fashion for these gentlemanly accoutrements was almost past. She had to admit, though, they lent him elegance and made him dashing to a degree that quite knocked her breath away. What her governesses would say, if they knew her musings, she dared not think.

"That is one up for the books! I declare you are not listening!" Miss Deveraux was jolted back to the present by her charge. Presently, the two were to be found comfortably wrangling about the relative merits of honey and aloe with respect to blemishes of the skin. Miss Deveraux was deemed to be a veritable goldmine of essential information, if somewhat wanting in the more usual attributes of governesses.

* * *

Lord Randolph held a small chess piece in the palm of his hand. He appeared to be considering it for quite some time before it was replaced, along with several other pieces, in the fine buckskin pouch he used for such trinkets. There was a knock on the door, and he answered wearily. No doubt Pinkerton with the *Gentleman's Gazette.* A fine man, Pinkerton, but with an annoying habit of intercepting one when one most wanted cool reflection. Still, his work with a brush and a lick of champagne was commendable. Randolph reflected with a wry grin that his boots were now no doubt sparkling in their usual impeccable fashion.

Pinkerton had preserved a stony silence that said much when he'd observed the mud-stained state of the top boots. Randolph smiled and moved to the decanter, from which he poured himself a large decoction of brandy before bidding his servant enter.

"Randolph!" It was not Pinkerton, but the Honourable Grantham Davies who strode purposefully into the room.

The Viscount Trent set down his glass and shook his head. "Ever the same, my dear Grantham, ever the same! At least you had the goodness to knock, but how on earth did you get past Masters? He must be losing it. I'd not have thought it possible!"

"Oh, I did not announce myself. Not a good time for calling and all that!"

Randolph raised his eyebrows. "Quarter past eleven? If it were the *day*, I daresay it would be perfectly acceptable!"

Grantham grinned sheepishly and moved to the decanter.

"Oh, come off your high horse, Randy! You are not such a gudgeon as to be as top lofty as all that!" He grinned endearingly.

"Old Baroness Stowecroft, now. What a tartar. Paid a morning call on her daughter at ten, and she had the effrontery to tell me she kept town hours!" His voice was indignant.

"I presume it was ten in the *morning?*" Randolph's tone was dry.

Grantham laughed. "What a lark it would be to arrive in the evening. She'd call in the watch, I daresay."

"As I should do. What do you mean by breaking and entering like this anyway?"

"Oh ... I felt like company. Sick of my sisters forever harping on about lord this and lord that. My townhouse is beginning to look like a flower boutique. You've no notion how many posies they each receive." His tone turned gloomy. "Wish I'd never invited them. And their chaperone! A tartar, I tell you! She actually titters!"

The viscount extended his due sympathies.

"Perhaps you should escape to India like me, Grantham! Return when the season's over and your sisters are all safely settled. At least they're all going off together!"

"Yes, I couldn't stand another season of this. Amelia's had three offers and Augusta no less than four. Five if you count that infernal man milliner Antonio Sedgington-Blair!"

"I *don't!*" Randolph shuddered. "So I should diligently read my *Morning Post?*"

Grantham's gloom returned. "They'll have none of them! Augusta has always set her sights too high. She'd set her cap at *you* given half a chance!"

His lordship, austere in a perfectly fitting evening jacket of deep maroon with little edging beyond a faint hint of ruby thread, set his glass down with decision.

"All respects to the lovely Miss Davies, but I am afraid, Grantham, I really must decline!"

Grantham laughed. "Bother! You'd save me a lot of aggravation screening all these beaux of hers! Besides ... I'd rather like you as a brother-in-law."

"Perish the thought." Randolph made a small grimace. "A fine song and dance you'd lead me. Don't think I've forgotten all your childhood scrapes!" He paused, in two minds, debating whether to tell his young friend about the success of his caper as a highwayman. No! That could wait.

"I can't help reflecting what prank you are now up to, young man! Have you thought more on your end of the ridiculous contest you dreamed up between us?"

Grantham's eyes gleamed with ill-suppressed excitement. He perched himself at the end of the viscount's leather-embossed desk and clicked open the drawer.

"Certainly I have, Randolph! That is why I have exerted myself and come calling this evening!"

"Oh?"

"We did not discuss the terms of our little engagement. What, if I may be so inquisitive, is the *prize* to be?"

Randolph looked at him squarely. "Why do I get the distinct impression you have something in mind?"

Grantham chuckled. "Because I have, Randolph! Perry is up to his ears in debt and is dipping, now, into the famous Lanarch cellars. They are starting bidding tomorrow."

The viscount smiled.

"I collect you have a mind to the finer things! What is it you are after, my little connoisseur? Bakingham's rum will last me a lifetime. You can have a few bottles. Anything else of interest?"

"I hear you can pick up a pinot noir seventeen-hundred-and-eighty-three. Bottled for the French court. Good year, they say."

"No! The grapes were too sweet. Are they selling an eighty-four?"

"I can find out."

"Good. Make sure it is of Montagne de Reims origin rather than the Côte des Blancs. If you have no choice, I'll settle for either, though I feel the Reims to be slightly superior."

"It is settled then?"

"It is settled!"

Grantham grinned. "I'll lay it down at the country estate."

His lordship shook his head, a decided twinkle lurking in his deep, dark eyes.

"Counting your chickens, my stripling? Don't be so sure!"

Grantham shook his head mysteriously as he withdrew the viscount's inkstand and paper from his desk.

"What, a promissory note? You *are* getting stuffy!"

"Give over, Randolph! Let us do this thing properly."

His lordship the Viscount Trent shook his head ruefully. He scribbled his name across the page without even glancing at the words. Then, with a pointed glance at the ormolu clock upon his mantelpiece, he firmly ushered his good friend out.

"Wake up, Henrietta!"

"What?"

"Wake up!"

The Lady Henrietta Stenning rubbed her eyes and rested her face on one hand, still warmly ensconced in the coverlet. She gave a sleepy yawn before checking the shadows behind her drapes. Her senses had not deceived her. It was still dark! She felt she really ought to protest, though knowledge of her unpredictable instructress did not afford her much hope of a reprieve.

"Wake up? It is still the middle of the night!"

Clementine's eyes twinkled. "Exactly so! And if we don't hurry, we are going to miss the sunrise."

At this, her charge sat bolt upright. It must be reported that her cap sat sadly askew and her long, lace nightdress fell in rumpled cascades all about her.

"Are you possibly mad, Miss Deveraux?" she asked politely.

Clementine preserved a straight face, though the laughter was bubbling up deep within her. "Undoubtedly, Henrietta Stenning! I give you fair warning! You'd better get up and humour me before I do something wild and unfitting in a lady not so demented as I!"

Lady Henrietta lay back provocatively. "What can *that* be, I wonder?" Her eyes were weary as she watched her companion advance towards her.

"Tickles, my dear Henrietta. Tickles!" Her fingers wriggled threateningly. Her charge was out of a bed in a trice. Maria was already at hand with a warm sponge and a bowl of newly heated water from the kitchens.

As Henrietta washed, Clementine reflected with pride that her charge had come a long way in just the one month that she had been resident at Inglewood.

Her ladyship had lost her listless demeanour and pasty cheeks. Her hair was gleaming, whether from the use of fresh chamomile tea—a favourite receipt of the redoubtable Miss Deveraux—or from the invigorating results of a daily brushing that made her scalp tingle, she did not know.

Suffice it to say that changes not hitherto thought possible by the house servants had been wrought. Even the hated pianoforte had come to life at Miss Deveraux's light and competent touch. Where previous tutors had nagged, threatened and punished, Miss Deveraux smiled. She'd drawn up a chair and insisted on interpolating with her own brand of humorous, catchy and thoroughly droll variations on well-known themes.

With practiced ease she had looked pointedly at Henrietta, shut her eyes and commenced playing seemingly infinite sets of scales in all chords and combinations, backwards. Henrietta laughed till the tears came and could not remember such pleasant evenings at Inglewood.

Lord Oscar never appeared after dinner, but rather retired with his port to the library and was not seen again until morning. Occasionally, some gentleman friends joined him in poker and macao, but Henrietta, not out, was always well above stairs when they arrived. Consequently, the nights at Inglewood had not previously been very edifying.

The governesses had forbidden reading anything but the heaviest of works, deemed by them to be suitable and of an improving nature. Henrietta longed to read *Guy Mannering* and *Frankenstein*. She'd glimpsed snippets of *Sense and Sensibility* and been intrigued beyond measure.

Unfortunately, the serial had been deemed "frivolous" by Miss Houghton-Fish, who had replaced the novel with a good dose of *Pilgrim's Progress* and an admonishment to pay more heed to the lessons she taught.

Since Henrietta was at that time engaged in deciphering the more lugubrious passages of *Paradise Lost*, she could not feel that Milton was a fair or reasonable substitute for the charming Miss Austen.

Clementine had changed all that. With her usual resourcefulness she had ventured into the library, where she'd found hidebound copies of Shakespeare, Lord Byron and even a smattering of Keats. Henrietta had been entranced.

They started with a light, romantic Shakespearian comedy, each taking a turn to read the characters. Though it was earthy stuff—and some high sticklers believed Shakespeare a little too fast for the tender ears of young ladies—no lasting damage appeared to accrue to Henrietta. The long evenings suddenly flew by. During the day, Henrietta was kept so busy with medicinal decoctions she began to think Clementine a witch.

After that, there were the long rides on the estate, accompanied by the Inglewood groom. He was greatly heartened by the advent of Miss Deveraux. Up until then, he'd had just cause to grumble. Lady Stenning's mare was growing fat from inactivity.

Stitching in the afternoon. Gone were the endless samplers with their fiddly little patterns. Miss Deveraux, mimicking the governesses of yore, had deemed embroidery of this nature an "idle waste of time." Henrietta had gaped openmouthed in astonishment. She'd been taught that it was every gentlewoman's destiny to stitch a fine sampler.

Miss Deveraux asked her what the sense in this was. What was the use of endless pieces of cloth that served no function? No, out came the fashion plates and the rolls of velvet and the fine Indian cotton. Clementine—a font of all wisdom it seemed—showed Henrietta the art of the invisible stitch, the knack of turning a seam without effort or ruching, the exact manner of gleaning every last vestige of material without wasting an inch. Scraps became pockets, reticules, gloves. It astonished Henrietta. What was more, she felt genuine pride in her handiwork.

The first time she'd presented herself at dinner in a handstitched garment, she had not raised so much as an eyebrow

at the dinner table. She had been crushed until Clementine
pointed out to her what a compliment she'd just been paid. Her
work was as fine even as that of Madame Fanchette's. The
earl, though not usually observant, would certainly have taken
notice of inferior workmanship. Anything less than what was
due to Henrietta's consequence as his ward would seriously
have displeased him.

They worked out how much money had been saved by the
homemade garment. That saving was used for new material
and another gown of equal calibre. Soon, Henrietta's pin money
seemed superfluous. Clementine made a mental note to take
her through some of the impoverished cottages on the Inglewood estate. A young lady blessed with a fortune ought to
know and care for what is in front of her eyes.

In this, Miss Houghton-Fish and her ilk would again strongly
have disagreed. A young lady of quality was to be spared such
painful sights, they believed. Indeed, many were the times they
admonished Henrietta to keep her nose in the air and her pace
fast if she was unavoidably exposed to such unpleasantness as
a babe in tatters or, worse, a thieving beggar.

Clementine had no such qualms. From her father, a noted if
improvident philanthropist, she had developed other notions of
what was befitting a young lady of consequence. She was
becoming steadily aware that there was more substance to
Henrietta than initially had met the eye. In truth, it needed
nurturing and guidance, but that was the work she had been
employed to do. And do it she would!

She suspected the earl might not be well pleased by this
curriculum, but she cared not a whit. For the first time, she felt
that her personal misfortune had some reason, some just cause.
She meant to make the best of it.

Thus it was that the Lady Henrietta was slowly eased into
the art of household accounts. Where savings were made, a
mark against the ledger on the credit side was affixed, the
savings set aside either for investment in new spangles or
ribbons or for future expenditure on a project yet to be determined. Clementine was certain that, in time, Henrietta would

learn to do more with her pin money than purchase frills and furbelows. In the meanwhile . . . invisible math lessons. Miss Deveraux congratulated herself.

Henrietta, for her part, could not remember the last time she'd had so much pleasure. The breakthrough came when she had first reluctantly sat down to play. Instruments were the bane of her life. She was tolerable on the harpsichord, but the pianoforte gave her nothing but the most severe of megrims. Clementine, knowing this, had drawn up a chair to join in duets.

This was novel to the young girl, who'd never before thought of music as anything but an annoying duty. Her halting fingers had stumbled over the keyboard and Clementine had gently corrected, showing her what a great difference rounding her fingers could make. The slight adjustment greatly enhanced Henrietta's ability to stretch to an octave, sometimes even more. The confidence gained in these improvements was like a balm to her soul.

Slowly, the girl opened out. She even allowed Clementine to translate some of the reviled works of Cicero and Plato she was used more to copying out as penance than to studying for content.

Clementine made it all seem effortless. What Henrietta *particularly* liked was that she was not prosy but practical.

When Miss Deveraux smilingly asked her to sing a Handel aria, Henrietta wailed in despair, confiding that she had no singing voice whatsoever. Clementine was not so certain. Henrietta had thought she'd little aptitude for the pianoforte and see how they'd progressed! Henrietta could not be convinced, describing the agony inflicted upon her by Miss Hartley-Dale and Miss Ridgely, who had both deemed it necessary for her to sing at a few select parties and neighbourhood routs. She'd cringed at the time and she cringed now at the memory. Clementine coaxed her to give it her best try. Surely, she argued, her singing voice could not be that bad?

When Henrietta had finally obliged, there was a moment's silence as the notes hung in the air. Then, to Lady Stenning's astonishment, the governess's face had lit up in unholy laughter, and she'd laughed till she was crying. Wiping away the tears, she'd doubled up yet again, then apologised.

"*Never,* Henrietta, never I say, will you grace another soirée with your unique brand of song! Whatever were the old tabbies thinking to let you stand up and sing?"

A smile rose to Henrietta's lips. A true friend, she knew, would bring honesty to the relationship. Clementine had done that and, what was more, she'd enabled Henrietta to own to her failings and laugh. A rare thing, that! She remembered the agonies of mortification she'd suffered and wondered, in surprise, why?

Why had she simply not smiled a refusal and been done with it? In the future she would certainly not lose her poise over a request to sing. She would smilingly decline and offer another young lady, more blessed in this particular social grace, to sing in her place. Deft and gracious. Clementine made the world seem suddenly simple.

Face fresh from the warm sponging, Henrietta now indulged in a long, luxurious stretch. Her gown of yellow organdie trimmed with sensible florets of blue was already laid out. It was no more than ten minutes later that two ladies, a groom, an abigail and a hamper full of breakfast treats were seen setting off in the direction of Halibut Creek. The sky was streaked in shades of brilliant red.

"Well met, my dear!" Clementine's heart did a swift, unnerving and extremely unpleasant somersault. Curse it! She *would* have chosen that moment to hitch up her skirts against the damp soil of the herbaceous garden. She drew herself up straight, however, and mentally prepared herself for the tête-á-tête she'd been dreading from her first arrival.

"Sir Andrew!" She drew a hand across her face and felt, to her chagrin, a spatter of mud streak her cheek. She did not like to appear at a disadvantage with this man. For a moment she pondered on the advisability of curtsying. No! The very thought was too mortifying to contemplate. Sir Andrew was taking in her disarray with the eye of a connoisseur. She found this galling in the extreme. The gleam in his eye was as disconcerting as it was unpleasant.

"His lordship is within. I was not aware you were calling?"

He lifted his glass, the better to survey her legs. She flushed.

"Were you not, my dear? So much *nicer* to arrive unannounced, don't you think?" His tone never altered, but his face became bland as he continued.

"I just may, otherwise, have missed you again." Miss Deveraux did not lose his meaning. She was guiltily aware of how long she'd spent cooped up in the schoolroom, mentally willing Sir Andrew Cunningham from Inglewood. What was worse, contrary to her brief period as governess, she had conspired to keep Henrietta from his clutches too. One look at the loathing in that lady's eyes had told her enough on that score.

"I fear, though, you are under a misapprehension."

"I am?" Clementine arched her brows coolly.

The baronet's eyes narrowed at the insolence, but he continued nonetheless.

"You are. It was not his lordship I was wishful of seeing."

"No?"

"No."

"Lady Henrietta has the headache."

"Has she?" His lips curled unpleasantly.

"She—"

"Oh, bother Lady Henrietta! It was not her I wished to see either!"

"Then ..." Clementine stopped short. Sir Andrew was regarding her with a malicious gleam at the back of his steel grey eyes.

"Ah, now I see we have come to the nub of it! Is it so very dreadful that it is you I was seeking out?"

"Yes, unless it was an apology you wish to be making!" Clementine lost her temper. Bother her employer and her lowly servant status! Her eyes flashed a vivid, startling green.

Sir Andrew smothered a sneer. "Apologize to a slut? Do you not realize I know you spent the night with a common felon? You could be had up for aiding and abetting! Not to mention your precious virtue! I hope you enjoyed yourself, my dear. You will certainly pay for it!''

Clementine's hand shot out to deliver a ringing crack to the gentleman's face. It was caught in that hated, viselike grip.

"Not so fast, young lady!" The words were uttered sarcastically.

"Do you wish to speak with anyone other than myself or not? If not, let me be. I've nothing further to say to you.'' She turned her back on him, and Sir Andrew changed his tack.

"How is the Lady Henrietta anyway?''

"She is fine, sir. She has much to learn, though, before her debut.''

"From you?'' He gave a crack of rude laughter. "I wouldn't *trouble* yourself! Her ladyship will have no use for a debut once we are wed. She will reside in Derbyshire where the customs of London society can be of little account!''

Clementine was seething, but she vouchsafed no reply. She would not give the man the satisfaction. He looked at her with a grim smile that did not quite reach his eyes. He was not used to being slighted by little slips of serving girls no better, in his opinion, than they ought to be. When the settlements were signed, he'd be back to teach her a lesson or two. Or three. She was, after all, extremely handsome, in her own way. He made her a mocking salute.

"Pardon me for not averting my eyes, dear lady, but as I think I've told you once before, you have remarkably well-turned ankles.'' Miss Deveraux reddened at his brazen insolence and in shame for the position in which he'd found her. Curse her hems! She bristled as she patted down the folds of her calico day dress and removed even the tips of her half boots from his view.

"I've learned not to expect the gentlemanly from you, sir!'' Her voice held scorn. Sir Andrew Cunningham, baronet of the realm, felt his fingers itch. He'd teach the slut! He studied his hand. Time enough later. His voice, though, was full of venom as he once again insulted her.

"Oh, I'd never think to address a *lady* in such a fashion!"
Miss Deveraux seethed. The inference was clear. To him,
the upright governess-companion was no more than a fallen
woman. A bit rich, Clementine thought indignantly, since it
was he who had first sought to bring about her downfall. She
straightened her back silently. It would be beneath her dignity
to afford the man any more of her time. Sir Andrew surveyed
the countless pearl buttons running seamlessly down her spine
with interest. He had no doubt—none whatsoever—that it
would be his fingers doing the unfastening that night.

He licked his lips in lascivious pleasure. But first, an interview with his betrothed.

Chapter Five

"Have you stoked the fire in the east drawing room, James? His lordship complained of a smoking grate this morning and the draughts are prodigious! I trust I will not need to speak with you on the subject again?"

The second footman looked abashed. He was greatly in awe of Curruthers, whose every word was law to the lower servants of Inglewood Manor.

"Surely I have, sir! Stoked them meself I did!" He tried very hard not to fidget with his gleaming white gloves. Curruthers was bound to notice and reprimand him once more. The butler vouchsafed a nod.

"Good. Have you seen Biggins this evening? I most particularly want a word with him!" Curruthers's tone was ominous and James, for once, was glad he was not Christopher Biggins, second under groom to the Earl of Inglewood.

"I reckon 'e's gone on 'ome, sir! I seen 'im rubbing down Lady 'Enrietta's mare gone on an hour ago! The chestnuts and the greys are all in their boxes, and I reckon the new foal 'as 'ad 'is victuals all right and tight!" His eyes lit up. It was ever his wish to be assigned to the stables. He always felt like squirming in his smart livery and scratchy pantaloons.

Curruthers brought him up short. "If I were interested in the state of the stables, James, I would have asked! He has gone home you say?" The words were disapproving.

James nodded. "It be gettin' dark and all, I reckon 'e wanted to be off right and early. Powerful far the village seems on a night like this!" There was a moment's hesitation. " 'Is wife be carryin' again, she is!"

Curruthers allowed himself a faint snort, the meaning of which James could not quite fathom.

"If you see him in the morning, you may tell him I wish a word with him." James nodded. He, too, was eager to take his leave. The wind was up and there was only a sliver of moon to light his way down to the dower house where he took up his lodgings.

Cook would have made a gammon pie from the leftovers from the evening meal. He knew he would have to hurry if he was to get his fair slice. The under butler was a sight too greedy for his reckoning, and there was no saying *what* he'd get for his dinner if he did not make good his escape this instant.

Curruthers seemed oblivious to these musings. "Light the tallows in the hall before you take off, James. I believe six will suffice, as his lordship is not expecting company tonight." The footman sighed inwardly. Six tallows! He'd have to get them from the store. No doubt it would be nothing but turkey gruel for him. He clicked his tongue in botheration. Curruthers looked hard at him.

"What was that?"

"Nothing, sir!"

The butler looked unconvinced. James bowed awkwardly to his superior and moved towards the servants' entrance.

"James!" He stopped again, with an ill-suppressed sigh. What now? His irritation was quickly changed to a cough. "Sir?"

Curruthers was on the stairs, inspecting the handiwork of the third and fourth housemaids. The smudge on the shiny brass knocker was quite evident. James heaved a sigh of relief. At least that could not be set to his account!

"Not wax, do you hear? The tallow candles will *more* than suffice! Amy wasted an entire box of white wax last week. Lighting the east hallway, if you please! Just when his lordship has taken to economising, too!" His voice was positively grim. Whether this was due to Amy's negligence or the earl's economizing, James did not quite like to inquire.

He was only too thankful to escape the beady eye of Curruthers as he nodded and disappeared into the dim hall. It was not long before he was running through the scullery, whistling at a volume that, had the butler been within earshot, would have brought down the wrath of heavens.

"Silly old toad!" was all he said.

Curruthers remained standing outside for quite some time. His sharp ears were certain they had caught a sound. If it was one of the housemaids dallying with the new Norwich groom . . . he listened. He could hear nothing, though his head was cocked like a little robin's when it was listening for the call of spring. Presently he shrugged. A rare nip of his lordship's brandy was stowed securely in his chamber. On a cold night like this, there was no better restorative. He adjusted his cuffs and made a stately return indoors.

Grantham Davies smothered a sigh of relief. He had been hidden in the shadows at least an hour, and his limbs were numb with frost and inactivity. He'd watched with impatience as a mincing pink of fashion had stealthily called out the grooms. His carriage had rumbled off long before Grantham thought to gingerly test his foot and slowly curse as it buckled beneath him.

Hell and damnation! He wiggled it slowly till the circulation returned. Unlike Randolph, who had had the forethought to secure for himself a greatcoat against the winter chill, Grantham wore only a thin jerkin and a swallowtail coat of fine lawn cambric. He shivered, then made his way slowly from out the shrubbery at the end of the long, west-wing patio.

The household was all long abed. Only the odd servant was still to be seen straggling here or there. Curruthers had been correct about the Norwich groom. . . . He'd flitted in close on twenty minutes ago and was even now busily occupied in the shelter of the east atrium lawns. Grantham grinned at his impunity. He could have done with an armful like that himself, he could! Still, he had better tread carefully. He would be hard pressed to explain his presence at Inglewood if challenged.

Grantham hoped his memory had not deceived him. If all was as it ought to be, there was a secret stair that led from the nursery to the second book room below stairs. The door to this was situated to the right of the manor's west-wing entrance. He knew for a fact that this remained unlocked at night, one of the strange aberrations of the very wealthy.

Only a sleepy sentry stood guard over this little-used passageway into the manse, his lordship preferring to have access to the night air without the necessity of alerting his staff. Thus it was that for as long as Grantham could recall, the odd oak doors had stood permanently open. He trusted that things had not much changed in his absence.

The unwelcome thought now struck him that the earl might just choose this night, of all nights, to proceed with his nocturnal ambulation. He swallowed hard. Not likely, if the thin sliver of a moon was anything to go by. Besides, he'd seen with his own eyes the flickering light of the earl's chamber darken to nothing more than the glow of embers in the grate.

Not a chance he'd be caught. Grantham Davies was too fly for that! He grinned. He loved the adrenalin rush he was now experiencing. It brought back some of his more daring escapades at Cambridge. No, breaking in would be a mere bagatelle. He and Henrietta had done this countless times in their salad days.

He moved forward slowly, stopping to crouch behind a pillar as he heard the call of an owl. Stillness. He crept forward again. For an instant, the half-sad, half-ebullient countenance of his

youthful playmate flashed into view. She would be around
seventeen, now. Quite a young lady, in fact. He half sighed for
the old days. He wondered whether her existence was less harsh
and friendless. Funny he should not have thought of her more
than he had.

He resisted an impulse now to pick up a stone and aim it at
the last window but one on the left. He smiled a little when
he imagined what her reaction might be. Not a freckle-faced
sprig, eyes alight with mischief and—yes, he knew it—adora-
tion. No, that was certain! Probably more like to be a very
unexceptional young miss with no thought to answer so
improper a call. He sighed. For a moment he regretted the past.
Then he continued on.

The sentry was just returning from a turn around the garden.
His red and gold livery gleamed a suitable warning to Grantham,
who froze once more. He sighed and resigned himself to another
long wait in the lengthening night hush. Frustrating! He was
so close to the house now, he could almost touch the stucco
pilaster and cold iron railings. With little else to do, he watched
the footman look first left and then right before pulling, from
his immaculate pocket, what looked like the remains of some
pasty of sorts. Grantham sympathised with the man, but could
hardly control his annoyance. Couldn't he have chosen to have
his little nocturnal feast somewhere away from his post? Evidently not! Mr. Davies's thoughts returned, once more, to his
quest.

The object of his ruminations was hanging quietly in the red
salon as it had for a generation at least. When the fourth Earl of
Inglewood had commissioned the portrait for his wife, Thomas
Gainsborough had been the little-known artist employed for
the work. The earl had noted his elegance of touch and had
responded greatly to his use of oils and light. A family portrait
for the Marquis and Marchioness of Asprey had settled his
determination to commission something along similar lines for
himself. His inclination had first run to a landscape, where
Gainsborough's genius for brushstrokes was striking in both
its realism and faint romanticism.

On second thought, however, he'd decided on the portrait. The gallery at Inglewood would be incomplete without an image of his beloved countess. Obligingly, Maria Malvern De Lacey had posed for several weeks before the artist had finally set down his palette and deemed himself satisfied. Grantham reflected with a wry smile that the birthday gift had been a fine one indeed. The painting, by one of the most lauded artists of Europe, was now worth a small fortune.

A fortune the current earl, Lord Oscar, was about to be relieved of. Grantham grinned. His conscience smote him not a bit. Like as not, Oscar would not even notice the theft. His inclinations did not run to finer things, least of all art.

Hidden in the shrubbery was a calico bag containing a long swatch of blue velvet. The theft going as it ought, Grantham would have just time to secure his prize firmly against the elements and possible damage before first light. His curricle was well hidden from view, his horses in fine fettle, thanks to the good offices of Grimes, who even now walked them slowly up and down somewhere on the boundary of the Inglewood estate. Since Grantham's own lands bounded with the manor's, the journey home should not be long even if it was fraught with a degree of tense excitement.

Grantham thrived on such excitement. He squinted now at his fob. Too dark to see. He cursed three times in his head. Unlike his good friend Randolph, he was not known for patience. Somewhere in the distance, a cricket began its shrill night call.

Lady Henrietta Stenning tossed in her sleep. Her dreams were filled with strange voices calling, calling. . . . She could not escape. Everywhere she looked, there were mirrors. Mirrors and mirrors. In them, one face. That of Sir Andrew Cunningham, her husband-to-be. She woke up with a start and was surprised to find she was hot despite the long-extinguished fire and the slight draught from the windows which were never properly sealed against the elements. Her heart was hammering and it took her some while to adjust to the fact that she was awake.

Once she had, of course, she could not get back to sleep. She lit a candle, but the shadows that fell across her bedstead still filled her with a needless dread. Everything was as it should be. Her pelisse was carefully laid out with her gloves, bonnet, slippers and riding dress of green merino. On her night stand, a glass of cold milk, a pearl-handled hairbrush and a much-treasured copy of Grimm's fairytales, illustrated by an unknown artist in pastel watercolour.

She picked up the book and thumbed quickly through the pages. Even the fairy godmother plate had lost its power to entrance. She sighed and quietly placed the little book in a sandalwood chest beside the door. A small voice in her soul was telling her that the time had come to put away childish things.

Down the corridor, Miss Deveraux was having a similarly fitful night. Her dreams had unconsciously darkened when the handle of her old, carved door had silently been turned. She'd not heard the smothered curse as the door had refused to yield, nor was she aware of how canny she'd been in making the decision to lock it that night.

As Cunningham's footsteps disappeared down the corridor, she continued to dream, but the dreams lightened to gold, then red, then pink, then became dark again ... dark as a silken kerchief and deep, fathomless eyes, dark as a highwayman. . . . She turned and her breathing became easier, her face flushed with the gentle beneficence of true rest. Little known to her, it was to be a night of dreams.

Many miles away, at the London townhouse of no less a person than his lordship the Viscount Trent, sleep was pursuing that peer in a pleasant parody of what Clementine now experienced. As the valet tiptoed in to lay out seven starched cravats and five quietly frilled shirt fronts of dazzling, impeccable white, he could hear his master's breathing deepen to a light snore. The viscount's lips were curled in such an open-hearted manner that even the redoubtable Pinkerton did not have the heart to move him.

The figure-hugging jacket of starched superfine would have to suffer inevitable creases. He sighed and hoped the dream was as pleasant as it looked. As he quietly closed the interconnecting door, he thought he heard the words "emerald queen" on his master's lips. He shrugged. Perhaps the viscount was dreaming of jewels.

Henrietta donned her thin night shift of organza and lace. She did not mind the cold! It seemed to shake the demons from her and she needed the fresh air. She considered waking Clementine, then swiftly put the thought aside. Why should her sleep be troubled simply because she was having strange, unwelcome dreams? She needed to think.

The best place for that was the old tree house at the end of the south promenade. Little used now, she imagined. She and Grantham had spent some fine times together up that tree. They'd pelted unsuspecting gardeners with apples, then smothered their giggles with little snorts of satisfaction.

When either had the need of comfort or quiet contemplation, they'd used that tree as their succour. Useful, since it was situated quite near the boundary of Inglewood and Dunstan, Grantham's family estate. Henrietta smiled as she recalled her childhood hero. When he'd found the time, he'd been really good to her. They'd spent many a fugitive hour secretly gazing at the stars. Once, Grantham had brought her a large, yellowing almanac as a birthday gift. She'd learnt the name of every single star in the northern sky.

Still, it was too dark to venture out now. Full moon was essential for nocturnal visits without benefit of a lantern. Besides, it was too cold. She decided on the second book room.

She took the corridor down to the nursery and opened the little-used door.

The sentry licked his fingers guiltily and looked round quickly. Good! No one had seen his light supper. Curruthers would have his head if he knew, but he could not help being peckish on such a long, dull night. The chill was quite severe now, so it occurred to him to take another stroll. The walk should warm his bones. As his red and gold trim disappeared into the shadows, Grantham seized the moment.

He made it to the house and in before the sentry had reached the flower beds so carefully landscaped by Nash. The corridor was dark and rather eerie at this time, but Grantham was made of stern stuff. True, his heart was pounding in his chest and the adrenalin was pumping through his veins, but these physical phenomena did not deter him in the least.

Confidently, he made for the second book room that would gain him access to the secret passage to the upstairs nursery. From there, he would have to watch his step. The red salon was five doors down and a turn in the corridor. He did not wish to be seen.

Henrietta stepped competently from the panelling that acted as the secret entrance. If anyone had seen her, they would have been startled into fits at this sudden apparition. Fortunately, though, there was no one at hand. The servants were sound asleep by now, only a handful awake in the kitchens against some unknown contingency. Mrs. Mullet would be baking bread, or old Adams stoking the great ovens, but that was all. The fresh ice baskets would arrive much later. For now, there was little to disturb the quiet peace.

The candle flickered uncertainly, and she set it down at a Queen Anne table close by. She'd had the foresight to bring another in case her original burned down too soon. She was not worried, though. She was almost certain she knew which volume she wished to select.

She passed over the Horace and Plutarch, dusty with age and lack of use. Her fingers hovered lovingly over the crisp edition of Scott's *The Lady of the Lake,* before settling with finality on *The Castle of Otranto.* Horace Walpole was one of those poor unfortunates whose work had been deemed anathema by her governesses. She'd managed to sneak in several pages of the romance, but not, until now, had she felt able to take the whole work back up to her bedroom.

Her ears alerted her to the muffled sound of footsteps. The sentry? Her heart pounded. He must not find her thus! She grabbed her candle and made for the panelling. To her horror, the door creaked open. For an instant she felt she'd been hurtled straight into the pages of the Walpole. How Gothic! She steeled herself to remain calm. Perhaps, in the half-light, she would not be noticed. She toyed with the idea of blowing out the flame, but the thought of an enveloping dark with an unknown intruder did not appeal.

Grantham walked in swiftly and quietly. Unlike Henrietta, he did not stop to peruse the shelves of tomes that accorded the room its status of second library. Instead, he moved with unerring precision towards Henrietta herself. She gasped as his hand began feeling for the panelling. He seemed to startle out of his skin when what he touched was warm, human and infinitely soft.

"Don't scream!" His voice was stern. Henrietta recognised it at once.

"Grantham!" She ploughed into him with all the excitement of a young puppy. He extricated himself and looked down at his childhood playmate with bemusement tinged with no small measure of amazement. His eyes had adjusted enough to the light to tell him that his little Hen had grown into quite a swan. As his eyes moved down to her scanty attire and the fresh, creamy promise of her bodice, he felt a stirring that he'd not before experienced in his dealings with the Lady Henrietta Stenning.

She, for her part, was aware of the hot flush that suffused her as she disentangled herself from Mr. Davies, and she hoped most fervently that the darkness would reveal little of it.

"Still up to your pranks, little Hen?" His voice held amusement and a surprising degree of relief. She'd not been transformed into so proper a little miss after all! Of course, there was no trace of the puppy fat and freckles. . . .

"Pranks?" She was indignant. "I came merely in search of a book! What, if I may inquire, are *you* up to?"

He ignored the question and took the novel from her hand. His eyes lit up in merriment.

"Ah, *The Castle of Otranto,* I see! How very edifying! And you tell me no pranks! The governesses must have changed their tune indeed if they've placed this on the reading list!"

Henrietta poked her tongue out at him. He noticed with interest that it was very pink and quite charming, despite her ignoble intentions.

"Brat!"

She glowed with happiness. It was a long time since she'd been called that.

"As a matter of fact, Grantham, I've got rid of Houghton-Fish *and* the Adams woman! My new governess—"

"Heavens, woman! We're not going to stand here in the musty, freezing half-light discussing governesses, are we?"

Henrietta looked doubtful.

"No. . . ."

"Shhh!" She was pushed back against the panelling. "The sentry's returning. Damn him!"

The footsteps were unmistakable. Either he was now taking a turn indoors out of the cold, or else he was actually doing his duty and had heard something. They couldn't afford to take a chance. Henrietta would be compromised utterly if she were discovered with him. He blew out the candle and opened the catch of the panelling.

"Inside! Quick!" Henrietta responded to the voice of authority and scrambled within. Grantham followed her, heaving the calico above his shoulders with dexterous agility. The panelling slammed shut just as the door was opened suspiciously with the sentry's foot.

"Hello?" The voice was cautious.

Henrietta hardly dared breath. Not that it was easy with the calico cloth squashed in her face and the warmth of a man impinging tumultuously upon her senses.

The sentry stood quietly, his ears cocked. The Lady Henrietta could hear her heart beat. The Honourable Mr. Grantham Davies experienced stirrings he could not altogether honestly set down to the earlier adrenalin rush.

The man could be heard fumbling with papers in the room. Henrietta prayed he would not notice the smoke twining from the newly extinguished candle. He did not. The dark was engulfing, but she felt curiously safe. She moved, slightly, but a restraining hand fell upon her. It was warm and smelled of fresh soap.

"Hello?" The sentry repeated his earlier remark. He must have heard something.

They remained stock-still on the passage stairs. Presently, they heard the welcome sound of footsteps receding. Under the footman's breath, they could just make out the word "rat."

"He must mean me!" Grantham released his hold reluctantly, his eyes bearing a merry twinkle.

"You?"

"Yes, I'm a positive rat to get you embroiled in my prank!"

Henrietta beamed. "A prank? I declare I've been starved of them since you left!"

His eyes melted. "Have you, little Hen?" She felt like crying at the familiar, careless words of endearment. Instead, she nodded, not trusting herself to speak. He took her in his arms and held her there for a moment.

The moment was a revelation to him. He knew for certain, there and then, that the lovely Miss Farring, the adorable Lady Sophria and the not-so-angelic Miss Patterson were about to lose out. He was holding in his arms the one lady who was destined to become his wife. He felt sure that Randolph would applaud his choice.

"*Leave* that, chicken!" Henrietta was fumbling with the folds of her gown, trying to achieve a semblance of modesty through the transparent organza. She flushed. He shook his head apologetically.

"Won't fadge, you know! Too much lace!" She blushed crimson, and he took pity on her.

"Here! Drape this around you!" He extracted the swath of velvet from out the calico. Gratefully, she covered herself in capelike fashion.

Grantham grinned, giving her the old, familiar, cheerful smile.

"I should banish you to your bedroom now!"

She looked indignant beyond belief.

"And miss out on the adventure? Not likely!"

"Game as a pebble, I see!"

She looked at him squarely.

"Would you have it any other way?"

He acknowledged the hit with a flourish.

"Bulls-eye, Lady Stenning! And the answer is . . . no, I would not!"

She beamed at him.

"So what are we up to?"

His voice dropped to a deep and wicked baritone. She smiled.

"We, my dear Lady Henrietta, are about to steal the famous Gainsborough oil!"

Chapter Six

Miss Deveraux was looking particularly well in the morning, thanks to the beneficial effects of an excellent sleep sweetened by dreams beyond her conscious control. She took up her brush and enjoyed the sensation of ridding the curls of their tangles and setting order to chaos. Her scalp tingled delightfully. She felt exactly, she mused, as a prize mare must feel after a good grooming. She made a tongue to the glass at her own humour. Heavens! She must not let the housemaids see her thus. They would think her gone quite, quite mad.

Henrietta appeared at her door dishevelled and yawning. Her cheeks were pink, and Clementine could only congratulate herself on the meritorious effects of daily exercise. Her charge was positively blooming, despite the decorous yawn that was issuing from her lips.

"Good morning, your ladyship!" Clementine often addressed her by her title.

Henrietta responded in kind, offering a polite curtsy and extending her hand a trifle haughtily.

"Charmed, I'm sure!"

Clementine laughed.

"Not bad, my dear! Not bad! But you would not wish to address the Lady Sefton or Mrs. Drummond Barrel in that manner!"

Henrietta hastened to reassure her. "No, ma'am! Nothing but a court curtsy for them, to be sure!"

She yawned again. Clementine looked at her suspiciously.

"Late night?" Henrietta flushed. She could not even tell dear Miss Deveraux what she'd been up to the night before. Her heart gave a little leap.

"Yes. I found a copy of Walpole to keep me amused."

Clementine's eyes lit up in amused comprehension. The mystery was explained. Even she could not sleep for a week after having read that particular tale!"

"Dreaming of dungeons, were you?"

Henrietta laughed guiltily. In truth, she had not read a page. Reality was much more exciting! Grantham had extracted the portrait with ease, replacing the empty space with a lesser picture hung in the small gallery next door. It was doubtful that the substitution would be missed. In any case, the measure would only be temporary.

Henrietta's heart beat faster at the thought of his return. He'd promised to be back in no more than four days at the outside. He would then switch the gallery painting to its original position and place a print of the Gainsborough in the red salon. With any luck, the theft would never be discovered. It had not so much crossed her mind as to why Grantham would wish to effect such an exchange. If it had, she would have been very certain it was not for money.

Grantham, as every one knew, was blessed with a considerable fortune of his own. Not so much, it was rumoured, as her prodigal cousin Lord Randolph, but still, Mr. Davies was known to be warm enough.

Her mind wandered to Randolph. She'd been a little slip of a thing in his time, but she remembered his good-humoured smile and his endearing way of allowing her to follow when others would have banished her forthwith.

He was old, of course . . . quite thirteen years her senior, but still, not so top lofty as to refuse her a ride on his gelding or to slip her a coin for some sugar candy when the peddlers made their rounds. Such a shame he'd committed those forgeries. So unlike him, with his honest eyes and upright manner. He was forever prosing on about good works and heaven knew what!

The old earl had thrown a fit, of course. He'd banished Randolph to India without so much as a penny to his name. Everything he had, he'd made out in the colonies. So far as she could gather, the viscount had also made some powerful friends out there. He'd invested in a mine, of sorts, and never looked back.

She wished now he was received at Inglewood. He was not. Lord Oscar refused even to contemplate the connection. His own brother! Henrietta shook her head in disbelief, then promised her governess to be ready in less than ten minutes.

Clementine nodded. ''Ten, no more!'' An early morning ride would be just the thing to shake the cobwebs. As she looked at Henrietta's retreating back, the familiar aspect of dark eyes and an aquiline nose crowded her thoughts.

''Daydreamer!'' she scolded herself crossly.

Lord Randolph had dispensed with the services of Pinkerton and his staff. They were less enthusiastic at their unexpected half-day than they might have been, for as the valet uttered confidentially to the resident butler, their master had that glint in his eye. That glint, they knew from past experience, boded no good.

The last time my lord had looked as if the cat had got the cream, he'd returned from his adventures travel soiled and dusty. Actually dusty! Pinkerton whispered this in horrified accents to the avidly listening Masters.

Masters nodded solemnly and added his own awed account of their mutual employer's unaccountable misdeeds. Shaking heads, they whispered with meaning that Santana had been called out again. Not a town horse, that Santana! Swift as the very devil and as black as night. My lord was up to his tricks again. Like as not he would return with bloodstained cravat and greatcoat as he had the last time.

Mrs. Lambton, her hands floury from dough, heaved a large, sentimental sigh. Though Masters's words had not been directed at her, she felt inclined to join in the discussion, having heard salient snippets on the way to the scullery.

"Oh, but there is no telling with gentry folk, now is there?"

Neither Masters nor Pinkerton deigned to reply. Undeterred, Mrs. Lambton towelled off the last of the flour and sat down at the large, heavy table she'd oiled only that morning.

"And he is so handsome!" She clasped her hands to her bosom. Masters and Pinkerton exchanged looks of disgust. Women! They set down their mugs and began preparing for the day's holiday.

His lordship, the Earl of Inglewood, crumpled the bill in his hand in disgust. Whatever was the world coming to, that he could be dunned by his own tailors? No proper respect, those people, *that* was what! He sighed. He supposed the bill—and others like it—would have to get paid somehow. No good for his credit to be in queer street, and that is what would happen if he did not cough up soon.

Damn it! He stood up. Nothing for it, but to dip deep into the De Lacey heirlooms. He'd not be the first to sell off the odd family treasure and surely not the last. His conscience stirred a little uneasily, then was quashed.

That was the unfortunate aspect of the earl's nature. His conscience was weak. Sinfully so. Even now, he still harboured moments of bitter regret about the estrangement between Randolph and himself. Were those forgeries really worth the agony over all these years? He vividly remembered penning his father's name, then shuddered. No, he could not then have faced his wrath. Randolph was always so much the stronger. Besides, India had been the making of him if all he heard was true.

For an instant, he half envied his brother the wealth and

freedom. He shook himself mentally. He, after all, had the earldom and the entrée into society. He may have had the one by birth, but the other would certainly have been shut to him if ever the truth came to light.

His heart gave a faint leap that seemed as cold as a shiver. That Cunningham . . . That infernal Andrew Cunningham! With his soft tones and his insinuating smile. Why must it be *he* who held proof of the truth? If only the past could be the past. This constant sense of impending exposure was sheer mortification. Hell! As for Henrietta . . . she'd been entrusted to his care and he was loath, indeed, to hand her on like a parcel to that blackguard.

He'd be inhuman not to have qualms, even if he was to receive a kickback from her capital. Unfortunately for her ladyship, the qualms were weak.

More salient a point was that he'd lose the annual interest off her capital the day she married. It was not in his interests that she marry so young. Lord Oscar swallowed bitterly. From the day he had committed those forgeries, life had never been simple. He felt bitter and ill used. A small part of him felt guilty, too.

Randolph could not have had an easy time of it either. He heard tell his brother was not received in the best salons. A pity. He bore him no real malice, only the constant dread of exposure wrought an unbreachable chasm between them. Randolph knew the truth. Randolph, with his perceptive eyes and cynical, upturned mouth . . . The earl shuddered.

"You rang, my lord?" Curruthers hovered at the door, impeccable as ever in his evening garb of black and white. Unlike the rest of the servants, the butler affected an austere colour scheme that added greatly to his consequence. He would have been surprised and more than a little displeased to learn that the earl, in his more humorous moments, often likened him to a penguin.

"Curruthers! Fetch, if you will, the blue jewel box currently housed in the library's safe. I entrust you with the key. See that it is safely back in my possession before the night's end."

Curruthers bowed. It flashed across his mind that the earl must be contemplating marriage. The jewels he referred to were family heirlooms, out of the ordinary way. He chided himself. Good butlers did not think. They simply performed what was required. He closed the door gently behind him.

The transformation was miraculous. The Viscount of Trent cocked his head to one side and smiled. The wig made all the difference, of course. Even without the patch he now meticulously affixed to the right side of his cheek, he'd have been unrecognisable but for the deep, dark eyes. There was not much he could do about that, but the kerchief went a long way towards the masking of his features—in particular, the distinctive, aquiline nose that had been the mark of a De Lacey for generations. He nodded in satisfaction, his cool eyes alight, suddenly, in anticipation.

This time there'd be no mistakes. It would be Lord Oscar he held up if it was the last thing he did. Several days of riding through that particular terrain had made him aware—almost too acutely aware—of the comings and goings of the household. He told himself that such diligence was necessary to procure himself the right quarry.

In truth, his mind more than once flitted to the Lady Henrietta and her oh, so beautiful companion. Even at a distance he could catch her eyes dancing as she addressed his cousin by marriage.

Certainly, at a distance, he was afforded a splendid view of her tumbling fair hair that glinted like gold in the sunshine. Gold, honey, sunshine . . . his dreams were full of it. He brought himself up short. Unbecoming thoughts in a gentleman.

Even in one soon to be wed? The thought hovered like a wisp of air, too light to catch hold of, but real nonetheless. He smiled to himself. Time would tell. Time would tell.

In the meanwhile, there was the pressing matter of the challenge to be won. Couldn't have someone of Grantham's untried palate gulping down Montagne de Reims pinot noir '84. Unthinkable! Besides—his eyes hardened—his brother still needed a lesson or two. Strange that there was still that unassailable pain of betrayal after all these years. He clicked on his cufflinks. Not his usual style, but gold nonetheless. When the day was done, he'd offer them up to the vicar along with the rest of the day's take.

The Earl of Inglewood sat looking at the box in front of him for a long while. He was lost in thought, none of it pleasant. When he roused himself, his eyes focused once more on the Inglewood heirloom. By rights his countess should wear it. It should dangle upon her neck in regal splendour, shimmering incandescently as she moved. He sighed. There was to be no countess.

Not now, when he was approaching forty and felt like fifty. No, there was no need of the opulent necklace with its huge, blue sapphires and encrusting diamonds that dropped like ponderous flowers from a bed of heavy gold. No need at all.

Perhaps, in his youth, if he had been less top lofty, less conscious of what was owing his rank, he might even now be wed. . . . The thought of Maria flashed into his head, then was gone.

She was way below him, his social inferior in every respect. It was not to be contemplated. He'd dallied with her, roused her expectations and then come up with a carte blanche. The wounded eyes still haunted him though the mark upon his cheek had long faded.

He wondered, for an instant, where she was, what she was doing. Then he hardened his heart as was his custom. The jewels should fetch a pretty price in Hazlett Street, a small catchment off Bond that dealt very well in exclusive exchanges of this sort. The place had been recommended by no less a person than Lord Harlbury.

He estimated he should be debt free and satisfyingly plump in pocket in no more time than the simple trip to the city. He opened his drawer and placed the last of his cash reserve into his pouch. The fact that many of his tenants could live happily off that sum did not weigh with him. The earl, in fact, considered it sufficient only for the hiring of a decent team of six, a tolerable meal at the Postilion Inn and perhaps a stake at one of the more exclusive gaming houses along Tenth and Sutton streets. He pulled out his snuff box and inhaled with pleasure. Excellent!

Across Inglewood Park, on the far side of the river bank, there runs a stream shaded by beeches and cobbled with tiny, smooth pebbles at its mouth. It is there that any man, with a mind to it, can catch sight of the traffic that ebbs and flows between London and the deep country.

It must be said, however, that this is by no means a common occupation. The arrival of the mail coach, the various accommodation chaises, the sundry landaulets, barouches and landaus, the curricles and even the occasional high-perch phaeton all render the pastime somewhat tedious. To one man, however, the vantage point afforded by this little known spot was found to be invaluable. The masked rider, alert upon his stallion, was determined to make no mistake.

He watched as the crested landaulet rolled into view. His heart lurched, but his hands were steady. This time he would wait. He would wait patiently until the bend was fully rounded. The trotting of hoofs was almost thundering in his ears when he caught a glimpse of the passengers.

Though his heart gave that same lurch, it was with quite another cause. The occupants were seriously engaged in discussion, but the highwayman's eyes could fix on only one. Her lips were pink, her gloved hands strangely expressive as she raised them in order to make a point. He could not be perfectly certain, but he felt sure he could hear a giggle or two emanating from the chaise. For an instant, he wished he could be with them, discoursing in perfectly ordinary fashion on perfectly ordinary things.

Then he felt compelled to quell the most absurd impulse to spur Santana on and hold her up again. He wondered if she would be pleased, if she remembered him at all. . . . He touched the emerald queen. It was his talisman. No, the chaise was allowed to continue on.

Several farm carts and a donkey were now seen to cross the path. The highwayman stepped back into the shelter of his lookout and resumed his wait. A little cogent bribery at the Four Horse Inn had led him to believe that his lordship would be travelling that day. Still, it took patience and some considerable strength of will to maintain the wait. Santana used the opportunity to take a quiet drink. He wished he could do the same.

Horses again! Instantly, he was at the alert. The Inglewood crest. Six horses and an outrider. He would have to be very cautious. He had five minutes to take the embankment and cut off their progress along the next stretch. He knew he could do it, but it was a matter of the outrider and groom. Could he cover three men? He thought not.

He waited for the carriage to pass, then carefully took aim. The shot was muffled by the wind and water, but the outrider's horse knew that its ear had been winged. It reared up, whinnying more in fright than in pain. The outrider did his best to steady his mount, but was simply not fast enough. Before he knew it, he'd been ditched.

The De Lacey barouche continued on its stately progress. The highwayman spurred Santana. The stallion responded gladly. Game to stretch his legs after the forced inactivity so alien to a creature like himself, his lithe forequarters moved effortlessly to full canter. The highwayman's superior skill was never so essential as at that moment. A lesser man, certainly, would have undoubtedly been unseated. In this instance, though, man and horse were of one accord. The highwayman's impressive form moulded to the saddle with graceful ease. The barouche never had a chance.

Lord Oscar was terrified. He looked behind him, expecting at any moment to hear the welcome shot of the outrider. None came. The groom was too busy with his horses to so much as look up, let alone take constructive action. With a plummeting of his heart, Oscar thought of the sapphire necklace and the purse full of money that he carried on his person.

Surely it could not be! He could not have such luck as this! Desperation made him draw his sword, though he realised it would be to no avail. A sword is no proof against a pistol, especially one that is levelled directly at your face. This one was.

"A very good day it be, fine gennelman!" The highwayman doffed his cap in mock courtesy. The earl was furious. Without thinking, he unsheathed the sword and pointed it at his adversary. The highwayman's eyes flashed before he skilfully parried the movement with a simple thrust of his barrel. The sword hovered dangerously, then fell impotently to the carriage floor.

"I wouldna 'ave made that move meself, fine gennelman!" The voice held a threat. The earl turned white, his hands, in their fawn riding gloves, visibly shaking. For an instant, the highwayman found it in himself to feel sorry for the man; then his resolve hardened. He could forgive his own loveless state and the ill treatment he'd suffered at his brother's hands. He could not forgive the state of Inglewood and its tenants, all but a hairsbreadth away from poverty and actual starvation.

" 'And over the goods, me man! And git a move on, then! I do not 'ave all day!" The highwayman glanced meaningfully behind him. The outrider would no doubt be extricating himself from the cold, dank ditch even as they spoke. He hoped the bend in the road would put the earl's predicament well out of sight.

Lord Oscar hoped that delaying would save him. He fumbled to pull out his purse and hoped against hope the highwayman would not notice the blue box at his side. Stupid to hope! The highwayman's hand stretched out and pocketed it even whilst the pistol remained trained on his face. He could have screamed in despair.

The heirloom! The priceless, irreplaceable heirloom! The fact that he, himself, had intended to hock it was quite beyond the point. He felt on the verge of a swoon. His pulse fluttered dangerously.

The thief was remorseless. In a hateful, deep baritone he demanded the antique snuff box inlaid with a rare cabochon ruby that had ever been the earl's pride. He seized, without regard for his victim's pleas, the purse full of money and a few minor trinkets that caught his eye.

Then with a doff of his cap and a small smile that was masked by the dark kerchief, he raised his hand in mocking salute and put his heels to his horse. When the outrider rode up, he could see nothing more than a cloud of dust. His lordship the Earl of Inglewood ordered his horses turned round.

The description, when she heard it, made Miss Deveraux clasp her fingers tightly in her lap. Her pulse fluttered unevenly as she heard the earl describe, in ponderous tones, the exact focus of her dreams and waking moments. The kerchief, the dark eyes, the baritone, the low, peasantlike accent.

In a fury, the earl described the upright bearing that so entranced her. His rage grew as he expounded on the very impertinence that made the highwayman so dear to her. Oh, yes, no question. It was her highwayman that had held up the De Lacey barouche.

A part of her was disappointed that so captivating a man should have so demeaning an occupation. Surely he was capable of better? She thought so. Still, life was never quite perfect. There did not exist the rose that grew without the thorn. The highwayman, at least, was chivalrous. She had seen that at first hand and took leave to give him credit where it was due. She hoped it was not just self-deception, but she was tolerably certain the man was not so sunk in depravity that he would harm or even rob defenceless wayfarers.

He had not, after all, held up the Riverton coach. That could have been his for the picking. No, she suspected her highwayman played by gentlemen's rules, and the earl was, after all, fair game.

Lord Oscar glanced at her suspiciously.

"You seem rather quiet, Miss Deveraux?" He was not

pleased by his unappreciative audience. By now, his tale of the highwayman had been embroidered to include several rogues and a great deal of physical injury done to them all. His quick wits and superior strength were, of course, the saving grace in the piece.

Miss Deveraux, shrewd as always, took note that his lordship's garb remained perfectly, if slightly outmodishly, intact. No sign of fisticuffs or even a minor scuffle. She suspected strongly that the original description had been the truest. She folded her arms demurely and cast her eyes to the ground. "I was just reflecting on your terrible ordeal, my lord!"

The earl grunted. She was not so bad, after all, this new governess. Still, his importance was piqued.

"I shall call in the runners! Bow Street shall have something to say in this!"

Clementine's heart plummeted. What hope could her highwayman have against the notorious Bow Street runners? He would be captured and hanged. For an instant his laughing eyes looked out at her, mockingly. The vision faded. Lord Oscar rose from his chair. "I'll alert them at once!"

He did not add that a family heirloom was at stake. It would not be at all the thing for society to know he was hocking the family jewels. Besides, there were still his creditors. They'd foreclose in a minute if they knew of the loss of such a thing. He would have to word his report carefully.

"My lord!" Clementine's fingers gripped the table, but otherwise she appeared cool.

"Yes?"

"The men. They were pockmarked you say?"

"Yes." The earl had got carried away with his own embroidery.

"Three of them?"

"Yes."

"All very *young*, you say."

"Not a day over twenty! It is a wonder I was able to resist them so! Young puppies!"

Clementine hid a small smile. "All on horseback, you say?"

The earl became impatient with this line of questioning. "Yes. What of it?"

Clementine looked down at her feet and concentrated fiercely on bringing a blush to her cheeks. Above all, she wished to appear demure.

"It is just, my lord . . ."

"Yes?" Lord Oscar was feeling testy.

"I'm sure you will give the runners *exactly* that description?" She smiled at him sweetly. Oh, pray God that he did! It would let her highwayman off the hook. He did not fit the self-serving ravings of the earl one jot.

The earl was silent a moment. Hoist by his own petard. He'd have to call the runners in, but the description they'd get was very different from the one he'd intended. Drat and drat his addlepated tongue! He bowed stiffly and left the room.

Chapter Seven

Lady Henrietta's flush worried Clementine. The rain had made it impossible for them to take their usual morning ride, but even so, the girl seemed more than unusually restless.

"I have the new bolts of muslin in from Salle Street!" That ought to arouse her. The new bazaar was much spoken of, and some of the fabrics were brought in from as far afield as China.

"Have you?" The eyes were dull and not quite as alight as Clementine could have wished.

"Are you finished with that kipper, or do you just enjoy dissecting it?"

"Pardon?"

Clementine repeated the question in some exasperation. Light dawned. Henrietta pushed the plate away as if it were distasteful.

"Oh, quite finished!"

"Are you well?" Clementine's eyes bored into those of her charge.

"Nothing that a turn outside could not mend!"

"You are certain?"

Henrietta blushed. How could she tell her governess that

she could think on nothing beyond the strong features of her childhood friend? He'd grown so handsome since she'd last seen him! Cambridge had certainly granted him the polish that had been wanting before.

"Yes. I am fine. Just fine."

"Good! I thought, since the clouds were clearing, we might take a walk down to some of the estate cottages. You've not been down there, I take it?"

Henrietta shook her head vigorously. Some of the brown curls fell to her forehead becomingly.

"The governesses would not countenance it! I think they thought I'd contract typhoid or some such disease simply by making the contact."

For once, Clementine did not laugh at the governesses's concerns. Lady Henrietta, indeed, was surprised to see that she looked quite grave.

"Not in the country, perhaps. But in the cities . . . yes. It is a real concern."

Henrietta felt shamed that she had hardly given it a thought. "Why?"

"No clear running water, my dear. All their washing, cleaning, playing and bodily functions contaminate the streams in which they live. Food is cooked and water drunk from those same sources. There is no place to isolate the infected."

She stopped to take breath, noting Henrietta's pale colour. She continued on.

"People live twelve to a room in many—indeed most— houses." She hesitated.

"Vermin is not uncommon. The warmth attracted from so large a concentration of bodies is very attractive to creatures used to the icy cold." Miss Deveraux took pity on her charge and did not mention that warmth was not the only attraction for these creatures. From her shudder, she divined Henrietta had guessed the truth anyway.

"In the country they are much safer? There is clear water, after all!"

"That is true." The tone was non commital. Henrietta continued her thoughts. "And game and pheasants . . . wild berries . . . plenty to eat."

"Not so, my dear."

"But there is the park. Lord Oscar hunts nearly every week, and he always brings home grouse of some sort."

"That is because the park is stocked especially for him. It is a hanging offence to be caught poaching game from the park. You know that! Why do you think so many gamekeepers are kept employed?"

There was silence as her charge digested all this. "I never thought—"

"Exactly so! You were never *meant* to think! Society believes young ladies should be spared such revelations. I don't happen to agree."

Henrietta continued along her own line of thought.

"Then the berries—"

"Belong to the estate, not the tenants. Most landlords overlook the gathering of wild fruit, but there are some who do not, or who at least demand a tithe."

"It is unfair!"

Clementine's heart softened. It was not an easy lesson she was dealing her charge, but it was one Henrietta, as an heiress, had to learn. If Clementine achieved nothing else, at least she would have achieved this. Henrietta one day would have it in her capability to make changes. The seeds must be sown now, before it was too late.

"Much is unfair, my dear! The thing is to be aware. If one has knowledge of the plight of others, it at least affords one the opportunity of helping where one may. In this way, knowledge gives one power. Ignorance is more comfortable, perhaps, but it removes from us the opportunity to do more with our fortunes than buy baubles or clothes."

Henrietta flushed at the thought of how much she'd spent on such trifles. Clementine guessed the direction of her thoughts and was comfortably prosaic.

"There is no need to feel so perturbed, my lady! There is a place for everything, after all! If one can achieve a balance, however, one may have the satisfaction of feeling one has attained both virtue *and* beauty!'' She smiled and rose from the table.

"Off you go, then. Stout walking boots and a warm pelisse. I had Dora dig out a serviceable muffler from the chest.''

"Thank you!'' Lady Henrietta left the room quickly. The proposed outing filled her with a sense of both misgiving and anticipation. Certainly the morning had lost its promised dullness.

Maria Lowenthal put down her scissors and knotted the last piece of thread on her hoop. The silks were perfectly matched and the design pleasing. She sighed, then set the work down. Another chair cover for her mistress's morning salon. She opened the drapes, the better to feel morning's gentle sunshine upon her skin. Somehow, even this action did not dispel the parlour's gloom.

Neatly, she folded her remaining corners of cloth and tucked them into the work basket. Her needles were scattered along the arm of the well-worn, but nevertheless carefully tended, brocade settee. She gathered them up carefully and walked from the room.

At almost the same instant a rush of cool air caressed her cheeks, the Earl of Inglewood sat in his library brooding. Though his weathered face showed the lines of age, his mouth still held the curves she had come to know and yes—with herself she had to be honest—love. Not for the first time she wondered if she had made the right decision. Surely mistress was better than nothing at all? The argument had almost spent itself in her mind. She was tired of it. The earl took up his quill and began to write.

"Ladies! What an unexpected pleasure!'' The vicar opened the door and stood aside. Henrietta entered the hallway and looked about her in some surprise. Small, but definitely cosy.

The windows were open and sun streamed in, although the day was still mild.

Lady Henrietta allowed her coat to be taken from her before exclaiming over the fresh posies that graced the mantelpiece and small occasional tables in the parlour.

"We do our best, we do our best!" The vicar beamed.

"Do you take tea or lemonade?"

The ladies disdained but the vicar was insistent.

"Mrs. Oldfield will *never* forgive me if I let you go without. Do, I pray you, have pity on me!" They laughed and accepted with pleasure the lemonade.

The vicar hustled about looking flurried for a moment until he caught sight of Betty. The parlour maid was quickly adjured to see to the refreshments, and the vicar's calm returned. He beamed at his visitors as he begged them to take a seat.

"I am *so* sorry Mrs. Oldfield is not within. She will be most particularly upset to have missed you. She has taken up a warm posset to poor Mary Jenkins, who is quite fatigued with ague. And Gwendolyn Morphy is with child again, her twelfth in as many years, I fear. The children need fattening up, but there is so little to spare. Still, we do our best, we do our best. . . ."

"I'm sure you do, Mr. Oldfield." Henrietta's voice was quiet. Clementine could tell she was moved, and in her heart she was glad. She had known from the start that the girl had a warm, loving nature. It had just needed nurturing. And direction. Miss Deveraux held strong views on the ways young ladies were reared. She did not hold with the cosseting and protection from reality that too often occurred. It made for beautiful girls, but shallow ones. She wanted Henrietta to grow into something more than a woman in a lovely dress. She wanted her to grow into a lovely woman. Henrietta was halfway there already.

"Miss Deveraux has been teaching me the art of ancient remedies. Perhaps I can assist in some way? I can make them up at the manse and bring them down in the mornings if it will be a help."

Her lovely voice was diffident now.

"I know that it is sometimes difficult to procure the right herbs. We have a herbaceous garden at Inglewood that may prove very helpful."

The vicar positively glowed.

"Thank you, my dear! A great help that will be. Matilda is always complaining to me that she needs a hint of thyme . . . a dash of rosemary . . . essence of yew. So difficult to come by at times." His voice was apologetic. Henrietta flashed a glance at Clementine. She wanted to ask if the vicar would take it amiss in her if she offered a donation. Unfortunately, she could not very well ask when he stood, so politely, at their side.

Miss Deveraux thought she detected the meaning behind the glance, but she, too, could not be so rude as to discuss the quandary out loud. In the event, the dilemma resolved itself most satisfactorily, for Mr. Oldfield was called away on parish business. He made his excuses and promised to return as soon as he was able.

Over the very refreshing lemonade and finger biscuits, Henrietta put her question. It was the obvious one, and one that had occured to Clementine on several occasions when she'd ridden through the estate. The houses were in an apalling condition, many roofs rotted quite through and serving very little as a barrier against the elements.

The occasional child chopping wood had several times been noted to be barefoot or improperly clad. Henrietta had been saving a great deal of her pin money lately, putting it all aside towards some hypothetical project. Here, now, was that project. A drop in the ocean, perhaps, but an opportunity for Henrietta to develop a community spirit whilst at the same time righting, in some small way, an obvious wrong.

The pin money willed to her on a quarterly basis was a sum large enough to enable most families to live comfortably for a year. Since her ladyship had taken up her own needlework, vast sums had been saved and meticulously set on the credit side of her ledger. Clementine did not see that the earl could possibly object to her charge spending the money in the way his own should have been spent.

Such objections would be churlish in the extreme, especially since Henrietta would not suffer any lack. Her gowns would be just as modish as previously, even at half the price. She nodded her agreement to Henrietta, whose eyes lit up in rare delight. Miss Deveraux smiled. How providential that the one remedy for Henrietta's listlessness should be so beneficial to the Inglewood parishioners.

The ladies were just beginning to wonder whether they should take their leave when Mrs. Oldfield, their absent hostess, broke in on the scene. With exclamations of delight over the visit, she relentlessly carried the duo off to inspect her rose garden.

A rambling patch of scented colour, it was guaranteed to have pleased even the most jaded of palates. Clementine noted with amusement that the term "rose garden" was a bit of a misnomer, for in truth, the lovely patch of green was filled with honeysuckle, lavender, primrose and morning glory. Not to mention the occasional hollyhock sprouting from under a tree stump.

There were, in truth, a few roses—yellow, pink and the occasional scarlet—but these were not ordered in the obligatory rows and labelled as in the majority of formal gardens aspiring to the name. Indeed, for the most part, a veritable riot of motley specimens abounded, each vying for space and creating a heavenly, if disordered, aroma of spring.

Clementine got the distinct impression of life. Bees, insects, slugs—they were all present and accounted for. The ladies were charmed. Mrs. Oldfield beamed at them and determined at once that they were true ladies of quality. Though she was not ennobled, or of the social class to which Clementine and Henrietta were accustomed, she had a definite eye. That eye had stood her in good stead as a vicar's wife. It stood her in good stead now.

"Miss Deveraux!"

Clementine smiled her answer. "Yes?"

"I hope you will not think me forward, but I know that my

husband would be greatly appreciative of some advice and you may be just the person to help.''

"I'd be delighted, if I am able." Clementine did not seek to hide her astonishment. In what manner could she, of all people, possibly be of service to the vicar? It had her in a rare puzzle.

Mrs. Oldfield noted her surprise. "Forgive me if I seem forward, my dear! It just seems providential that you choose to visit us today of all days.''

"Today?" The tone held an interrogative note. Clementine was at a loss to guess why today should be different from yesterday or the one following.

"I must apologise. I talk in riddles!" Mrs. Oldfield smiled her warm, comfortable smile.

"Come inside, dears, and we will see if the vicar cannot enlighten you a little.''

Lady Henrietta followed them in, more than a little curious herself. Her thoughts took on a new direction, however, when Mrs. Oldfield referred to her earlier offer of herbs for medicinal decoctions. Mr. Oldfield must have briefed her before continuing with his parish business.

Henrietta was delighted to be taken up on her offer. Before she knew what she was about, she found herself engaged in the most lively discussion on the best ingredients for liniment and the extraction of essence. Mr. Oldfield's return to the parlour and his subsequent discussion with Clementine went practically unnoticed.

Maria Lowenthal's hand trembled as she fingered the seal. She would have recognised that handwriting anywhere, even if its identity had not been confirmed by the clear, crested frank of his lordship, the Earl of Inglewood. A ghost, a voice from the past. What could he possibly want now, after all the years? Wasted years of longing, of repining, of anger and finally of simple, unspoken regret.

Not regret for her decision. Regret for what could have been and was not. The missive beckoned to her, yet she could not open it. She placed it on the mantelpiece, then thought better of it. Not the sort of thing she would like to leave lying around, even in the privacy of her own small but decorous chamber.

She heard the bell pull tinkle in the parlour. Sighing, she placed the unlooked-for communication in the capacious pocket of her serviceable morning gown. The navy kerseymere cradled it there the whole day, the occasional crinkling as she moved the only indication that the day was not to be an ordinary one.

Maria smiled at her employer and opened the drapes. "May I get you a shawl, my lady? The blue paisley is very fetching!"

She was rapped on her knuckles, but she could tell her employer was pleased. At five and seventy, Mistress Ellen was still a redoubtable old soul.

Mr. Oldfield removed his glasses and polished them carefully. He would trust his wife's judgement at any time, but he was a little surprised that she deemed Clementine to be suitable for the type of confidence he had to impart. Still, he had to say that she seemed a very levelheaded young lady, and she was certainly held in very high esteem by the Inglewood servants. That, he knew, was no small thing.

Her connections in London settled his slight misgiving. Short of a trip to the city himself, he had no way of eliciting the information he required without her help. It seemed he had little choice but to divulge as much as he knew of his strange bequest and hope that she would be of some small assistance.

"I wonder if I could trouble you to step into my study a moment?" The vicar looked anxious, and Clementine became more mystified than ever.

"Certainly, sir!" Her well-bred voice held none of the surprise she felt.

"I have no fear for Henrietta. I see she is well occupied!"

The vicar smiled. "Ah, yes, I am afraid when dear Matilda starts on her favourite hobby horse there is no stopping her!"

"It is fortunate, then, that she has found a kindred spirit in

Lady Henrietta!'' Certainly, that lady was now in her element, regaling her hostess with snippets from *Mr. Landau's Recipes on Physique and Good Health* that she had chanced upon in the Inglewood conservatory. Some of it was hopeless quackery, and the stifled laughter of the two ladies was a tonic to hear.

The vicar indicated his intentions to his good lady, who acknowledged him with a slight nod of her head. Clementine found herself led below the landing and down a long, cold passage. Like the rest of the house, it was spotlessly clean, but she noted that the carpet was frayed and very worn along the edges. The vicar caught the direction of her glance and apologised.

''A bit threadbare, I'm afraid, but one gets used to it. So many other necessities, you know.'' Clementine thought she did.

''Here we are, then.'' The room was in much the same style as the parlour, only where there had been flowers in that room, there were now tomes scattered everywhere and spilling from the desk. The vicar pushed a number of the volumes aside to make space and bade Clementine sit down.

''Now then, Miss Deveraux!''

Clementine looked full at him. ''How may I be of service, sir?''

The gentleman wrung his hands and wrestled with his conscience.

''The matter I am about to impart is strictly in confidence, you understand?''

Clementine nodded, and he seemed relieved.

''The good Lord works in strange ways, Miss Deveraux, and none so strange as the communication I received only yesterday.'' He clasped his hands impressively.

''As you may know, the tenants of Inglewood have had a hard time of it lately. I do not like to cast blame, and that is certainly not my immediate business or intention, but under the present earl rents are preposterous and there is little time to do the necessary harvesting or sowing.'' As Clementine nodded her understanding, the vicar continued.

"Housing is deplorable, and although we are fortunate enough to have many fresh running streams in the vicinity, we are ever aware of the dangers of contamination. Already this season there has been one outbreak of whooping cough, and with winter coming. . . ." He stopped. He held Miss Deveraux's full attention.

"If truth be told, we were all at our wits' end. Matilda has worked herself to the bone with her remedies, stitching blankets together from scraps, taking on the odd darning, but a lot more has been required than that." He took a breath.

"Yesterday, we received what was required." He looked pleased at Clementine's lifted brow.

"A parcel arrived on our doorstep. The parlourmaid thought she heard a faint knocking and went down to investigate. When she opened the door, all she found was this." He pulled a package from his drawer. Clementine could not see its contents, but noted that the wrapping had no mark upon it.

"What is it?" She asked the obvious question, and the vicar relaxed back into his chair.

"*That,* my dear Miss Deveraux, is enough to see my parishioners through a miserable winter and on, at least, to the hope of spring. It is enough to see that the worst of the houses are mended and that a chicken goes into every pot. It is enough to see the young ones are clothed and the older children provided with sound boots against the winter chill. It is enough to purchase seed for planting and to procure ploughs for farming. In short, Miss Deveraux, it is enough. It is enough."

There were almost tears in his eyes, and Clementine was moved to silence. She folded her arms and waited. The man managed a wan smile. "You must think me a regular watering pot!"

"Not so, Mr. Oldfield! I think I would feel the same if such a miracle happened to me."

"A miracle. Ah, yes. That is what I, too, think. As a man of the cloth I can only say that it is gratifying, Miss Deveraux. Most gratifying."

"I can imagine that! May I ask who your benefactor is?"

A cloud descended over the vicar's face.

"There is the nub of it, my girl! Mrs. Oldfield and I have spent a sleepless night over it. We would not wish to show ingratitude."

"Do you not know, then?" The surprise in the governess's question was almost palpable.

The vicar sighed. "No, I'm afraid we do not. One may hazard guesses, but then, they may be so wild, may they not?" He reached into the desk.

"There was a note of sorts." His hand fumbled before arriving haphazardly upon the missive.

"See here! See what you make of it!"

Clementine stretched out and took the note from the vicar's hand. She was as bewildered as he and more than interested to see what the deliverer of such largesse could possibly have to say. There was silence as she read slowly, her brain a whirlpool of ideas.

> To the vicar Oldfield. Please accept this donation in the spirit in which it is intended. I entrust it into your care in the certain knowledge that you will distribute it wisely and with great fairness. From the bottom of my heart, I wish the tenants of Inglewood well.

It was signed with an indecipherable flourish and had an addendum attached.

> There is no need of thanks or other signals of good will. Neither my name nor my face is of any consequence If I ask any boon at all, it is that my privacy be respected.

Clementine turned the sheet over in her hand. There was nothing more.

"He makes his wishes clear, does he not?"

The vicar sighed. "He does and I wish to God he did not. It is hard to accept such a gift and not offer up thanks."

"Perhaps he knows. I'm sure he does. In any event, the

gentleman will be sure to see the changes you effect and be pleased. The best way you can repay him is by making sure the money is used to the best possible advantage.''

The vicar beamed. His wife, as always, had been right. Clementine's brain was acute.

''Exactly so, Miss Deveraux! Which leads me on to why I seek your advice.''

''Yes, Mr. Oldfield. Any help I can be in this regard will be the utmost pleasure, I assure you!''

The vicar opened the bag.

''The bequest has come in a strange form. It is not merely comprised of gold guineas and bank notes, although of that there are a few. It also comprises jewellery. Of some value, we surmise, but the pieces need necessarily be sold in order to serve our purpose. There are also a few promissory notes. . . .'' He coloured.

''Let me see.''

He handed the package over to her. ''We thought since you are recently arrived from London you would be able to direct us to a reputable jeweller or solicitor at the very least. It is hard to know who is suitable, after all. I am very aware of the trust that has been invested in me and am wary of being fleeced by a town shark. I believe there are many, if one is not sufficiently careful.''

''Indeed there are!'' Clementine bit her lip thoughtfully.

''I know of several reputable dealers, however, and will oblige you with their names . . .'' She stopped short. In the palm of her hand lay, quite unmistakably, Sir Andrew Cunningham's ring and fob. Deeper inside lay a snuff box inlaid with a brilliant cabochon ruby. It was undoubtedly gold. Her hands were shaking as she further explored the parcel. Two purses. One she was almost certain she recalled as belonging to Sir Andrew. The other contained the exact sum lost by the Earl of Inglewood.

In crisp bank notes was an inordinate sum of money. She did not count them, but noticed instead a piece of twine. Attached to the twine was a small note. It read, ''Proceeds of the sale of one sapphire and diamond necklace. Marquisite style. Origin unknown.''

The room swam before her, and for the first time in her life, Miss Deveraux honestly thought she would faint. The vicar noticed her pallor and rushed to her side with alacrity.

''Is anything amiss, my dear?''

Clementine could only weakly shake her head. The self-mocking eyes of the highwayman flashed into her head. The face had haunted her dreams, now it mocked her waking moments. The benefactor was undoubtedly he. The highwayman, masked in supposed shame yet ennobled in real glory. *Her* highwayman. She knew her instincts had been right. The man was playing a deep game, but he had not a base bone in his body. Her heart rejoiced.

His actions may have been criminal, but his intentions were of the highest order. He had risked life, limb and a hanging to see justice done. He had not kept a solitary item for himself. All the stolen goods were accounted for. No gain, none whatsoever, to himself. She stopped short and a dull red crept through her face. Her heart was hammering in her chest, and for the life of her, she could not quell it. She placed her hand in the package once more and felt around urgently. Nothing! She tried again. The vicar looked at her curiously. ''Are you looking for something, my dear? I think that was all.''

Miss Deveraux realised with a secret smile that that was, indeed, all. She packed the items back into the packet and handed them on to the vicar.

Not once did she mention the emerald queen. The void in the chess set had come to mirror the void in her heart. She could only dream that *he* would someday return, to fill both of these and perhaps make her consummate in the noble game.

Chapter Eight

"I won't have it, I declare!"

The two ladies dropped their eyes and continued eating their morning repast of welsh rarebit. Lady Henrietta was particularly hungry as she looked longingly over at the fresh strawberries laid on by the hovering footman. Clementine shook her head subtly. Now was not the time to be drawing attention to herself. Henrietta sat back and tried to make the most of her rarebit. She was heartily sick of hearing about the highway robbery.

Lord Oscar was in fine fettle, now, recalling all the acts of daring he had used upon the felons, embroidering, to Clementine's distinct amusement, each time he spoke. The strange thing was, she actually thought he believed the tales himself. It had taken only a slight prompting on the earl's part for both the groom and the outrider to agree that three people at least had set upon them. How else could anyone have got away with such out-and-out robbery?

Still, the loss of the heirloom had been a severe blow to the earl, who found himself in a most uncomfortable position. Whilst he wanted the treasure found and restored to him, he had no wish for society to get wind of the fact that he'd intended putting it up for hock. Such an admission would surely deflate his credit with the *ton*. That would be unthinkable!

His entire life, the earl had lived by his pride. Were it not for his overweening sense of what was due his position, he might even now be married. As it was, he remained a bachelor, unable to discover in any eminently titled young lady all the attributes he'd found in Maria. Maria, Maria. The thought of her put him in an even worse mood.

"I am going to call in the runners. *That* is what I will do!" He put down his coffee with decision. Clementine, delicately drinking from a steaming cup, suddenly felt that her tongue was scalded. The Bow Street runners! It was what she knew would happen, what she had feared and what she'd most tried to push from her thoughts.

She calmly nodded to the lackey and helped herself to the strawberries. Henrietta, on cue, did the same.

"The runners, sir? Surely that is quite a large step?"

The earl glared at her thunderously.

"And so it should be, girl! I am several hundred pounds out of pocket and I'll be damned if I am going to sit back and let that happen!" Miss Deveraux noticed that he never mentioned the heirloom necklace. Not even to his kin would he acknowledge such a calamity.

Mr. Grantham Davies walked Upper Kensington Street in some confusion. For the life of him, he could not remember whether he had been directed to number ten, number twelve or number fifteen. Whilst he looked debonair as ever in a light morning suit of flecked green, he was aware that he must present a somewhat foolish picture strutting up and down the street with a large, calico-covered canvass under his arm. Not even the comforting thought that his cravat was tied perfectly in the modish mathematique style could rid him of this uncomfortable impression. Quite simply, he was making himself ridiculous. But what to do? Short of rapping impudently on every knocker, there seemed to be no real solution to his problem.

He cursed yet again that he had called up a hackney coach to take him to the Upper Kensington address. If he had taken his own chaise, he would even now be making good his escape. As it was, he stood, a ridiculous figure, out in the drizzling rain.

The door to number ten opened. He half started in that direction when he noticed a rather buxom lady disappear within. From the style of her skirt, the cheeky wide brim of her bonnet and the extremely interesting décolleté, Mr. Davies suspected that the tender young thing must either be a bird of paradise or the next best thing, an opera dancer. That being the case, his task was now reduced to discovering whether his destination was number twelve or number fifteen.

Number fifteen had an artistic-looking knocker, but that, he knew, could be misleading. The painter probably led a drab existence, surrounded by dull, lustreless things. On the other hand. . . . Grantham cursed in vexation. The Gainsborough was getting heavier by the minute and the rain was a real concern. He hesitated only a fraction of a second before making his decision and taking the steps of number fifteen two at a time. He had quite a five-minute wait before his knocking was answered.

Curruthers held the card out on the very tip of his genteelly gloved fingers. In normal circumstances he would have closed the door in their faces. Now, however, he directed them to the servants' entrance with a faint air of distaste. His nose was tilted as far in the air as was possible, given the deplorable necessity of actually having to see as he walked.

The men were left in no doubt that they were regarded as creatures too lowly to be dignified by the acknowledgment of the butler. Indeed, they found they were exactly right in their surmise when they were released into the definitely inferior care of the under footman, who in turn led them into a small, distinctly cheerless antechamber.

Marlon grinned and winked at his colleague. They were old hands enough to take not the least affront at this cavalier treatment. If truth be told, they were somewhat amused. Gentry folk and their airs and graces! Even the servants were the top loftiest set of pontificating gudgeons they'd ever come across. It was amusing, that was what it was. Jobbins removed from his capacious greatcoat a sandwich sliced thick with butter and filled with great dollops of his favourite apple cider jam.

He grinned and broke it in half. Marlon took the proffered snack with a broad smile. Came prepared, Jobbins, that's what he did! They were waiting on the dubious pleasure of his lordship the Earl of Ingleside. They bit deep and munched steadily. They both knew it would be a long wait.

The letter had nestled in her pocket all day. Maria was shocked to think that even now, after all the years, it could have the power to make her tremble and lose the gentle art of conversation. Even her indulgent employer, herself beyond her prime, had been forced to draw her from her obvious reverie half a dozen different times that day.

Still, it was not often that she received anything remotely likely to relieve the tedium of her existence. Not that she was unhappy, exactly. She was content in a dull, unanimated kind of way. She had forged a life for herself. Under the circumstances, she had done well. Still, the letter beckoned. On impulse, she decided she would use wax candles that night. Tallows were well and good, but this once, just this once, she wanted full illumination.

"Good night, Miss Ellen, dear. You are comfortable? You do not wish a hot brick under your feet?" Her voice was amiable and a little anxious.

"God bless you, dearie! Any one would think I was at my last breath the way you pamper me so! Get along now! There is still time to make Miss Huntingdale's card party if you wish it so! She was most specific in her invitation to you."

Maria was touched by her employer's concern. Indeed, all her acquaintances were most kind.

"Thank you, ma'am, but no. I am a little tired. Besides, I have not a thing that is suitable to wear."

Miss Ellen looked disgruntled. "And whose fault is that, pray? When we have bolts and bolts of fabric lying in the attics going to rack and ruin!"

Miss Lowenthal perceived that tact was going to be required.

"Ma'am, we've been through this before. I cannot possibly accept—"

"Bah, girl! And what is to happen to all those silks? Am I to take them to my grave?"

"Don't talk like that, pray!"

"And why not? In my day we were never so prissy mouthed we could not say what we were thinking!"

Maria laughed. Her voice was suddenly melodious and light.

"You win, ma'am! I'll take the bolts down in the morning. Maybe we can make up a day dress or two. . ."

Miss Ellen smiled in triumph. Then her head sank back upon the pillow and she fell into a restful, dreamless slumber.

The two men had fallen into a companionable silence. The ormolu clock on the mantelpiece ticked the hour, but still there was no sign of his lordship. The last vestiges of the apple cider jam had long since been disposed of. Neither man appeared perturbed. In their game, waiting was an all too familiar occurrence.

The door to the anteroom clicked open. The men looked at each other, then stood up with alacrity. His lordship was announced, in stentorian tones, by Curruthers himself. He walked in without so much as a glance in their direction.

"Be seated, will you?" The door was closed behind them. The men respectfully drew up chairs close to the earl. They would need to spend quite some time eliciting details. Though they looked somewhat shifty, they were actually very good at what they did. Marlon, the more senior of the two, drew out a sheaf of papers and a long, pheasant-quill pen.

This was to be the first known report of highwaymen

operating in the area. It was distressing that it had come to this pass. The man named Jobbins shook his head sorrowfully and asserted that up until now the Inglewood countryside had been notably free of the criminal element.

He was rewarded with a glare from the earl and subsided with alacrity. Still, he thought, the spoils of London palled when people were becoming more conscious of danger, when open curricles were being replaced by more circumspect barouches, when outriders had become the vogue rather than the extraordinary. No, London was become too hot for the rogues. Well, if they sought to destroy the peace here, they'd reckoned without Bow Street.

Marlon Witherspoon gave a grim nod of satisfaction.

* * *

My dear Maria,

I do not know why I write, only that I have to. I owe you an apology. One I make too late and after too much angst has passed between us. I hope, my dear, that you are not as bitter as I am become. I hope that you have lived your life to its fullest extent as I begin to see I have not. I have many such hopes . . . all of them futile.

Perhaps it is their very futility that drives me to write. Perhaps you are a demon that can exorcise my conscience. It seems that things have not been well with me since you left. No, I will be blunt. Since I drove you away. I do not expect forgiveness. Forgiveness implies cleanliness, and I do not feel clean. It appears every considered action I have taken—and still take—has led me further down the path of self-destruction.

Queer, is it not? Well, here is a turn up for the books. I sought to wed nobly and have wed not at all. After you, my dear, the interest palled. That is not to say, of course, I do not keep my high fliers and opera dancers. I do. I am not sufficiently noble to be forbearing. To think I was once monstrous enough to place you in the same class! It is a strange world, Maria. A strange world. This missive comes by Julia. She has occasionally dropped word of

you, though often, I suspect, to her regret. I am neither
gracious nor grateful.
                    Yours ever,
                    Oscar De Lacey
                    Fourth Earl Inglewood, Baron Severn

The candle was gutted before Maria gently placed the letter
down and lay with her thoughts in the darkness. It was a hard
letter, a strange one and one long overdue. It filled her with a
sense of foreboding and at the very same time a tiny incandes-
cent, glimmer of hope. It was not romantic. It was not even
remotely pleasing. It was, however, a signal.

What she was to do with that signal would be the subject
of her thought for some days to come. She watched the moon-
light play shadows on the curtains. She heard the street crier
call the hour and the linkboys shout their services. She turned
onto her side and buried her head in Miss Ellen's soft, down
pillow. For the first time in ten years, the very proper, very
pragmatic and ever so lonely Miss Lowenthal cried.

Clementine knew it was wrong. She knew it was wrong and
yet, like a naughty truant, she did it anyway. The Lady Henrietta
would have been stunned and quite possibly exultant to see a
governess listening at a keyhole. And that, precisely, was what
the redoubtable Miss Deveraux was doing. It was annoying,
indeed, that the gentlemen had seated themselves on the far
side of the room and that her figure was such that she was
forced to endure long moments with her neck straining to reach
the proper angle. Still, she considered it worth the risk.

Knowing what the dreaded Bow Street runners were about
would be one step towards thwarting them. And thwart them
she would. She was not her proud, fiery father's daughter for
nothing. Even if she were never to have the rare, tumultuous,
dizzying joy of an encounter with her mysterious benefactor
and robber ever again, she would treat his life as if it were her
own.

Miss Deveraux clung to no illusions. Her eyes were well open to the fact that she was dealing with a hanging offence. Well, he would not hang. Those dark, impudent, knowing, mischievous, loving eyes would not know the disgrace of a hangman's hood. She'd save him if she died doing it.

It had been an inspiration, indeed, to lead the earl on at dinner as she had. She prayed he would not revert back to his original, more accurate account. That would be fatal! Almost breathless with anxiety, she concentrated her energy on hearing every nuance of the discussion within.

Unfortunately for her, the Bow Street runners were not deemed of a class the earl felt particularly inclined to impress. Whilst he did not waver from his assertion that it was three men who attacked his person, he appeared more inclined to place an accurate description of the primary suspect. He had dropped the story of the pockmarked face, she noted to her disgust, and had described the kerchief exactly as she herself had encountered it. Fortunately, the highwayman's eyes had not had the same devastating impact upon the earl's awareness as they had upon her own. He was vague on that point, describing them impatiently, as "slate green or some such thing."

Clementine shook her head in amazed delight. That anyone could not notice the sartorial, dark, depths of his eyes! Slate green indeed! She was overjoyed, though, at the error. Her pleasure was curtailed soon after by the earl's accurate depiction of the man's attire. He'd noted the cut of his inexpressibles and greatcoat, venturing the opinion that the felon was outfitted by Weston at least.

The runners exchanged significant glances at this point and Clementine's heart plummeted to the depths of her very boots. Hell and double damnation! Could he not have recalled common rags? So much harder to trace than the elegant perfection of the highwayman's garb. She must listen harder.

"Miss Deveraux!" Clementine started, high colour upon her cheeks. Lady Henrietta stared at her first in disbelief, then in gathering amazement. Her palpable sense of astonishment ended with a hearty crow of delighted incredulity. The governess was mortified! Then Clementine remembered the gravity both of her position and of the man she loved. Her qualms vanished, and she indicated that Henrietta was to be still. At least she could rely upon her for that!

An attempt to rid herself of her charge failed utterly. By dint of frantic gesticualtion to and fro, Miss Deveraux was given to understand that Henrietta was not budging an inch. Well, so be it, then. Clementine could only pray the servants had better things to do than lurk in this particular, little-used wing of the house. The spectacle they would present would be farcical. Quite, quite ludicrous.

" 'Ow much did yer lor'ship say yer be losin', then?" Marlon had quick wits and knew at once that the earl was hedging on certain scores. He was too vague by far. The man cast a knowing glance at his colleague. Yes, that was ever the way with the gentry! They wanted matters attended to, but never at the expense of a scandal. To avoid scandal, they lied.

It was the sorry lot of the Bow Street runner to sift the lies from the half-lies and the truth from those again. It was a long and laborious process, but they settled to it with resignation. Before the interview was over, they would have extracted the essence, at least, of the truth, if not the whole of it. Already, the image was taking shape. The earl did not say it, but the runners detected there was more than simply money at stake.

They would push, prod and gently pry until they had the truth of it. They were right. By the end of their interview, they knew much about a certain diamond and sapphire necklace. They swore, in their line of duty, to be as silent as the grave.

When the earl expounded at length about impudence and horse whippings and such, Mr. Marlon Witherspoon passed over a note to his junior. It took Jobbins less than a flicker of an eyelash to digest its contents. "Guinea for a groat there were not three men. One, most like. More flash than foolish." Jobbins nodded agreement. He was awake on most counts.

The earl had not made so much as a push to describe the so

called accomplices. His blustering nature would have made such a description obligatory if he had one to offer. Clearly, he had not. Marlon marked the fact down in his book. Clementine burned for a sight of the page. A heavy step on the landing distracted the ladies. Of one accord, they straightened their backs and ambled to the far side of the corridor. Curruthers had no inkling of the spectacle he'd missed as he knocked with aplomb.

"What, I would like to know, are you going to *do,* gentleman? I warn you, I am going to have a word with my good friend Sir Graham Ballantine about this! He, you know, is a justice of the peace!" The earl glowered at the runners. They remained undeterrred. They were used, in fact, to a lot more than mere bluster. Marlon could have wagered his morning pay the earl would start mentioning his connections. That was ever their way, ever their way.

"We are going to set a trap, yer lor'ship!"

"A trap?" The earl looked eager. Mr. Witherspoon was encouraged to continue. "We 'ave found, yer lor'ship, that in these instances, attack is the byword. We lure the 'ighwayman on, then we catch 'old of 'im and arrest 'im red 'anded. Red 'anded!"

"But how do you know he will return?"

"Oh, 'e always returns, yer lor'ship! Always!"

"Do you sit upon the roadside and keep watch in constant, fatuous hope?" The earl could not keep the sarcasm from his voice.

The duo did not blink. They were used to odd humours.

"Almost, yer lor'ship, almost! In some cases, though, matters may be 'urried along a bit. What say you, Jobbins me man?"

The Bow Street runner's boon companion nodded his head sagely. "Reckon we can this time, Mr. Witherspoon sir! Reckon we can!"

The earl lifted his eyebrows in little disguised contempt. "Oh?"

"The 'ighwayman always strikes twice. First, 'e surprises ya. When that is successsful, 'e gets emboldened. Nearly always they come back for a second swatch at an easy lay.'' The earl did not look gratified at hearing himself so described.

"Easy lay, am I?'' His tones were arctic.

The runners exchanged glances.

" 'Course not, your honour . . . er . . . beggin' yer pardon, yer lor'ship, sir!''

The earl folded his arms. "Well?''

"Well . . .'' For the first time the men looked uncomfortable. The earl looked resigned.

"Oh, stop fidgeting so! You have a plan. Better tell me what it is. And you can cut the theory. I am not particularly interested in the descriptions of the criminal type.''

Witherspoon decided to drop his usual speech to the gentry. A canny one, this lord. Mighty canny. He expounded, at length, on the skeleton of their plan. When he was done, his lordship was heard to grunt in reply.

Marlon, long experienced with the upper classes, took this to be assent. He stood up and made his bow. He glared at Jobbins, who belatedly did the same. They were ushered out before even the earl had the chance to tug at the bell pull.

Clementine's fingers ran over the octaves with consummate ease. She was one of those few, fortunate women to whom music came as naturally as breathing. No one present in the room—and there was quite a little party, since the Andovers and the Jenkinsons had decided to grace the evening with their presence—would have realised that Miss Deveraux's thoughts were anywhere but with the melody. In fact, she was hardly aware of her long, slender fingers as they flew across the keys, nor of the hush in the room as she weaved her own magic.

In short, Clementine's thoughts were with her dark, enigmatic stranger. The keeper of her heart, the holder of her emerald queen. The net was closing in, and there was no way to warn him. What irony that she'd been informed—ordered, one might say—that it was to be *her* chaise that acted as the bait.

She and Henrietta were to commence daily trips into Inglewood. Not on horseback, as was their custom, but in a closed, crested barouche. It was hoped that the highwayman would strike by the end of the week. Bow Street runners were to be posted night and day against the possibility it might be some other private chaise held up. The runners, from long experience, however, thought not.

The ladies had been assured there was nothing, whatsoever, to be afraid of. The highwayman would be cornered like a rat before ever he had an inkling of the trouble he was in. Caught in the act was so much neater for the judges at the assizes. He would undoubtedly hang. The runners uttered this cheerfully and with due confidence. It is not surprising, then, that sleep did not come easily to Clementine that night or any other.

Chapter Nine

"Perhaps it will be today!"

Lady Henrietta spoke the thought uppermost in both ladies' minds. The daily ride to Inglewood was becoming irksome to say the least. Thus far, to Clementine's considerable relief, there had been no sign of the highwayman. She wondered how much longer she could endure the suspense and the agony of not being able to find or talk to him when she needed him so.

Yes, she was honest with herself. She half expected that the highwayman, warned of impending disaster, would merely laugh off the danger. Her need of him stemmed from far more than a mere warning. Was she wanton? Probably. Did she care? After much careful consideration of all the facts to hand, not one whit.

She was guiltily aware that Agatha and her other faithful retainers would ring a peal over her head for this attitude. Again, she cared not a jot. "Just let me see him again!" she bargained with God. Over and over, the same litany.

"Don't let them capture him. Dear God, don't let them." Henrietta stared at her curiously.

"If you wring that reticule any further, Miss Deveraux, there will be nothing left of it!"

"What?" Clementine was recalled to reality. Henrietta's eyes danced.

"Here was I thinking I was the daydreamer! Where *can* your thoughts have wondered?"

Clementine flushed up and looked out of the window. "Are you perchance being impertinent, my dear?"

Henrietta laughed. By now, she knew Clementine too well to take affront.

"Impertinent? No! Nosy is a better word!"

"If I were to tell you the truth, your ladyship, you would not believe it. Therefore, I hold my peace."

Clementine's formal tone was joking, yet Henrietta nonetheless caught some glimmer of truth peeking out from under the surface. She decided, virtuously, not to pry. Grantham would be proud of her when she told him. She was developing restraint! He dared not call her a hoyden again. Or almost not, she reflected with truth.

"What shall we purchase today? I never thought shopping would be wearisome, but so it has become! We have exhausted the milliners, the jewellers, the mantua makers, the modistes, the library—how I wish I may see Hookham's! . . ."

"Shush, child! You shall! When you are presented to His Highness, you will stay for a while in London. I will speak to Lord Oscar about it. He cannot refuse."

Henrietta's eyes shone, her momentary petulance all but gone in the sight of this promise.

"Well, then? What shall it be today? I cannot honestly say I need ribbons, although I suppose we could stop and get a jar of cod liver oil. . . ."

"You must surely jest!"

"Just checking that you were still listening to my ramblings!" Clementine smiled. She held up her hand. "You've forgotten one important establishment."

"Which?"

"The confectioners!" Henrietta grinned. "You really *are* a

bang-up companion! I cannot think how Lord Oscar came to employ you!''

"He was at his last stand, I think! You have quite a reputation for sending governesses along their way. No one respectable enough was interested in the position, unless I miss my guess.''

Henrietta had the grace to look a little ashamed.

"But they were all such *bores*, Miss Deveraux! Any more straitlaced and they would have swooned!''

"Still, no reason to terrorise them so!''

Henrietta continued as though she had not been interrupted. "Some of them did,'' she added conversationally.

"Did what?''

"Swoon, of course!''

Miss Deveraux shook her head. The child, at least, was enlivening.

The highwayman pulled down his hat and adjusted his wig, which was faintly noisome to him, unused as he was to its use. This would be the third robbery. In his mind, the third and final one. Grantham could not, surely, wish for more? In theory he knew he need not do it. Any day he could demand of his young conspirator in arms a bottle of pinot noir 1784. From the Montagne de Reims. A most superior vintage and one that he was looking forward to enjoying.

Unfortunately, though, a point of honour still bothered him. The sapphire and diamond necklace, the most bounteous part of his loot, he had not sold. Truth to tell, he had divested Oscar of it with just that intention. When it came to the sticking point, however, he found he could not do it. Why not? Two reasons.

First, the principle of the thing. He could not be party to the selling of gems that had been in the De Lacey family for generations. Had Oscar bought the item as a trinket for one of his demi reps, he'd have had no qualms. The necklace, however, had been the property of the Countess of Inglewood by tradition. He found, strangely, he could not set that tradition aside as easily as his brother.

Secondly and more sentimentally, the necklace had hung upon his mother's neck. She had looked splendid in it. Randolph remembered vividly receiving his good-night kiss from the tall, slim, dark beauty. The jewels had flashed brilliantly, for some reason burning themselves into his memory. He'd been young then, but not too young to remember.

No, on an impulse he had kept the jewels, drawing the exact sum of their worth from his bankers in London. The notes that Vicar Oldfield so carefully locked away were not, strictly speaking, procured on their sale. Instead, they had been offered as a token of the value of the gems. He'd scribbled the note of their origin out of impulse rather than strict veracity. Randolph did not have any qualms about using his own funds for this. His intention was, after all, to help the estate of his father and his father's father.

What bothered him about this arrangement, though, was that he might, inadvertently, be playing Grantham false. If he returned the gems—and he intended to—he would actually have divested the earl of far less than he ought to have. For this reason, a third incursion into his personal fortune was deemed imperative.

Grantham, he was certain, could make no complaint. He chose the morning for his next attack, for he knew the ladies were out riding. Whoever rode inside the crested barouche, it would not be them.

Messrs. Lumsden, Partridge and Pinn, Confectioners, offered a rare selection of sweetmeats, French bonbons and candied fruit. It quite made the ladies sigh. Such a selection was all well and good, but sooner or later choices had to be made!

The green- and white-striped mints were an instant selection for Clementine, who had not indulged in such fripperies since she'd forsworn her rightful place in society. Still, the guineas in her purse jingled invitingly, and she knew it would not be long before she could draw on her first salary. Henrietta, however, simply could not make up her mind. She wavered, she dallied, she pointed Clementine's attention to this, to that, until the smile on the serving maid's face had become quite fixed.

Finally, a compromise was reached that was most amiable to the ladies and exceedingly farsighted of Mr. Pinn himself. He suggested that her ladyship take a selection of each to the daintily bedecked table set aside for the purpose and consider the trial a compliment from the house.

Henrietta was overcome, but Clementine, a little shrewder, understood that the patronage of an heiress about to come into her fortune was no small thing. She held her peace, however, allowing Henrietta to thank the man prettily and carry her treasure over to the window.

"Oh do have some, Miss Deveraux! I shall make myself sick!" Despite the words, Clementine could see her charge looked unrepentant. She smiled and sat down.

"Serve you right if you do!" Despite her severe tone, her eyes twinkled.

"Not if you help me, I won't! Want to try a sugar plum?"

"Don't mind if I do!" They smiled at each other in perfect amity.

It was gone on quarter of an hour before Miss Deveraux thought to call for a dish of bohea tea. She was just pouring, when a shadow fell over their table and a most unpleasant sight besmirched their eyes.

Sir Andrew Cunningham. A trifle overdressed, but nonetheless debonair if you liked the type. His cravat was starched so high his neck acquired a giraffe-like stature, but since this was the mode, none could think the affectation at all remiss.

"Ladies!" He made his bow, removing his gloves as he spoke. Clementine noticed that his eyes did not meet hers. Nor, when he raised Henrietta's hand to his lips, did the trace of a smile soften his demeanour.

Instead, he took in Henrietta's carriage dress of pale peach, becomingly complemented by feathers of the same shade, and regarded her assessingly. The magic of the day evaporated in an instant. Miss Deveraux noted her charge flush and became confused, stammering something as incoherent as it was foolish.

"You are not thinking of growing *fat,* my dear? Bonbons can be quite unbecoming to the complexion and figure, I am told." Sir Andrew seated himself. Clementine was too stunned to say anything.

"You are dismissed, Miss Deveraux. My fiancee will return to Inglewood under my escort." Clementine did not miss the implied insult. He meant to treat her as a common servant. Well, they would see! Her emerald eyes flashed dangerously as she dreamed up a suitably biting retort.

To her surprise, she found it was not herself, but her charge that championed her cause.

"You are impertinent, sir! Miss Deveraux has been kind enough to accompany me today, and I will *certainly* not repay the kindness by leaving her to her own devices now!"

"Will you not?" Sir Andrew played with the silver fob that had replaced the one stolen not long before. His tone was not amiable.

Henrietta blushed. Lord Oscar would haul her over the coals for insubordination, but she stood her ground.

"We are not yet wed, sir!"

"We are betrothed. That accords me the right to see you home safely!"

Clementine broke in on what seemed likely to become an undignified brangle. She was aware of curious eyes upon their table.

"It is not gazetted, sir! I would be remiss in my duties if I allowed her ladyship to travel unattended in your chaise."

The words were impeccably polite and unequivocally socially accurate. Sir Andrew, however, was no fool. He read Clementine's mind like an open book, and to that end, she may just as well have slapped his face.

You old lecher! Hell will freeze over before you subject Henrietta to the importunities to which you subjected me! She may just as well have voiced the thought out loud. His lips thinned. Well, she'd won the first round. He was a patient man. There would be more rounds to come. He stood up.

"I won't bother you further, ladies. Tomorrow, Lady Henrietta, I shall call for you at ten o'clock sharp for a turn in my curricle. See that you are ready.'' He turned on his heel and walked out.

There was an uncomfortable silence between them. The morning was quite ruined, and both agreed it was time to return to Inglewood. Henrietta made a quick selection, more as a courtesy to the manager than anything else, and the carriage was called up.

The highwayman felt his pulse quicken. He had not been mistaken. The sounds of hoofs were already barely discernible in the distance. By the pace and the fact that the groom was not sounding his yard of tin, he surmised it was neither the stage, nor the mail coach bound for Hatherington. That being the case, it was possible, if not likely, that the coach was a private chaise. He hoped it was the right one. His eyes squinted into the morning sunlight. It was hard to see, beyond the fact that the carriage was closed and crested.

He waited a while longer, scanning the horizon as he did. He did not wish to be caught by an unexpected outrider. There was none. He nodded and whispered something softly to Santana. The horse edged forward slowly, his ears well pricked up against the sound of the approaching team.

In the bushes not far to the left of the highwayman, several men waited. They were perhaps not as alert as they should have been, but then, this was their fifth fruitless day on the same king's business. They began to tire of their task. Not so two men along the roadside a small way down. Mr. Marlon Witherspoon and his junior waited in breathless patience. They were on the hunt and knew it was just a matter of time before the trap closed in on its prey. In the meanwhile, they were happy to split a mutton pie and a side of cold ham. They both agreed there was no better cook than Mrs. Jobbins Bingham. Jobbins smiled.

The Viscount Trent watched the chaise rise over the hill with calculated logic. Two minutes . . . one . . . He kicked in his heels urgently. The horse sprang to life, every muscle etched against his fine, well-groomed skin. The tension in the air was palpable. Something did not feel right. Out of the corner of his eye, the highwayman saw a farm wagon approaching from the north. He reined in before his horse had taken the ditch and appeared on the level of the road. The stallion's reflexes were precise, if confused. His ears twitched.

"Shhh. . . . Easy does it. . . ." Randolph soothed the horse, his sharp ears ever on the road. The two vehicles nearly collided, the path not being wide enough for the certain safe passage of both. The wagon providentially was filled with farm pigs grunting at every turn. They grunted now, snorting and squealing in so frenzied a manner that the highwayman took advantage of the noise to turn his beast and position himself further along the wide, deep ditch. He cursed. The new position would mean a long, fast sprint for Santana instead of an easy right-angled approach on the chaise. Still, it was an opportunity not to be missed.

The barouche had slowed almost to a crawl and the fit was prodigiously precarious. He did not know that the occupants inside both equipages were holding their breaths, each expecting at any moment to scrape against the other vehicle and thereupon cause the debacle not infrequent—but certainly lamentable—upon narrow country roads.

"My dear lord—" Once she had begun this rather uninspired greeting, Maria could think of no more to add. She grappled with herself for perhaps the tenth time that day, wondering whether a reply was necessary. Certainly, it was not *comme il faut* for a single lady to be writing letters to any gentleman not her guardian or immediate family. But then, as she wryly forced herself to admit, she was not in the first bloom of youth after all. Some would say past her last prayers, and they would have to be forgiven such an assertion. She sighed. If this point of decorum were her only obstacle she would find herself well satisfied.

Unfortunately, there were greater, probably more pertinent issues at hand. The primary of these—and she smiled at herself rather mockingly—was what to say. After all these years, his lordship had offered the apology she knew was due her from the start. The question this begged was why?

The letter of self-abnegation burned into her soul, but still offered no clues. Was he merely putting his conscience at rest? Did he wish to put the past behind him in some indefinable way? Was he simply suffering a fit of the blue devils? Or did he wish to clear the path for a future? A new future? Together? The thought was as novel as it was unsteadying.

Certainly, there was no mention of the proposal that ought, strictly speaking, to go hand in hand with such a letter of confession and apology. It was owing to her as a point of honour if not as an instance of desire. Yet, no matter how often she read the by-now crumpled missive over, she could not see words to that effect.

How then to answer? How much of her heart to reveal? This latter gave the much-tried Miss Lowenthal pause for thought. She replaced the pen neatly in its ink stand and began, slowly, to take stock. She needed to be sure that her heart, after all the years, did not play her false. So many eons of pushing unbidden wishes from her mind may have made some imprint on those very wishes. Like the farmer's wife who stores her good linen away for some occasion and, when the occasion arrives, finds it is all yellow and moth eaten.

She allowed her upright carriage to sink back a little into the comfort of the armchair. She closed her eyes, but not for one moment could she have claimed to be sleeping.

The moment was upon him. There was no stopping Randolph, Viscount Trent as he lightly touched his kerchief and urged Santana from gallop to canter. It was a time that would have lengthened the odds at Brooks's, Watier's and even White's. The notorious betting books, however, were not, at that moment, uppermost in his lordship's mind.

For an instant, Santana whinnied and looked about to stumble. With the consummate skill he was famed for, the viscount set him right. It was not a hair's breadth later that the dual forms of man and horse made their dark appearance on the country road.

The men waiting in the cool morning shadows cocked their pistols and glanced meaningfully at each other. The long wait had not been in vain. Mr. Witherspoon held up his hand and all around him silent bands of men took note. They sank back into their designated hiding places, but their eyes were watchful and wary. None more so than those of their leader, whose every nerve tingled with the exhilaration of the hunt. The man they stalked was almost level with the chaise.

Marlon again signalled, and again the men remained stationary. Each knew that it would only be minutes before the trap was sprung. Even now, an arrest could be effected with ease. Still, patience was ever the way with Mr. Marlon Witherspoon, who so far had a reputation in Bow Street for never letting even the most hardened criminal slip his wily net.

No, the runner's tactics were as well known throughout Bow Street as ale in a common taproom. If Mr. Witherspoon said, "Give him enough rope to hang himself," they did.

Unaware of the danger closing in around him, the highwayman raised his pistol straight above his Mantua beaver and fired the two obligatory shots. The carriage halted even before he had time to utter the age-honoured phrase,

"Stand and deliver."

The curtains of the barouche were cast aside before he had so much as dismounted. Inside, he caught a glimpse not of his brother or his brother's minions, but of the object of his dreams, his thoughts, his every waking fantasy. His heart quickened and his breathing altered more palpably than it had during even the most taxing of his exertions at Jackson's Boxing Saloon earlier that week.

He smiled, allowing his practiced eye to linger over the charming jade dimity and wide-brimmed bonnet, to run over the tumbling curls threatening to escape their severe coiffure.

He shrugged and grinned lopsidedly. Today it would not be guineas that he stole. Today it would be a kiss. His eyes glinted as he approached the chaise with a steady step and a decided twinkle in his deep, fathomless eyes.

"Good day t' yer, ladies!" For an instant Clementine forgot the terrible danger. Forgot all else, in fact, except the heady presence of this man, more suave, more excruciatingly debonair in his wig and top boots than ever her wildest dreams had allowed. Again, the smiling wildness of his eyes. Again, the dark kerchief that hid his features and the sensuous lines of his mouth.

Though she'd never seen his lips, Clementine knew they would be maddening. A thrill of shocked excitement shuddered through her. She blushed crimson as his eyes bored into hers with a certain impudent sparkle. He knew exactly what she was thinking! He grinned.

Henrietta, looking from one to the other, was bemused. She had set out on this errand fully expecting to be frightened, panicked, importuned. She was none of these. Instead, she sensed the electric element that passed between her esteemed governess and the common, albeit exquisitely garbed, felon she had thought to fear. She had not time to ponder this strange development, for Miss Deveraux had regained her scattered wits.

The runners, she knew, would be closing in. It could be a matter of seconds. Life and death. In the face of such adversity, her heart did not misgive her. Her actions were instinctive and took both her charge and her mysterious stranger by complete surprise.

With a swift movement, she leant over Henrietta's modest lap and wrenched the kerchief from the highwayman's face. He was startled, but his mouth was every bit as enticing as she could have wished, though this was no time for such reflections. She hissed a warning to him to be silent. The urgency of her tone startled him into brief submission. Then, turning, he understood.

At a signal from Witherspoon, the men had silently stood

up, revealing themselves as still, motionless figures in the morning sun. Even as he looked, Randolph could perceive men in drab trench coats emerge from the thickets. The sight was numbing. To Randolph, it was especially so. To the last man, they were armed.

He realised, a trifle ruefully, that for him, the game was up. He glanced at his one, true love and his heart misgave him. Her emerald eyes were flashing, her guinea gold curls were loosened and falling about her face. Adorable little curls, he noted, as his life flashed by before him. Her eyes, green, green; her lips, red, urgent, appealing. Appealing. What was she saying?

Clementine gave up words. Her highwayman was clearly dazed. Instead, she lunged forward, invading Lady Henrietta's personal space yet again in her effort to salvage the situation. She grabbed the smoking pistol from his motionless black-gloved hands. The runners were upon them as the catch of her reticule clicked shut.

"Good mornin t' yer, ladies!" Similar words to the ones the highwayman had used, but a lot less welcome. The captain seemed cheerful as he thrust the viscount's hands behind his back and began a thorough, if not particularly gentle, body search.

"Apologies for alarming ye, but as ye can see, all's well that ends well and no 'arm done! It be the nubbin'-cheat for 'im an' make no mistake!" The man made a slight bow before cocking his head in his captive's direction. The viscount remained impassive, so his captor turned back to the occupants of the chaise.

"I be thankin' ye ladies, for all yer 'elp in this business. Without the bait I reckon it wouldna 'ave been this easy." The highwayman's eyes flickered for the first time. Something in the way he looked at Clementine made her heart ache as it had never ached before.

He thought her a willing party to this foul plot against his life and limb. Well, she would do her best to prove him wrong if she died doing it! Certainly, she risked open disgrace, but that no longer seemed important. They might even arrest her for conspiracy. She cared not a whit.

She drew herself up straight and summoned every semblance of dignity she could muster.

"Alarmed, gentlemen? Why *should* we be?" Her face took on a puzzled, blank look that would have appeared slightly imbecilic in anyone other than a governess. The runner reddened, loath to point out to her her danger, yet compelled, by her mystifying manner, to do so.

" 'E be a 'ardened criminal, ma'am! No saying what 'e might 'ave done given 'alf a chance!" He looked at her meaningfully, expecting a ladylike shudder, even a swoon. He always instructed his men to carry sal volatile on their persons for just such instances.

Miss Deveraux surprised him. She neither swooned nor screamed.

"Hardened criminal? I think, sir, there is some mistake!"

The runner allowed himself a confident laugh.

"Mistake? No mistake, ma'am, or my name is not Marlon Daniel Witherspoon!"

There was a moment's silence as Clementine's green eyes rested upon him. For some reason, he felt uncomfortable under that gaze and found it necessary to shift his weight onto the other foot.

"I am loath to dispute your name, sir, but I feel I must enlighten you. You seem to be suffering under the misguided impression you've apprehended the highwayman. You have not. You are merely incommoding my brother. It is fortunate he is so good natured."

For an instant, the runner looked as if he had been struck. Then astonishment changed to disbelief in his eyes, and he regarded Miss Deveraux a little more shrewdly. So! The oh so prim and proper upper servant was in cahoots, was she? Well, he'd soon send her the rightabout! No flies on Marlon Witherspoon, there were not!

"Yer bruver, ye say?"

Miss Deveraux nodded. Her chin had acquired a degree of

hauteur hitherto unknown to her charge. Henrietta, struck dumb, was silent during this interchange. Then she looked into the face of the prisoner and was, herself, mesmerised.

The man who looked back at her had aquiline features and devilish good looks that were the exact duplicate of the subject of the portrait that hung in the gallery at Inglewood. Older, maybe, but unmistakable nonetheless. The odd, mocking gleam was more familiar even than that. She had been a mere child when he had left; yet she remembered. There could be no mistaking his lordship, the Honourable Viscount Trent.

Chapter Ten

The prisoner was silent. Clementine could only be thankful for this demonstration of good sense on the highwayman's part. She realised, of course, that as soon as he opened his mouth the game would be up. It was up to her to make the encounter as brief as possible, the necessity for speech being thus obviated. It was unfortunate, indeed, that the man could not speak pure king's English, but such was their plight and she was only too awake to the predicament. She flashed him another of her warning glances and demanded that he be unhanded.

"The error has gone too far, gentleman! My brother is over-set, as you see, with the surprise. Release him at once that he may take up the rest of the journey with us. I'm sure your men can see to the stabling of his horse." She added darkly, and with great poise, that it was the "least they could do, under the circumstances."

Her grandiose manner gave Mr. Witherspoon an instant of pause. What if he were in error? He'd never live the ribbing down in Bow Street, he'd not! All the same . . . He went with his gut instincts. They'd never failed him before.

"Bruver, is 'e? An' I distinctly 'earing pistol shots in me 'ead!"

Clementine maintained her sang froid. Lady Henrietta determined to say nothing at all.

"Very likely, my good man! The earl is forever complaining of poachers on his land! Is it not tiresome, your ladyship?" She appealed to Henrietta and her eyes were speaking.

The Honourable Lady Stenning arched her eyebrows in what would otherwise have been a comical imitation of her great-aunt Aurelia Fotheringham and yawned delicately.

"*Such* a bore, my dear! You can have no notion how often the earl has cause to speak with the gamekeepers! I fear at *least* a grouse and a partridge may have gone astray. I distinctly heard two pistol shots so I fear the worst. They never miss their aim, you know."

She sank back into her pillows, as if exhausted by the exertion of this speech. The runners looked decidedly nonplussed. The governess an accomplice, but surely not the Lady Henrietta? There must be some mistake!

"I'm afeered you be mistaken, ma'am! The shots were from this 'ere gennelman's gun!" He afforded his lordship a steely glare. He was rewarded with a stony silence.

"What gun?" Clementine contrived to appear sweetly puzzled. The runner pointed in the direction of the highwayman, then found his eyes narrowing.

"Lord a mercy, 'e must 'ave dropped it then!" He emitted a shrill whistle, and two of his underlings stepped forward. " 'Ere you! See if ye can find this 'ere 'ighwayman's weapon. Dropped it unner the carriage 'e must of!"

While the men effected their fruitless search, he turned a more than disgruntled back on the prisoner and turned to address the ladies once more. His voice took on a cajoling tone that they were not fool enough to mistake.

"Sure 'e's yer bruver, then? Doesn't *look* like yer bruver if ye'll pardon me sayin'!" Clementine cursed her bright shining locks and creamy complexion. So different from those of the highwayman! Although she could not see the colour of his hair

under the white wig, she could tell that he was dark by his
honey tones and the black stubble that lent a dark haze to his
chin. Also, she noted, his brows were as black as night. She
felt she knew every inch of his visage, and she also knew he
was as unlike her as ever he could be. She sensed his gaze
bent upon her and she looked up, her skin edged with a tiny
blush of pink. He smiled then, and the smile was dazzling. She
knew he understood. Even if it was hopeless for him, he knew,
by the very risks she took, that he'd not been betrayed.

The smile gave her courage and comfort. She lifted her brows
in disdainful contempt.

"Indeed not, sir? How very curious! It is not, however, a
topic I find preeminent at this moment, although at a future
date I might find myself more inclined to discourse on great-
aunt Aurelia's genetic aberrations. They appear to have been
passed on to me, although my brother, as you see, has *escaped*
that fate! If you will please be so good as to make passage for
us, we will be on the way. The team grows restive."

"Not so fast, young lady!" Marlon had the most lowering
suspicion he was being hoodwinked, but he could not quite
place his finger on the problem. Suddenly he whirled around
to the silent prisoner and barked out a command to speak.

Fear flashed into Clementine's eyes. Marlon saw it and was
triumphant. Miss Deveraux's world was collapsing. Still, she
remembered her father's stalwart words to her that attack was
always the best means of defence and set to with passion.

"My good man, there is no need to harangue my brother
so! I have a good mind to recommend that he write to the home
office about this. Call your men off and have done. This has
truly gone beyond the bounds of acceptability!" She paused
meaningfully.

"Admit your error, I beg you, and let us hear no more of
this unspeakable nonsense. Even as we speak, the real highwayman may be lurking at the ready!"

This last gave the runner pause. Consider his mortification
if he'd held up an innocent gentleman and allowed the criminal

to slip through the net! No, he'd still go with his gut. The prisoner was suspiciously quiet, after all.

"No one is going anywhere until the gennelman speaks."

There was a deathly hush. Emboldened, the man continued. "Speak, do you hear me, or I arrest you in the name of the king!"

There was a moment's silence in which Clementine truly experienced the sensation of having her heart stop. Beads of perspiration, quite unbidden, dampened her neck and dripped from the inner brim of her bonnet. Her hands clenched and unclenched convulsively, but her back remained rigid. Still, she was a credit to her endless training in deportment.

Lady Henrietta, too, held her peace. She would not reveal the highwayman's identity. The scandal would be too great, and she was certain the gentleman would not wish it. She wondered if she could just tamely let him be led to the gallows. It was a hollow thought and one on which she did not like to reflect. If only Grantham were at hand! He would know what was best done in these circumstances! Gentlemen, she knew, had such strange ideas of honour.

The runners advanced upon him. Mr. Witherspoon, evidently, had waited long enough. When he first laid a rough hand on the captive's arm, he received such a glacial stare that he almost released his grip. The words, when they came, were arctic.

"Unhand me, my good man. You are creasing the folds of my greatcoat. My valet will be *severely* displeased." His formidable aspect left the runners in no doubt that he, too, was severely displeased.

"Beg pardon, sir!" Mr. Witherspoon's mouth was agape, and he could no more finish his sentence than he could swallow a pig. The prisoner was looking at him as if he were no more than a stick insect, and indeed, if he were to wake up to find he was, he would hardly be surprised.

"I trust we have had enough of this rather tiresome debacle? Amusing as an interlude, I believe, but the jest wears thin."

"Sir . . ." Mr. Witherspoon stammered, and looked appealingly at his friend. Jobbins stood stock-still as though he'd taken leave of his wits. There seemed, at that moment, no more appalling a predicament to be in.

The highwayman turned to the much-maligned runner. From the pocket of his greatcoat he produced an elegant box of snuff, from which he proceeded to help himself. He appeared more absorbed in the aroma than in the sight of a dozen men at least all foolishly dangling weapons.

When he had taken his fill, he stretched out one leisurely arm and took Santana by the reins.

"Gentlemen, I will not keep you. I understand you were merely performing king's business. How you came to make so cretinous an error is beyond my powers of judgement, however, I am prepared to overlook the brief insanity for the sake of my stomach. I am told they provide a tolerable repast at the next posting station. It is your good fortune, indeed, that I find myself formidably hungry."

He swung himself onto the saddle and did not deign to wait for a response. Instead, he bestowed a broad, most unutterably dazzling smile upon the two conspirators within. With a pleasant doff of the hat, he made a passing bow.

"Ladies, I bid you good day." Then he was gone.

"Good day to you, Grantham!"

"Peter Stratham by all that's holy! Where have you been hiding all these months?"

His grace the duke looked at Grantham Davies and grinned. "Better you not know, my lad! Slipped the leash I did and a very good time I had too!"

Mr. Davies laughed merrily. "I'll wager you did! And the dowager duchess? Dare I ask?"

The duke produced a comical grimace.

"Poor mama! Nearly apoplectic she was and that's a fact! She has too strong a notion of what is owing to my consequence. A mere valet, chef and assortment of lower servants in attendance was not to her taste, and so she told me until I was obliged to return to put an end to the brangling!" He chuckled.

"And how goes it with you, Davies? Leg shackled yet?"

"Not yet, Peter! Not yet!" His eyes twinkled mischievously. 'But I have hopes. I have hopes indeed."

The duke looked at him appreciatively. "I won't ask further, ny friend. You're looking annoyingly smug as usual, but be ure I'll be scanning my *Gazette!*"

Grantham afforded him an impudent, lopsided grin.

"You may have a small wait, your grace. The lady in question has no notion of my intentions—"

"Neither does her father I'll be bound—"

"Don't interrupt!"

His grace looked down at him with an affectation of haughtiness. "I apologise, to be sure!"

Grantham was unmoved by this sally. "Good! So you should. As I was saying . . ."

Behind him, there was a murmur as a well-heeled lord tried to make his way into Hoby's before them. Mr. Davies moved inside, his grace following suit.

"Let me guess! First the bootmakers, then a trip to Weston. This will be followed by any number of excursions to exclusive establishments on Bond and Conduit Streets before you put in your illustrious appearance. Miss my guess?"

Peter Stratham, boon companion, took the wind out of Grantham's considerably inflated sails. Mr. Davies looked at his companion suspiciously.

"Are you a mind reader, your grace?"

Peter afforded him a wide but charming smile. "No, gudgeon! I'm up to the same rig, myself! You may felicitate me in due course."

Before they could discourse much more, each man found himself the solicitous subject of Mr. Hoby's attentions. The imperative matter of the manner, fit and sheen of the footwear to be purchased occupied all of the rest of the morning. The afternoon, of course, was taken up with Lobb and Lobb and a lengthy but considerably important appointment with the hatters.

Grantham Davies looked well satisfied. He had a plan in

hand that, if successful, should outshine even that of Randolph's latest escapade. A trick, perhaps, but one that he was willing to play. He declined a chair and made his way to Brooks's, whistling softly under his breath.

The ivy was sparse, and the midnight caller was certain he would go tumbling to a quick and very likely ignoble death if he persisted. Nevertheless, he tested his foothold gingerly as he edged his way round to the far corner of the west wing. How annoyingly diligent the servants were, shuttering all the below stairs windows and missing never a one! Well, he was not one for giving up mid mission, and "mission" was what he called this latest act of folly.

Two missions, actually. The thought entered his head unbidden, and he quelled it with dampening precision. He would leave a certain Miss Clementine Deveraux out of this little escapade, thank you very much! As if she hadn't suffered enough on his account, for one day.

He smiled until his boot lost its grip ever so slightly and he was forced to grasp a stray root for balance. He did not fall to his death. The thought pleased him, but not so much as the memory of his own true love's actions earlier on in the piece. She could not be indifferent to him, she could not!

The thought was as balm to his soul. He had never realised, until then, how very valuable a good opinion could be. He suddenly had an overwhelming, endless and quite unbidden desire for Miss Deveraux's good opinion. If only she did not think him a common highwayman ... What a coil! A coil indeed.

At the same moment that his lordship, the Honourable Viscount Trent was engaged in shinning the drainpipe, his young friend, Mr. Davies, was taking an easier, far less perilous path into the manse. He had considered bribing the sentry, for if the man was so lax as to indulge himself with Cornish pasties and

hip flask of some unnamed beverage, he would surely see
ought amiss in taking an unscheduled stroll through the gar-
ens at some specified and opportune moment.

On reflection, however, Grantham vetoed this plan to cut
hort his long, cold wait in the shrubbery. The man may not
e trusted after all, and he would not like his plan to go awry.
lot now that the mistress Henrietta had become involved. Well,
would be a wait then. He grinned as he looked down at his
isselled hessians and creamy pantaloons. Figure hugging and
ll the rage, he'd been assured. No need for padding in the
leek black driving coat that looked almost as good on him
s several such garments appeared on his friend and mentor,
andolph, Lord Trent.

He blessed the fact that he had learned his lesson and dressed
p warmly in a greatcoat complete to a shade. It had an outra-
eous number of capes. He was warm, this time, at least, as
e watched Curruthers do his rounds and had the dubious
elicity of witnessing the footman's evening snack.

The calico sack was suspiciously full as it lay on the grass
eside him. He had to admit, the artist had been a master. It
vas hard, indeed, to pick the difference between print and
riginal, although he fancied that Gainsborough's brushstrokes
vere slightly more subtle, his evocation of poetic melancholy
imply by the use of faint light inimitable. Still, if the portraits
vere not held up side by side for inspection, it would take a
iscerning man, indeed, to note that there was a difference.

The print had divested Grantham of a considerable sum, but
e considered the lark worth the blunt. He was scrupulous,
hough, to deduct the figure from the value of the painting he'd
tolen. He was to divest the Earl of Inglewood of a great sum
f money. The return of the print must be considered the return
f some small capital gain. He felt certain Randolph would be
n agreement on this issue.

His patience was rewarded eventually, when the guard, find-
ng his feet a trifle numbed by the cold, decided of his own
ccord to take a turn in the garden. "Doing his rounds" he
vould have called it. Grantham grinned. He had the luck of

the devil! He stepped towards the entrance, then stopped. No, this time he would have an accomplice. He drew in his breath and picked up a small, smooth pebble from one of the formal flower beds.

He aimed, keeping his ears open for the return of the sentry. All was quiet, although he fancied he heard something overhead. He looked up in surprised disbelief. Surely the sound could not be coming from outside? Outside and above? On the roof, on a patio? Surely not? He listened. All was quiet once more. It must, he decided, be a figment of his overzealous imagination.

Twenty yards from his head, his bosom friend the viscount grinned and shook his head. Grantham, by all that was holy! Up to his old tricks, he could see. He found himself rather curious as to the contents of the calico bag. Then his precarious position was recalled to him. It was only by dint of intensive skill that my lord saved himself an undignified tumble. When he had regained his foothold, he found he was close to a ledge. Merciful heavens! The window was open, contrary to his best hopes. He pushed the damask drapes aside and crawled in cautiously.

Mr. Davies aimed the pebble once more. He'd done it countless times in his youth, much to the concern of his parents and the horror of the governesses, whenever they found out. That they did not more often was a credit to Mr. Davies's enterprising ingenuity. He gave a small smile of satisfaction, then discharged the pebble with practiced skill.

Lord Randolph, were he not otherwise occupied, would have laughed. The stone missed its mark and neatly bounced off the window of my lord the earl. Or that of his dressing room, if one were to be exactly accurate. Fortunately for Mr. Davies's composure, his error was not witnessed, the viscount being greatly occupied in his intrigue.

Grantham cursed inwardly, admiring his restraint. If it were not for the cursed sentry lurking somewhere in the vacinity, his epithet would undoubtedly have been stronger and out loud.

As it was, he silently cursed himself for a gudgeon and any sort of witless fool before bending for another stone.

Time was not on his side, as he was all too aware. He could not rely on the footman not suddenly suffering an unaccountable fit of duty. He aimed with greater care this time, and the pebble hit its mark with consummate ease.

Lady Henrietta lay awake and worried. Four days, he had said! She had counted them by impatiently and knew for a certainty they were long past. Had he changed his mind, after all? Was she not sufficiently interesting to merit a second call? Had Grantham turned top lofty and decided not to embroil her in this latest adventure? She hoped not. Sincerely, she hoped not. It was bad enough having to endure the morning drives with Sir Andrew, having to watch his leers and listen to his prosy, hypocritical strictures of what he expected—no, demanded—in a wife.

It was bad enough having to countenance an engagement not of her making and entirely abhorrent to her being. But this! To be made to wait when patience had never been a virtue, to withhold confidences when she longed to confide, to stay awake night after night in case of a pebble fall that never came, this was the outside of enough! Self-doubt turned to anger and self-righteous indignation. Just wait till she got her hands on Grantham, she'd tell him a thing or two!

As quickly as it arose, the anger subsided. Hands on Grantham . . . The picture that her mind conjured made her blush in the darkness. She put her hands up to her cheeks and felt they were hot. She wished, more than anything, that he could be with her now.

Earlier, her curiosity had been the most dominant power in her brain. It had urged her to question why Grantham was doing what he was. She knew as surely as night followed day that it wasn't for the money. Grantham was well heeled in his own right, as everyone knew. Besides, she *knew* the man. He had not a mercenary bone in his body. Why, then? The only possible answer was for a lark. But why this particular lark? It was all such a puzzle.

She had determined to unravel it at the first opportunity. Now, her cheeks flushed with the warm glow of some sweet, new and very intimate stirring, she knew it did not matter. Only let him come. Dear Lord—she found herself hardly breathing— let it be tonight!

It would have astonished her how soon her prayers were to be answered. In precisely the same moment she was reflecting on her newfound feelings, Grantham was aiming his pebble. He did not have a long wait before the window was flung open and a faint flickering of light was discernible within. Not much longer before the door to the secret stairway was pushed open. Having sauntered casually into the second book room, Grantham now did the same with the passage. The door had clicked shut long before the sentry made his return.

"My, you look a regular Corinthian!"

Grantham did not know whether to become puffed up at the compliment or to take affront at the surprise in her tone. He decided, incongruously, on both.

"Do you think me such a poor fellow I cannot cut a dash if I wish?"

Henrietta thought nothing of the kind, especially as she took note of the muscled thighs shown off to full effect beneath the tight inexpressibles. She did not add to his consequence, however, by voicing these thoughts. Instead, she said rather dampeningly, that his head was in danger of becoming swelled up.

He laughed his utterly charming laugh and looked at her in such a way that all thoughts of depressing his spirits fled instantly.

A thought occurred to her, and she felt the colour rising. "Do you?"

"Do I *what?*"

Now the colour became a full, rosy blush. He had deliberately misunderstood her! He'd think she was fishing for compliments. She stood her ground, however. She had ever been a game one.

"Do you wish to cut a dash?"

He grinned.

"Stop being so provoking, Grantham!"

"Provoking? When I must have spent half a lifetime with my hatter, my tailor, my bootmaker, my—"

"Candlestick maker?" She smiled sweetly.

He stopped, exasperated.

"You always were infernally impudent!"

"That never worried you before!"

"It doesn't worry me now!"

"Good, for I doubt I can hold my tongue with you, you know!"

He looked at her searchingly. "I'll take that as a compliment. Has it been very hard, my poppet? Holding your tongue, I mean?"

She warmed as he used the special term of endearment he had fallen into the habit of calling her in their salad days. She nodded.

"Not easy, I can tell you! Especially when that infernal popinjay Sir Andrew Cunningham subjects me to his advances!"

Grantham's eyes narrowed and he felt a sudden, oversetting stab of jealousy and nausea.

"I'll kill him!"

"You cannot!"

"I'll call him out, that is what I'll do! I'll call him out and kill him." He had never been so certain upon a point.

Henrietta appreciated the sentiments, but was herself more prosaic.

"He trains at Manton's shooting gallery!"

"Confound it, woman, so do I! *And* Jackson's Boxing Saloon, not to mention fencing with Senor Du Prez—"

"You're a regular out and outer!" Henrietta could not conceal her surprise. Grantham had been quite green when she'd last spent time with him.

"Yes . . . well . . ." he flushed, the heat taken out of his manner. "Nothing like Randolph, of course. . . ."

''The Viscount Trent?''

''Yes! He is a member of the Four Horse Club . . .'' He stopped. ''I am surprised you know of him. His name is as black as mud around here.''

''I remember him well.'' She did not mention her latest encounter with the intrepid Randolph De Lacey. Grantham nodded, satisfied.

''Great good gun is Randolph! I wish . . . But no matter! We'd best get on with it.''

''You brought the print?''

''I have indeed! Took the artist far longer than the stipulated time, but, by George, you would never know the difference. Excellent!''

''I thought you'd changed your mind and decided not to come.''

''Not come?'' He looked blank. ''On a matter of honour? You're losing your marbles, Hen, and that is all I have to say to it!''

''You never mentioned it was a matter of honour.''

''Did I not? Oh, that explains it then!'' He grinned. Henrietta felt a tiny disappointment that the reason he'd returned had nothing to do with herself. On the other hand, she was more than happy to learn that the theft was caught up in one of those mysterious and incomprehensible quirks known as ''gentleman's honour.'' That term at once explained much and nothing at all. She was satisfied, however, that Grantham acted from no base motives.

''No one noticed the substitution. I could have died laughing when Sir Andrew made some remark about the painting needing a good dust.''

Grantham's eyes darkened. ''Sir Andrew again? Does he run tame in this house? How come you to be so often in his company, Hen? I had not thought you out, never mind entertaining gentleman visitors! Certainly not gentlemen of *his* ilk! Why, he has several ladybirds in town and rumour has it . . . But no! I am shocking you. Confound my tongue. I never was a one with the ladies!''

"Pooh, Grantham! Don't think to still it for me! You know I'm a hoyden!" The tone was laughingly mournful.

"That's what I love about you, Hen! You don't care a rap for the conventions. You can have no notion of the high sticklers I've had to dance attendance on. It is regular drudgery, I assure you!"

Led on by Henrietta's expression, he continued on his theme. "Some even demand poetry written in their honour." He looked a trifle sickened, and Henrietta smiled at his expression, though she could not quite like the idea of his dancing so much attendance on other ladies. He'd not yet finished, closing his eyes rapturously and issuing forth.

> "Cecilia of the wondrous eyes
> How stunning, how beautiful, what a surprise.
> I think you are gorgeous, wondrous fair.
> Your lips are like cherries and as for your hair . . ."

He opened his eyes as Henrietta started to chortle. He closed them again, much encouraged.

> "Rosalind, thou art divine
> Thy teeth so fine, thy skin like silk.
> There's none so fair, none of thy ilk.
> Rosalind thou art divine.
> Rosalind be my Valentine."

"You don't, Grantham! Oh, *say* you don't!"

He smiled. "But I *do*, your ladyship! Endlessly! Over breakfast I am forced to attend to these paltry sonnets. This one, for example, was composed over kippers this very morning!

> "Lady, I dare not utter your name
> In fear I may worship in vain.
> Thou alone hold'st the key to my heart
> Turn the lock I implore thee
> For we never should part."

"That is *terrible*!"

Grantham looked affronted, but his eyes twinkled. "Not so, my lady! Just think how clever! I attached no name, so I can—"

"—use it forever!"

He positively beamed at her perspicacity. "Exactly! It will do for Lady Sophria, Miss Pembleton, Miss Castle, Lady Jane—"

"Stop roasting me, sir!"

"Sir? You were never so formal!"

Her eyes clouded.

"No, but then I was never affianced before."

Chapter Eleven

The Honourable Mr. Grantham Davies looked as though he had been struck.

"Affianced?" She nodded miserably.

"Who the devil . . . ?" A terrible thought occurred. "Not that twisted, good-for-nothing, fortune-hunting, lazy product of an interesting connection between a shewolf and a—"

"Grantham!" There was a plea in her eyes.

"It is Sir Andrew, isn't it?" His voice, for a change, was sober. Henrietta nodded. Mr. Davies clenched his teeth. "I *will* kill him!"

Lady Henrietta, nodded positively. "If only you can, Grantham! He is supposed to be prodigious light on his feet!"

It is to be noted that she showed no ladylike squeamishness at the idea of a duel. In fact, her face had brightened considerably.

"To blazes with lightness of feet! My only concern is the scandal! I shall have to leave your name out of it, of course. I will insult him. I will slap his face with a wet kerchief, that is what I'll do! The man cannot ignore an insult like that."

The thought was borne in on Henrietta that even if her

beloved did kill his man, he would be obliged to leave England under a cloud. She frowned.

"There must be a better way, Grantham! I have no desire for you to be exiled!"

"No?" He looked strangely smug.

"No!" Suddenly, she felt shy. Though she'd taken care to throw over her shoulders a heavy, striped brocade gown on this occasion, she might just as well have been in the confection of organdie and lace she'd been caught in the last time, for the way she suddenly was feeling.

Grantham, too, felt hot. He detected, beneath the folds of her gown, the most delightful curves that began to play havoc with his reason. They had better apply themselves to the business at hand before he so far forgot himself as to apply himself to her. He picked up the package with decision and indicated that she lead the way.

Randolph cursed as he dropped from the sill to the floor of the interior. A greater fall than he had anticipated! Still, he was in one piece even if his ankle ached and his superfine needed dusting. He straightened himself and looked around.

A small room, one of the lesser bedchambers on the east wing, he reckoned. The late countess had always deplored the number of vacant rooms in the house. Not even the largest house parties were ever sufficient to justify the wastage of so much precious light and space.

She'd called for holland covers over the whole of the east wing at one time. The decision had saved a great deal of dusting, but, as far as Randolph could make out, the current earl must have reversed the edict. For here he stood, at odds with the low ceilings, small bookshelf and delicate occasional table to the right. He smiled. Fashion plates! A chamber for ladies, then.

He recalled himself. He had no business being here. If he were discovered, it would be like tragicomedy at the very worst. My lord had never enjoyed farce and did not intend to embroil himself in a real-life one of his own making. He could just imagine what the tabbies would say, trotting out all the old scandal and inventing devious and convoluted reasons for his presence on the estate. Better he arrange the business as quickly and keenly as he could.

As he stepped gingerly over the footrest and made a beeline for the door, he could not shake off the sensation that he was not alone. A sudden thought occurred to him and stopped him dead in his tracks. Surely not? But yes, there was evidence. The embers were still warm in the grate and my lord could detect, hanging over one chair, a froth of clothing laid out for the next day. Whilst his practiced eye could tell the items were not of the first stare, instinct told him they were impeccable if a trifle dowdy in colour.

He was confronted, in fact, with an amber velvet trimmed with black and a high poke bonnet of a matching but slightly lighter shade. Irreverently, he noticed that the bodice was to be tightened with dark satin ribbons. His breathing quickened. Surely not?

He, who disliked farce excessively, to find himself in the bedroom of his lady love? Having shinned a drainpipe and clambered into what he mistakenly believed to be an empty chamber? Not even he could effect so vile a scenario!

The gentle smell of rosewater and chamomile wafted through the room, eliminating all trace of its former mustiness. Further evidence of the unholy predicament in which the viscount found himself. In other circumstances, he might have found the situation a high jest. Had it been one of his notorious friends, he would have ribbed him to death.

As it was, he stood stock-still and at a rare loss. If he were discovered here with her, she would be instantly dishonoured. If he were to wake her . . . well, there'd be no telling what his treacherous, libidinous, worst self might do. No, he clearly had to get out of the chamber, and as soon as possible. He removed his boots as a precaution against waking her. As he made his way across the highly polished floor, he wondered idly and with a great sense of ill use why it was that floorboards only creaked when you wished them to be silent.

He was closer to the door, but also, now, closer to her bed. He could hear her rhythmic breathing and her soft sighs as she turned a little in her sleep. Though he could not see her recumbent form, he could just catch glimpses of the soft, shining mass of curls that tumbled from the nightcap as if they, too, demanded a rest. He felt a fool. Worse than a fool, as he stood in stockinged feet, rooted to the middle of the room.

Where, he wondered, was that top lofty, awe-inspiring man of the world Lord Randolph right now? All trace of the dashing, slightly wicked Viscount Trent had vanished. He felt like a truant schoolboy in the throes of being caught out.

It was no more than three large strides to the door handle. He willed himself to take them, but could not. His legs moved in quite another direction. Closer, in fact, to the crisp white sheets and well-starched pillows. Closer to the young woman whose acquaintance he had barely made, but who held his heart as if it were on leading strings.

The wicked Viscount Trent battled fiercely with the protective Lord Randolph. Sad to say, the viscount won the first round. He bent over the bed and felt the soft, pink skin beneath his hand. It was warm and soft as a baby's, the layers of long, blond curls a strange and striking frame for the very dark lashes that sheathed the hidden emerald eyes. The light that entered my lord's own eyes was not quite to the good Lord Randolph's liking. As he began a regular scold of his mischievous other half, the viscount bent to kiss the tips of the lady's lashes. Once, twice.

Lord Randolph was in a high panic. Outraged. As he began another homily, the viscount grappled with the urge to rouse the woman from her sleep and discover a passion quite equal to his own. There were hidden depths there, he'd known it from the start. He'd had many women in his lifetime, but none whose mind was as attractive as her indisputably delicious body. My lord's eyes darkened once more. He moved closer to the bed.

No! Lord Randolph, his better half, was becoming tiresome. And, he acknowledged ruefully, was quite correct as always. With hardened resolve he took the necessary three strides, opened the door and bent his mind to the real task at hand.

"Will I see you again? I *must* see you again!"

"I am betrothed!"

Grantham's eyes flashed. "The hell you are! I could stomach it—maybe—if it was to someone decent, someone upstanding. But Cunningham? I would rather eat dung!"

"Ughh!" Henrietta crinkled her nose. He found it charming after the ladylike airs he'd been subjected to since the start of the London season.

"I'll speak to the earl. The announcement is not yet gazetted, and though I have no title, I am surely to be deemed more eligible! My land marches with Inglewood, I am tolerably well off—*very* well off in fact." He grinned.

Henrietta grinned too. She was experiencing the first undiluted dose of true happiness that she had known for a long time.

"Quite puffed off in your own consequence, I see!"

"Quite!"

"We really should stop meeting like this." The lesser painting had been returned to its former position and the print was now hanging, for all the world, where it always had. The two had gained access noiselessly and quickly, there being no untoward incidents save for the barking of a dog that had nearly scared them witless. It had only been for a moment, however, and they were now confident the house and its occupants still slept the sleep of the deep.

"We should!"

"Should what?"

"Stop meeting like this." Mr. Davies absently nodded assent before taking up her ladyship's hand.

"You are awfully young—"

"Not too young to know my own mind . . ."

"I wouldn't like to press you. . . . ."

"I wish you would. . . ."

"Henrietta!" he sounded shocked.

"Well, I told you I was a hoyden!"

"It had better only be with me, then!"

"Quite right, Mr. Davies! You will need to protect me from myself at all times!" She glanced at him wickedly.

"Be serious! Seventeen is too young. Perhaps I should wait. . . ."

"And let Sir Andrew get in first?" Her tone, for the first time, was sober. Grantham looked at her keenly.

"I shall get a special licence tomorrow."

"Do that, Mr. Davies!" Henrietta glowed.

"It will mean a trip to London. . . . Aunt Tabitha has connections that might prove helpful. It has to be signed by an archbishop, you know. . . ."

"I know."

"Perhaps we should try for Lord Oscar's consent."

Henrietta frowned. "Hardly likely! He was set on it when he announced the betrothal."

"Perhaps I can change his mind?"

"You don't know the earl! Besides"—her voice altered in slight puzzlement— "I think the man has a hold, of some sort, on his lordship."

"I'll be bound! That scoundrel is the wiliest, vilest specimen ever to cross the doors of Watier's! If the earl had not sponsored his application, I doubt he would have been tolerated. Everyone who is anything knows him to be a cardsharp."

"You would not wish me to wed that!"

"I would not indeed!"

"Well, then?"

Mr. Grantham remained stubborn.

"I still feel you are too young."

Lady Henrietta leant forward. She felt dangerously bold and headily fast. She raised her lips unforgivably close to Mr. Davies's.

"Kiss me, Grantham."

It is regrettable that the upright young gentleman succumbed. Just sufficiently to rouse himself to the unshakeable belief that his dear Hen, young or no, had better be leg shackled. And that quickly.

It was some stupefying minutes before he slipped back into the dark of the shrubbery. He felt that his life had just altered momentously, but for the life of him he could not ponder on anything but the sweet taste of his lady love upon his lips. Mr. Grantham returned to London a man entirely changed.

Lord Randolph regained his scattered wits not long after temptation was shutoff, a heavy oak door, behind him. He made his way swiftly to the earl's private apartments, then stopped as he heard voices within. Drat! The man's valet had taken it upon himself to do a spot of pressing at the ungodly hour of past one at least.

He had called up a minion, too, by the sound of things. Poor man. Well—he sighed resignedly—it would have to be a quiet walk down to the earl's study. He wondered if it had changed much since his father's day. It felt strange to be walking the corridors of his ancestral home, the passageways of his childhood. He grimaced wryly, still bitter from a sense of ill usage. Well, he hoped Oscar had his fill of it!

His thoughts were savage as he took the padded stairs two at a time and found himself on the landing. From there, it was but a short step through the open door on the left. Well, he noted grimly, his curiosity was satisfied. Things had not changed in the slightest. The room was still hung in royal blue, although the draperies and furnishings were faded somewhat from the years of sun. Crystal candle holders still hung in a dazzling multitude from the ceiling, though the majority of tapers were unlit. The strong smell of tobacco clung to the rafters as of old. His lordship suspected, though, that cigars were probably more favoured these days. Still, such musings were not the point of this clandestine visit and he knew it.

He felt for the pocket of his crisp, form-hugging waistcoat

of French superfine. His valet would have fallen into instant apoplexy, for the lines were marred by a bulge. A *distinct* bulge! The viscount removed the offending bulge, and it glittered in his hand like a thousand twinkling stars. The dull tapers of the hall just caught the shimmer of diamonds before the drawer was opened and the gems were lost to the light for that night at least. The viscount nodded with satisfaction. Well, the evening's work was done at any rate. He suddenly felt hungry for the cold collation awaiting him at Upper Wimpole Street.

"If you would be so kind, sir, I will ascertain whether his lordship the Viscount Trent is at home to visitors."

The butler bowed briefly before divesting Mr. Grantham Davies of hat, coat, gloves and a rather peculiar-looking parcel for that time of day. If he thought it a trifle unusual that the likeable if rather harum-scarum young man, who had hitherto had the freedom of his master's house, now chose to be so formal, not a flicker of an eyelash showed it. Instead, he made his stately way to the master bedroom, where he knew his lordship still lay abed.

"What is it?" Pinkerton looked disgruntled in the extreme. He was holding aloft a much-soiled garment of Bath superfine and did not look pleased. What was worse, my lord's boots once again lacked for more than a mere lick of champagne.

"Mr. Davies to be presented belowstairs. Is his lordship awake?"

"He's awake, alright! I've just been questioning as to this . . . this . . . travesty!" Pinkerton held the jacket up in comical despair.

Masters had only one moment to breathe, "Diabolical!" before he was commanded into the room.

"Come in, Masters! I suppose you may as well scold me for entering my own home unannounced last night. You may as well *both* get it over with while I am shaving. That way, all being well, I may continue with my breakfast in peace. I have tolerable appetite this morning, and do not wish it impaired y the sight of your Friday faces."

Pinkerton threw a meaningful glance at Masters. His lordship as in that mood again, it seemed to say.

"I did not mean to scold, your lordship. I hope I know my lace quite well enough not to do *that!* However, now that you aention it, it is owing to your consequence that you be properly ttended upon your return. The drainpipe has never been, in ay opinion, a suitable point of entrance. I am sure the late ountess would concur."

Whenever the butler dragged his mother into matters, his ordship perceived the man was greatly displeased. He comosed his face into duly repentant lines, although neither of his aithful retainers were at all deceived, and promised to be better ehaved in the future. With this indisputable whopper they ere forced to be satisfied. Masters returned to offer the waiting Ir. Davies a copy of the *Morning Post*, and Pinkerton proeeded with the intricate business of the neckcloth. By the time e nodded his grim satisfaction, it was well past the hour.

"Interesting reading, Grantham?" The viscount bestowed a azzling smile upon his young friend before advancing into ae breakfast room.

"Interesting? Why, it is scurrilous! Still, I had nothing else) do whilst I was kicking my heels down here!"

"I beg pardon, but you *do* insist on arriving at the oddest ours!"

"Randolph!" Grantham was outraged. "I took especial care, iis time, to observe all the proprieties!"

"I would have wondered if you were sickening from someiing, had it not been such an ungodly hour. Don't be such a udgeon, Grantham! I'm only hoaxing you! Come eat a little Vestphalian ham. It is good for the digestion."

"I've already breakfasted."

"Then watch me! I am prodigiously hungry this morning." 'he viscount, in fact, was as pleased with the results of his latest escapade as ever he could be. The necklace was restored, his conscience need not prick him so. He was still one robbery short, but he was confident in his ability to contrive.

"I have news for you." Grantham was as excited as a young puppy.

My lord did not disturb himself. Instead, he took a long sip of hot coffee and extended his hand for one of the fresh-baked rolls that hovered before his elbow.

"Thank you, Matt. That will be all." The lackey bowed himself out.

"What may *that* be?"

"The pinot noir is to be mine!" He looked exultant.

The viscount drained his cup and looked at his young companion.

"Indeed?"

"Indeed! You can't think how *clever* I've been!"

"I am quite convinced, somehow, you are about to enlighten me."

"I am!"

His lordship sighed and put down his fork. "Well, do be quick, then! If I am to concentrate I suppose I shall have to cease eating and I am, after all, starving!"

"It shall not take long, your lordship."

Randolph grimaced at the formal address. "Oh, high in the instep today, I see."

Grantham coloured. "Oh, very well. Randolph then!"

"Much better! If I am to be parted from a bottle of the finest pinot noir from Montagne de Reims, I may as well feel I am on terms with you!"

Grantham grinned. "Oh, that you are! You'll never believe what I've done."

The viscount sighed. "I suppose you expect me to ask the obvious. *What* have you done?"

"I've stolen something of great value from Lord Oscar, and that from under his very nose!"

"Excellent, my good man. I suppose I shall have to concede." He took up his fork. "What did you steal, by the by?"

"You'll never believe it!"

Randolph, Viscount Trent sighed patiently. "So you've said. *Several* times, I believe."

Grantham beamed. "Patience, patience! Do you want to see it?"

"See *what*?" This last was a positive roar.

"I've stolen the Gainsborough oil! It will fetch a pretty penny, it will!"

My lord was silent. Utterly, utterly silent.

Grantham concluded that the blow of losing the contest had been too great. He began, now, to feel a little sorry for his mentor.

"Randolph?"

Silence again.

"I'm awfully sorry. The wine is not important, you know. . . . We could . . ."

He heard a sniffle. Then a chuckle. Then something suspiciously like a chortle. He was, understandably, a little bewildered.

"Randolph?" His lordship was now succumbing to a fit of hysterics. He was rolling in his chair in such mirth that Grantham thought him in danger of an apoplexy. Still, he had not laughed like that for many years, and Grantham, good hearted as he was, could only be pleased, even if a little puzzled.

The laughter was so infectious, in fact, that it was not long before the first snicker left his own lips. Another followed with amazing rapidity, until it seemed they were both caught in positive convulsions.

Masters was forced to close the door in outrage, for fear one of the lower staff should catch sight of their betters behaving in so undignified a fashion. He moved upstairs, the better to apprise Pinkerton of this latest lunar madness. For, as the butler said, such goings-on could only be ascribed to the moon.

Chapter Twelve

When his lordship had finally laughed his last, he handed his handkerchief to Grantham and proceeded to ask him a few salient questions.

"The Gainsborough of which you speak. Is it the portrait of my mother that hung in the red salon? The one primarily depicted in blues and greens? If I recall, the sky was romantically overcast, with just the hint of light to relieve what would otherwise be gloom."

Grantham looked suspicious. "That is the one, all right! Do you wish to see it? Masters took it from me when I arrived."

The viscount ruminated. "Yes," he said at last, "I believe I do!"

The portrait was procured, and Grantham extracted it with care from out the velvet and calico sheath. My lord looked at it a long while, touching it gently before nodding his head. Grantham noted, with surprise, that his eyes glinted with sudden, unwanted tears.

"Randolph! Are you all right?"

He smiled. The change of expression lightening his features once more.

"I am, you gudgeon! Thank you for your concern! But I have sorry news for you!"

"You have?"

The viscount nodded. "You've gone to a great deal of trouble for nothing, I find! You see, that portrait belongs to *me!*"

Grantham eyed him, openmouthed.

"You will note that my revered brother has not hocked or pawned it long ago. Why not? The answer is clear. It never was his to sell. The portrait was specifically willed to me by my late mother. It hangs in the Inglewood gallery simply because I did not have the heart to remove it from its place of honour. Also, I did not exactly feel like crawling to Oscar and begging him for what was rightfully mine. He never forwarded it on, and I never pursued it. That is the way of it."

"I should have known it was too easy."

"Perhaps." There was an indulgent smile in Randolph's eyes.

"What do you wish me to do with it?"

"It?"

"The painting!"

"Oh, that!" Randolph reflected a moment. "You smuggled it out. Is it too much to hope you can smuggle it back in?"

Grantham grinned.

"Not in the least! Consider it in the red salon as we speak!"

"It should be in the gallery, you know."

"Do you wish me to place it there instead? That would be a fine prank!"

Randolph shook his head.

"Sorry to disappoint you, my man. Better return it to its proper place. I have a mind to claim it in the near future."

"Right you are, then! I commissioned a print." He grinned. "You may have it with my compliments."

Randolph's eyes gleamed appreciatively.

"There is more to my sprig than meets the eye! Keep up the good work and I might even let you in on the secret of tying the oriental."

"Randolph!" Grantham could hardly credit his ears. The

secret of this particular neckcloth style had eluded many a frustrated dandy.

"Do not cast your hopes too high, I beg!"

"I won't, I promise you. Randolph?"

"Mmm?"

"The pinot noir is not yet yours. I still have one arrow in my bow."

"You have? Excellent! Then I need have no qualms in telling you not to rest on your laurels. You would not wish to be bested by me in this, and I intend to have a definite hand in events."

Grantham looked at his mentor with near worship.

"You are an amazingly good gun, Randolph!"

"Pooh! Spare my blushes before breakfast, I beg! Are you off to Inglewood this day?"

"No. I have private business first."

If my lord was interested in what that business might be, he showed no sign. Mr. Davies was forced to leave in high dudgeon, telling himself it was better that Randolph knew little.

The Lady Henrietta Stenning, it seemed, was to be his trump card in every sense. He smiled jauntily as he entered his hack. It was some time later that he realised he would have to return to the viscount's London address. In the excitement of all else, he'd forgotten the Gainsborough.

"I won't do it, Miss Deveraux! I won't!" Henrietta's mulish expression was back in force, and Clementine certainly sympathised, though she could hardly tell her charge as much. Henrietta sat down on one of the attractive alcove chairs that led to the stucco and marble portico outside.

"Lord Oscar insists that I wed him, but for the life of me I cannot see why I should. My portion is large, and I'm not such an antidote that I'm not likely to do *better!*" Far from looking an antidote, Henrietta appeared very fine in a pink muslin morning gown with rouched underskirt of matching tones. The slight hint of damask lace had been an inspiration, as had the notion to match the chip-straw bonnet with lace from the same swatch. Henrietta had been in alt at her own handiwork. Now she just smoothed the gown with irritated displeasure.

"Surely Papa would have been displeased? The notion to make Lord Oscar my guardian over dear Harry Tredbold has always confounded me!"

Clementine sought to sooth her.

"He probably thought his lordship's title would gain you entrée into circles Mr. Tredbold could not."

"Exactly my point! Why marry me off to Sir Andrew, a mere baronet, *before* my presentation?"

Clementine had her own theories on this, but it was not her place to say. The only thing of value she could really offer was advice. She proceeded to do so now.

"Henrietta, he is your betrothed. He has every right to make morning visits and take you for drives in his curricle."

The stubborn look returned. Clementine held out her hand. "Wait! If you truly hold him in aversion—and I can sympathise with that sentiment—you must say so at once! No one—not even your guardian—can make you marry against your will."

"You don't know Lord Oscar!"

"I know enough to be aware that society will regard him very strangely if he forces a noted heiress to marry so far beneath her! The Stennings are centuries old. You are lovely, you are titled and you are rich. Sir Andrew, if I may say so, has none of these qualities. I discount his rank. A baronetcy does not hold a candle to your impeccable lineage."

Henrietta sat up. "I'd not thought of it like that. Truth to tell, I've been a coward."

Clementine made her decision. "Henrietta, you are seventeen. A young woman with a mind, a life and a body of her own. You cannot marry Sir Andrew if he repels you." Her tone held a finality that could not be gainsaid.

"Think what it will be like living in constant company with someone you hold in aversion. You will have to be obedient to him for the rest of your days." Her eyes acquired a slight twinkle despite the solemnity of her words.

"You know how good you are at *that!*"

Henrietta smiled. "Not my best quality! Grantham has always said—"

"Grantham?" Miss Deveraux looked at her keenly.

Henrietta straightened. She trusted Clementine in a way she could not have dreamed possible. She blushed painfully.

"There is someone else ... someone for whom I have a great regard." Her tone was diffident. Clementine noted her flushed cheeks and sudden air of abstraction. She decided not to press her. There would be time enough later to catechise the young Lady Stenning on this development. She now chose the prosaic course.

"All the more reason to get this over with! Here." She held out a well-starched handkerchief from her reticule. "Sir Andrew is waiting—I imagine impatiently by now—below stairs. Go and send him the rightabout. Perhaps if you refuse him he will stop haunting Inglewood so much. His visits grow tedious!"

In other circumstances Henrietta would have giggled a little at this understatement. Now she choked back laughter in one of the multitude of handkerchiefs her governesses had forced her to painstakingly stitch. She handed Clementine back her own proffered kerchief and sniffed a little.

Miss Deveraux found herself pitying her charge with all her heart. It was one thing to be importuned by Sir Andrew, quite another to be expected to wed him.

"Tell him!" Her tone was urgent.

"I cannot!"

Clementine's voice took on its stern, authoritarian tone. She hoped it would have a calming effect on her charge.

"You can. Do you wish me to be present?"

Henrietta peered up at her through her lashes. "You'll do that for me?"

Inwardly, Clementine cursed herself for her good nature. Outwardly, she smiled.

"You goose! Of course I will!"

Henrietta let out her breath.

"Thank you! thank you! I can't stand to be alone with him. He looks at me so!" She shuddered. "I can't explain it. He makes my very flesh crawl . . ."

Clementine silenced her. There was no need for explanations. Though she'd never divulge as much to Henrietta, she knew exactly what her sensations must be. The man was more than a mere cad or "man milliner" as the highwayman had labelled him. He was actually sinister.

"Dry your eyes, then! I promise I won't leave your side. Thank the stars the betrothal has not actually been gazetted yet. Its end will raise few eyebrows among the *ton*. A good friend once advised me. 'Do it, do it now!' Sound advice, though I doubted as much at the time." Her voice softened.

"Just as sound now, mark my words. You are young yet." She took the ivory fan from Henrietta's fidgeting hands and smoothed down the ruffled overdress.

"Perhaps I should look my worst!"

Clementine was relieved by the returning humour. Her eyes glinted.

"No need, my dear! Have you thought of giving him his congé in song?"

The two ladies' eyes met. The second and third chambermaids, their ears pressed silently against the smoky glass of the adjoining room, were amazed to hear peals of laughter.

Sir Andrew lifted his quizzing glass and eyed Miss Deveraux with distaste. "I do not believe you are invited, madame."

"I should hope not, Sir Andrew. I find I do not enjoy carriage trips over much in your company. Is not that strange?"

Lady Henrietta, caught up in her own anxiety, did not notice the look of black anger that crossed the baronet's face at this rather innocuous sally. Clementine, however, was ashamed that she'd been so easily provoked. She wished to make the interview easier, not harder, for her charge.

"There has been a change of plan, sir!"

The words were Henrietta's, and her pallor was noticeable as she began the sudden outburst.

Sir Andrew surveyed her coldly.

"Indeed? And to what do I owe this sudden change of plan? To your governess, no doubt?" His look was poisonous. Clementine shivered.

Lady Henrietta stood her ground.

"You mistake me, sir! It is not the curricle ride I object to, though I admit, I will be happier indoors on a day like this."

"To what, then, do you object?" Sir Andrew's voice was icy and Clementine did not delude herself that there was no hint of threat to be detected. She only hoped the menace would not make Henrietta falter.

It almost did, but the thought of Grantham gave her strength. She needed to be free when he returned. Though she had not asked for the match, she owed Sir Andrew the dubious decency of jilting him firsthand. It would not be at all the thing for him to learn of her marriage through the *Gazette*.

"I cannot marry you, Sir Andrew!" She pulled at the hated signet that had enclosed her finger leadenly over the last few weeks.

"Here! You will be needing this." She removed the ring and placed it in the palm of her hand. Sir Andrew made no move to touch it. Instead, he said not a word. The silence was most awkward. For an instant he fingered the gold silk cravat, dotted in lavender, that he'd chosen to effect.

Finally, Clementine moved to say something bright and perky and not at all relevant to the tension of the moment. The pearls were not well received. Sir Andrew afforded her a withering glance before sweeping out of the room. Henrietta was left holding the ring in stupefied bewilderment. Clementine gently took it from her and led her up the stairs.

Lord Oscar laid down his ledger and gazed far into the distance. He wondered if Maria had been delivered his letter and, if so, how it had been received. He wondered, too, whether it was ever possible, after all, to set back the clocks. Some small part of him wished it was. How different his life would be then! Not for the first time, my lord choked back that odd stirring of remorse that threatened, at times, to engulf his sanity.

He picked up the ledger and began checking the arrears. He would need to put the rents up this quarter, and there was an end to it. If the neighbours became restive, he'd send them down to one of the magistrates. Bill Harlings could be relied upon to put an end to any unrest.

He picked up his quill and began to write. The ink blotted and he cursed in annoyance. He opened his drawer in the expectation of a large sheath of blotting paper. He found, instead, the family jewels.

Oscar was bereft of words. He could hardly credit the veracity of his eyes. Yet here it was, as bold as brass! The necklace had been restored to him. That it was genuine, there was no doubt. My lord had a discerning eye and could tell real from paste with absolute conviction. Who could have placed it there?

Not the runners, surely? If they had recovered such gems he would never hear the end of it. It would not be this silent, subtle return of priceless jewels. It did not make sense. It could not make sense. He paced up and down as his fingers lovingly threaded their way through the heavy, sparkling heirloom. He'd not sell it now. It had been unthinkable, really. A moment of madness. As so much of his life had been . . .

There was a scuffle at the door. His eyes darkened. Who could this be? Not Henrietta, surely? For all her hoydenish ways he knew she had more decorum than that. Who then?

He did not have to wait long. The door to his sanctum broke open as a breathless lackey looked apologetic and an irate Sir Andrew's eyes glittered.

"I'm sorry, your lordship. . . . I did try to tell the gentleman you were not to be disturbed."

"Without effect, I see." His lordship's tone was at its dryest.

"I want a word with you, your lordship!"

"Close the door, Higgins. And make sure I'm not again

disturbed. This day is beginning to take on farcical dimensions.''

The footman nodded and bowed his way out.

''Do take a seat, Sir Andrew!'' The sarcasm was palpable on Lord Oscar's lips.

Sir Andrew did not reply. His eyes were fixed on something glittering in the earl's perfectly manicured hands.

''Charming, is it not?'' The earl noted the direction of his gaze and laid the gems down. He did not think it necessary to enlighten the Honourable Sir Andrew in any way whatsoever. Inwardly, he despised the man, and he regretted the necessity that made him offer the Lady Henrietta up for barter. It was distasteful, whichever way you looked at it. Still, for a kickback of her capital . . . He eyed Sir Andrew warily.

''You must have some reason for breaking in on me like this! And do sit down! Craning my neck is giving me head strain which I find most unpleasant.''

Cunningham sat, but his eyes watched Lord Oscar like an adder's its prey. The earl began to feel uncomfortable under the intensity of his scrutiny. He decided to be a little more amiable, though it galled him to do so.

''Havana?'' He proffered a large, gold cigar box. Sir Andrew waved it away.

''I have business with you, my lord!''

Lord Oscar's heart sank. The man was not going to try and extract any more from him, was he? Instinctively, his hand covered the sapphires on the table. Sir Andrew noted the action, but made no comment.

''I've just come from an interesting little discussion with your ward, my lord!''

''Henrietta?''

''Indeed!'' The tone was silky.

''What does she have to do with anything?''

''Perhaps you can enlighten me, my lord! It seems my suit is no longer quite to her liking. The lady, I am informed, now holds me in disfavour.''

Lord Oscar turned pale. "But that is impossible! She is my ward and will do as I bid!"

"Nevertheless, my lord, the lady, it seems, has other ideas!"

"I'll speak to her."

"*Do* that, my lord." Sir Andrew smiled in bland satisfaction. "I shall expect a notice sent into the *Gazette* by noon today. I am beginning to tire of this business."

"She is too young! I have told you—"

Sir Andrew's eyes narrowed. "Told me what, my lord? There is no necessity for delay, and I have a mind to her dowry. You do not mind if I speak forthrightly? We do, I know, understand each other. Like minds and all that."

Lord Oscar felt as though he'd been slapped. He did not at all like feeling he had a mind in the gutter, as Cunningham undoubtedly had. Still, there was an unpleasant element of truth in what the man said. . . . He *did* understand the baronet very well. He tried to salvage what he could from the humiliating conversation.

"The kickback you mentioned from her capital . . ."

"Yes?"

"On the day she marries, her entire fortune will be transferred from the hands of her executor to your own. She will cease living off interest, and the capital will be yours to invest fully."

"I am aware of that, Lord Oscar."

"You mentioned I was to receive a lump sum from the released capital—to offset my loss of annual interest off the amount." Sir Andrew was silent. "I assume such a sum would be considerable, as the loss to me will be not insubstantial."

He licked his lips as Sir Andrew again did not respond.

"How much exactly are we talking about, Sir Andrew?"

Sir Andrew flicked some dust off his riding jacket of striped grey.

"I have reconsidered, your lordship. I have suffered consider-able inconvenience over the trollop and do not any longer consider it necessary for you to share in the proceeds of the capital. After all, you should be in a debtor's prison rather than in that comfortable earl's seat even as we speak."

Lord Oscar's eyelids flickered.

"Are you threatening me, Sir Andrew?"

Cunningham closed his lips smugly. His lordship could see from the satisfaction lurking in the man's eyes that he was, indeed, bringing the blackmail issue to light once more. He experienced an unbearable fury up in very being. Surely he had paid and paid again for that youthful mistake?

The folly of his life that had put him offside with Randolph and had poisoned him sufficiently not to offer for the woman he loved? Not to offer, that is, except the most perfidious of insults? Not for the first time, he wished he could have undone the moment he had set seal to his forgeries. There had been nothing but trouble since, there could be nothing but trouble now.

"I have promised you a fortune in a dowry. What more can you want?"

Cunningham's eyes darted to the necklace, then back to the earl's face. It was wizened, belying the fact that he was not yet even close to fifty.

"Lord Randolph will be interested, I'm sure, in the proof I have to offer! He is returned from India, you know. He is not received at Almack's or at any of the better salons. So sad, don't you think? I am perfectly certain he will be more than happy to purchase from me the proofs of your villainy. Why should he, after all, bear the shame of what his brother has done? I hear he is as rich as Croesus now. We should deal well together."

Lord Oscar closed his eyes.

Cunningham was deliberately taunting him, he knew. It was less likely that he would cut a deal with Randolph than that he would persistently torment him. Randolph, after all, could be expected to pay only once for the proofs. Lord Oscar would be expected to drip-feed the blackmailer for a lifetime. Of a sudden, his future rushed before his eyes.

A lifetime spent kowtowing to Cunningham, a lifetime of scrimping and scraping to no effect. In his heart, he knew the tenants could not sustain the increased rents any more than he could the increased stakes at Watier's and some of the more exclusive gaming establishments.

Devil take it! Sir Andrew was like the voice of the devil, luring him into more perilous waters, against the voice of reason. He stood for everything the earl despised about his life, everything he most regretted.

A little smile lingered on the demon's lips, and he yawned ostentatiously. He was in alt. He thrived on power games, on the delicious sense of leading people towards their baser selves, then dashing all hope with the lift of a finger or the curve of a lip.

Lord Oscar was being brought to discover that he would be receiving no financial reward for bringing about the marriage. The capital, if used, would certainly not go towards lining the earl's pockets! Sir Andrew laughed at the stupidity of the man who could dare hope such a thing. Then he made his first mistake. He voiced his contempt out loud.

Lord Oscar, already rendered unstable from the shock of discovering the heirloom returned, now lost all sense of decorum or reason whatsoever. In Sir Andrew he saw the incarnation of his lowest self, and he hated him for it. He loathed the laughing smirk; the cold, contemptuous eyes; the exultant abuse of power. He hated Cunningham, for Cunningham represented everything *he* had become.

He knew that if he could blackmail someone, he would. If he could extort money, he would. He knew it and he despaired. His will was weak, but this baseness of nature had never been what he'd wished for himself. His overweening pride in the earldom was merely a cover for his inadequacies. In that blinding moment he saw clearly. And with the clarity came anger.

He picked up a marble paperweight and aimed it at the smiling interloper sitting beside him. In an instant, Sir Andrew saw what he was about and sprang from the chair. The paperweight caught him, but to no effect. It was not his temple that was bruised, but his well padded shoulder. He looked about him and picked up a paper knife. There was something not quite sane about the earl's eyes. His lordship lunged towards him. It seemed a volcano was erupting in Oscar's very being and his energy was focused on one man and one only. The little, leering creature before him. He struck out wildly but was forestalled. The paper knife was plunged into his heart. He fell back, gasping.

Sir Andrew, white, could not believe the evidence of his eyes. He knew he had to leave the manse and leave it fast. He did not stop to check the earl's breathing or even staunch any blood. He simply stretched out his hand, removed from the desk the sapphires in their sparkling diamond setting and made his exit.

Chapter Thirteen

It took a long while for the Earl of Inglewood to recover.
Had it been a side sword rather than the decorative paper knife
that Cunningham had seized, it is doubtful whether he would
have survived at all.

As it was, it was close on half an hour before an under
footman discovered him in his reclining position and one hour
more before Dr. Melden was apprised of his condition. By the
time the doctor's trap was called for and the horses harnessed,
a good two hours had elapsed between the time of the injury
and the time of the examination.

It was fortunate, indeed, that Miss Deveraux was well versed
in the healing arts. The housekeeper, to whom the duties of
nursing should naturally have fallen, unfortunately was seized
by a fit of hysterics, being unused to the sight and smell of
blood. Especially blood of those belonging to the higher orders.
She was relegated, much to her relief, to the preparation of hot
possets and to the concoction of a reviving gruel.

Miss Deveraux removed the earl's outer garments and discovered the blood to have nicely congealed. Realising there
was no emergency and not wishing to alarm any further staff,

she arranged, between herself and the earl's valet, a kind of stretcher affair which was used to carry his lordship to his own quarters. Dr. Melden, when he arrived, confirmed her initial assessment. My lord had sustained a severe injury, but it was neither life threatening nor singular in nature. He would require time to convalesce, however all things being well, there was no need of too much in the way of alarm. He provided Miss Deveraux with some sound advice and nodded approvingly when he saw the bandages she had contrived.

"I have left a sleeping draught with my lord's valet. It tastes nasty, but should relieve some of the pain his lordship is bound to complain of. Do see that he drinks it, won't you?" The doctor's eyes acquired an exasperated twinkle. "I know the earl can be a trifle testy at times, but persevere if you may! Despite its abhorrent flavour, the decoction will undoubtedly help."

Clementine thanked him gravely for his help and personally led him down the stairs.

"Maria! You look beautiful!" The old lady looked at her companion in surprised delight. It had been a long time since the spinsterish Miss Lowenthal had put aside her drab fawns and greys in favour of such a splash of splendid colour.

"Come here." The obedient Maria did as she was bid, but there was high colour upon her cheeks and her eyes held an odd, secretive sparkle.

"I declare you are a beauty, my dear! A beauty!"

Miss Lowenthal declaimed, attributing her improved looks simply to the rolls of silk that had so long lain forgotten in the attics upstairs.

Her employer was not convinced, pointing out that if the Annersley twins were to get hold of the self-same swatches, they'd look just as dumpy and confoundedly pudding faced as ever.

"Madame!" Maria bit back her shocked laughter.

"Can you deny it? At my age I have no time to coddle the truth!"

"You are a mere spring chicken, Miss Ellen!"

The lady humphed in pleased disbelief.

"That may be and pigs may fly, but it is quite beyond the point! What you need, my dear Maria, is a good suitor."

Her companion blushed becomingly and began to scold.

"I am quite past my last prayers, ma'am. Come, no more of this midsummer madness. Is it not strange how a simple frock can lead one to such silliness? Perhaps I should retrieve my old navy...."

"Don't you dare!"

"Then have done with this suitor nonsense, I beg. Come. I believe there is a good deal of sunshine on the front porch. Let us see if we can find a patch that exactly suits us."

So saying, Miss Lowenthal took up her needlework and her little bag of oddments. If thoughts of the earl lingered in her mind overlong, she did not say, and Miss Ellen had the grace not to ask.

Grantham Davies was feeling very out of sorts. Despite an impassioned plea to the Archbishop of Batten-on-Sea he still had been unable to convince the man of the necessity for a special licence. Such a thing, he'd been told in no uncertain terms, was not to be granted lightly. The lady in question was young, and without the knowledge of her guardian, the clergyman could not find it in him to deem the chosen course appropriate. He suggested—kindly, of course—a suitable period of reflection, then an attempt, on Grantham's part, to follow the protocol in such cases. In short, he was to approach the Earl of Inglewood for Henrietta's hand.

Mr. Davies was not pleased. Even worse, he was obliged to spend a dreary afternoon taking ratafia with his great-aunt Tabitha. Ratafia! He could only hope the *ton* did not discover it.

He revised his plans for the following week, cancelling several matters of estate and business, one ridotto and one invitation to a masked ball. That done, he took up the Gainsborough masterpiece and ordered the horses back to Dunstan, his country estate. It would not be unfair to state that his servants felt he had run a little mad.

Lord Oscar opened his eyes and groaned. His head felt liable to split in two, and he had a strange, burning discomfort in his chest. These he felt moderately able to cope with. What he could not cope with, however, was the determined young lady in the muted green cambric who so persistently tried to push some vile-smelling potion under his very nose. Each time his feeble hand struggled to remove her noisome presence, he felt her draw a little closer. Her voice, he had to admit, was rather pleasant. Somewhere between a caress and a cajole. Her actions, however, were to be deplored. He knew of a certainty he did not want to taste the proffered liquid. She, it seemed, was too stubborn to take no for an answer. They were destined to stalemate.

The impasse was ended only because the sight of her stubborn, uptilted chin was too exasperating to endure much longer. With a curse he took the mixture and downed it in one draught. One gulp was enough, he told her fiercely. It crossed his mind that she was poisoning him. He relaxed. No poisoner could look so truly concerned. Or so delightful in the little chip-straw of amber. She was smiling now, he noted with a kind of grim satisfaction. Good! Perhaps she would fetch up something a little more sustaining than the nauseating broth that had been set before him. Was the world run mad? he wondered.

Miss Deveraux smiled blandly.

"Gruel, my lord! It is good for you!" He smothered a curse.

"Am I to be henpecked and mollycoddled in my own home?"

"Indeed you are, my lord." She smoothed down the pillows. Henrietta was indisposed, the result of her oversetting interview with Sir Andrew. When her abigail informed Miss Deveraux that she was sleeping, there had been no real cause to awaken her. Indeed, Miss Deveraux suspected that a strong case of the hysterics had been very timeously averted, and she could only be glad.

Lord Oscar, then, was entirely at her tender mercies. They were tender, and despite his lordship's professed loathing, Clementine suspected he was secretly glad of the little extra attentions that came his way. Certainly, he now appeared more human than he did set against the severe backdrop of his lordly office and dining halls. Clementine was led to hope that his heart, after all, might not be solid granite. Still, it was early days. Too soon to tell.

"After the dinner I will read to you. Do you have any preferences, my lord?"

"Dinner? Dinner? Do you have the temerity to call this unadulterated codswallop dinner? I have known the lowliest of servants to eat better than this broth! It is no more than vilified water, I tell you that now!"

Clementine forced two spoonfuls upon him. "Hush, my lord! I am perfectly certain your housekeeper would not be glad to hear you speak of it so!"

"Glad?" He glared at her. "She should be lucky she is not dismissed! By God, I've got a mind to give her her marching papers over this!"

"She was only following my directions, your lordship. The broth has strong healing properties, being concocted of all manner of healthful herbs and remedial ingredients. There is arrowroot, aloe—"

"Stop!" If my lord could bellow he would have. As it was, he was feeling comfortably mellow and more than a little drowsy. Clementine nodded in satisfaction. It would not be long now before he slept. Dr. Melden had suggested this as the wisest possible course.

His lids drooped, but every so often he would jerk himself awake and furrow his brow fiercely as his eyes came to rest on the governess-companion. She was not alarmed. She merely placed her hands in her lap complacently and smiled sweetly.

Drat the woman. Despite himself, the earl smiled. He'd lost a lot of blood and felt as weak as a kitten. For the first time in a long time, however, he felt a rush of warmth and kindness. His last thought, before he fell into a dreamless slumber, was that his wits must be growing addled with age.

The Earl of Inglewood slept peacefully. His watchful guardian remained at his side long enough to satisfy herself that there was no danger of fever or infection. When the snores deepened to positive thunder bursts, she felt able to hand over care to the respectful valet who stood in attendance. She outlined briefly where she could be found should her services be required. Then, with a lingering backward glance, she closed the door firmly behind her.

Miss Deveraux was a normal young woman. Being that, she also had a curiosity. That natural curiosity was now allowed to make its headstrong appearance, tired of being held in check whilst more important matters took precedence. What had happened in the earl's inner sanctum? One did not come by such a wound by accident, or for no reason at all. Had the house been burgled? Had my lord been maliciously attacked? Had he had some mad seizure and fallen upon the weapon? She discounted this last as a ridiculous rambling, but her interest did not abate any more for the foolishness. Why had the footman been the first to discover my lord? Surely, if it had been accident, the staff would have been notified earlier? Who had been closeted with the earl?

A terrible shiver of fear ran through her person. Not the highwayman, surely? And yet, the possibility rose before her with a terrible ring of truth. Perhaps because she was so aware of the man, her thoughts ran to him even when they least wanted to. He was known to countenance robbery with equanimity. Murder, too? She could not believe it. And yet . . . there was Lord Oscar abed and no more explanation than a garish wound to tell the tale.

Of course, there was Sir Andrew . . . A more appealing prospect, certainly. But what possible motive could he have? A man does not run a knife—albeit a slender paper knife—

through a man because he is jilted. Or does he? The psychological makeup of the baronet was notoriously complex. Clementine did not wish to press the earl for explanations, but she did feel she had a right to think—if not to express—her concerns. With difficulty she strove not to take the stairs two at a time. When she finally reached the landing, she made unhesitatingly for the first door on the left.

"Lord Trent! Delighted to see you!" The beauty that gushed at him and all but wrinkled his new Savoy buckskins did not notice the uncompromising set of his lips and the slight, haughty stare he directed at her person. Had she been slightly more sensitive to exquisite social nuances, she would have shrivelled up like an insect at the derision she commanded.

Instead, she opened up her ebony fan and fluttered it delicately in his face, all the while hoping that my lord's eyes would fall to the buxom cleavage tucked into the confection of silk and spangled lace. My lord did notice, and his lips curled all the more. Miss Bradshaw may be a diamond of the first water, but it was well known she was on the catch for a husband and none too choosy where she found him.

My lord found he did not quite like to be in the category in which Miss Bradshaw's attentions placed him. It seemed he was rich enough and titled enough to be the object of any marriageable miss's attentions. He was, however, de trop at Almack's, Benton's and all the most de rigeur of places. He had not enjoyed being given the cut direct by the Countess Lieven or the curtest of nods by some of the high sticklers. The fact that he was welcome at the Prince of Wales's pavilion at Brighton irritated rather than soothed the noisome condition. His royal highness was not noted for social discernment and was often quite vulgar in his choice of guests.

What, then, was he to do? Clearly the world had forgiven, but not forgotten, his youthful folly. He could live with that had he ever committed the terrible indiscretion of attaching his father's name to promissory notes. The fact that he was inno-cent, however, made acceptance all the harder.

It was not something he could simply refute. No one ever asked to his face whether he was a forger. Word seemed to waft around intangibly, always beyond the grasp of libel or even scurrilous gossip. My lord squared his shoulders. He would have to, he supposed, resign himself. But he would be damned if the ambitious Miss Bradshaws of the world would find him easy game. He bowed curtly, but did not take leave to kiss the lady's hand. Some of the hawkeyed dowagers watching the exchange passed meaningful glances. It seemed Randolph, Vis-count Trent, was to be as top lofty as his father before him.

Maria Lowenthal dropped the carefully scripted missive into the wastepaper basket. Though the lettering was exquisite, she could not help but be dissatisfied with the words. What, after all, does one say after the lapse of so many years? Certainly, she had no wish for a repeat of her youthful and shamefully humiliating folly, but by the same token, she would give much to cry end to the sorry business once and for all.

The earl had flirted with her, raised her expectations, romanced her. She had allowed herself to be enslaved, closing her eyes to the differences in their rank and fortune. She winced when she remembered the well-meaning words of warning from people, who, as it turned out, had known better. But no! In her first bloom of her youth, Miss Maria Lowenthal had fallen madly, surely and with deep sincerity in love with the Earl of Inglewood. It was the type of tale that should have had a happy ending. Should, but did not.

The selfsame evening she had anticipated a proposal, she'd been offered a carte blanche. It had taken some moments before the meaning of the earl's smiling words were born upon her senses. She was to have her own carriage, the finest team of horses available even to impeccable ladies of the *ton,* a town house to command as her own, a staff of servants and all the clothes, baubles and trinkets her feminine heart could desire. There was no proposal of marriage.

Instead of being offered the moon, she had been offered a cluster of rather dim, inconsequential stars. Even now, her face reddened at the thought. He must have thought she'd been courting such a suggestion. It had taken her years to appreciate the high price he'd placed upon her favours. Greater men were less generous, it seemed, with their paramours. She flushed again. Paramour! Well, after all these years, her virtue, at least, was in tact. She wondered if the misery had been worth so trifling a fact. Perhaps not. She took up the earl's letter again.

At first glance, there was not much to be detected in the huge, dark, room that imposed itself upon the senses with awesome grandeur. The leather-bound volumes touched the ceiling, and the room was encased all around with a small landing and a balustrade of oak. Nought seemed amiss or even mildly out of place. Clementine doubted whether the volumes were ever taken down and read, since they retained a curious uniformity that seemed to indicate they were bought simply as an adornment for the study. In this, as it turned out, she was correct. The previous earl had ordered them with the house, and Lord Oscar certainly had little truck with the Greek and Latin tomes.

The desk was tidy in its own way, although Clementine noted ash in the heavy venetian glass piece set there, presumably, for this purpose. There were none of the formal flower arrangements to be found at various strategic sites around the rest of the Inglewood manse. A couple of papers lay across the desk, together with a quantity of red sealing wax and a bottle of ink.

For the first time, Miss Deveraux had qualms. She should not be in here, privy to the earl's private papers and correspondence. There was nothing, after all, she could find that would enlighten her any further as to the general mystery of the situation. She picked up a heavy, marble paperweight that had somehow made its way to the floor. As she was closing the door, she noticed a wisp of gold spotted with lavender. It was caught on the frame of the open window. She breathed a satisfied sigh. It had been Cunningham, then.

The redoubtable Miss Lowenthal made her decision. With the choice had come not peace but a burning, glowing zest and energy. Peace she'd had in surfeit. Now, she knew, the moment had come for her to take a more masterful control of the ship that was her life. She would no longer be content to sail with the wind, charting unknown territory simply by default. The wind and the waves would no longer rule her, she would tame them with her will and her actions and her spirit. If this was at the expense of going against the current, of challenging the tide, then so be it.

Her employer sighed gently when she heard the news. In her heart she was not sorry, only thrilled that her dear Miss Lowenthal was finally to have a chance at happiness. If she sighed, it was for the times they would no longer share, the books she would no longer hear read in that gentle, tender, perfectly modulated voice. She'd always suspected that beneath the demure, dove grey petticoats, there lived a creature of passion. Passion, once unbridled, can never be tamed.

Miss Ellen, wise at her five and seventy years, knew this and was glad.

His lordship's eyes fluttered open then shut once more. He found the strange half-light curiously peaceful and peace was not an emotion he'd properly understood or even hankered after in the past. Though he was feeling sufficiently restored to sit up and possibly resume some of his more rigorous pursuits, he decided against the exertion.

The turmoil in his mind was immense, and the outer peace of his environs acted as a strange, unknown foil to his inner demons. He lay like this for quite some time, only dimly aware of passing shadows and quiet footsteps in his chamber. When it was warm, he felt the coverlets eased; when it was cool, he felt the feather-light down of a quilt laid upon his person. Beyond that, he was conscious of little else beyond his own thoughts and senses.

None of it pleased him. He'd known for a long time that he was little more than a bully and a coward. Add to that the folly of overweening priggishness coupled with the inability to see beyond the hauteur of rank and he felt he had the sum total of himself as a man. Unpalatable stuff. It was no wonder that the shadows lengthened and he still made no move.

The picture of Sir Andrew Cunningham, contemptuous, conniving, vilifying . . . that was a common thread that kept recurring in his deepest insights into himself. Sir Andrew witnessing his foulest moment . . . blackmailing him . . . holding it always above his head like a sword of Damocles . . . despising him for his weakness and knowing—nay, *profiting*. Sir Andrew, Sir Andrew . . . leering at his ward, insinuating, suggesting with a mere inflection, a raising of the brow . . . It was intolerable!

The earl was sweating profusely and those in the sickroom stepped forward to bathe his head with cool water. He knew nothing of it. All he knew, with a sudden shock of clarity, was that the baronet must be quashed. He must be destroyed so completely that the alter ego in the earl's inner depths would die. Inevitably and unmourned.

The earl's eyelashes flickered. Clementine moved closer, but could detect no visible change. His lordship's thinking had turned from a murky purple to angry hues of red slashed with orange lightning. Now it changed, suddenly, to a crisp, clear, uninterrupted shade of subtle sky blue. Where there had been anguish, there was now calm. And in the calm, the earl could see clearly.

He would remove, forever, from Cunningham's hands the tool the man used to destroy him. He would write a confession of his youthful sin and absolve his brother completely. Randolph would be returned to the bosom of society, and that, for him, would be enough. He found he'd lost his taste for the London set, in any event.

An earl's robe, though ermine, is nevertheless cold unless dignified by human warmth. The earl had felt no such warmth and had found that his rank palled as a result. What had once been important was no longer. He could bear, he found, to be given the cut direct by his peers. It would be no more cutting than the pain he'd hidden in his breast for so long.

When the confession was signed, all Cunningham's "proofs" would be as worthless as the paper they were written on. The man would not benefit by that means again. More importantly, he would not be allowed to corrupt the innocent. Lady Henrietta would be presented, as was her right. In the fullness of time she would no doubt meet an appropriate life partner and they would wed. The loss of the interest off her capital did not even feature in his musings.

Maria . . . Well, that was too late. She would not have him. Surely, if she would, she would have written by now? Or had he been too ambiguous? Had he again made the mistake of insulting her by not making his wishes plain? He half suspected he had not because he was terrified of rejection. Well, since this was to be an epiphany in his miserable existence, he would expose himself to her.

God knew, he'd doubtless inflicted enough pain. Maria would wear the sapphire necklace. Whether she wed him or not, she'd have it. It was a fitting token. Destined for his countess, returned as if by omen. It was a sign. One that he would not, any longer, ignore. And Randolph. Yes. Randolph, too, deserved a letter. The simple blue changed to crystal white.

He opened his eyes and was startled to find his curtains drawn back and the fresh, sweet smell of jasmine and violet entering the room. Light did not filter through the drapes. Rather, it engulfed the room, for Clementine had had enough of the gloom and had ordered the windows opened and the filmy barriers pulled back. My lord blinked. Then he called for a pen and some of the firm, creamy, crested paper he kept in the top drawer but one.

Chapter Fourteen

"By God you are not going to dish that sop up to me!" The earl's introspection was at an end. Clementine noticed that his pallor had abated and her patient was sitting upright in his sturdy, wooden rocking chair. He was still garbed in his dressing robe, but she deemed it would not be long before he would be calling for his demented valet.

That gentleman had been at pains to point out that the earl required a bath and a shave. Miss Deveraux was unmovable. She would see the colour returned to his cheeks and the veal at least half-eaten before she allowed him to be fussed over.

"It is not sop, my lord! It is perfectly delicious veal."

"Sop!"

Miss Deveraux took leave to ignore him.

"Veal, braised with excellent farm-fresh vegetables and served up as—"

"Sop!"

"—stew!" Miss Deveraux was undeterred. She smiled at his lordship sweetly and patiently. She proffered the spoon. He glowered, but took it up.

"See, sir? Delicious!"

"Humph!" Miss Deveraux did not appear to see anything amiss in this rather unpromising response. Rather, she smiled inwardly and was emboldened to offer the earl a draught of tart, fresh lemonade.

His eyes boggled. "Lemonade?"

She nodded. "Made up by cook this morning. I have a receipt that my own mother—"

"Take it away!"

Miss Deveraux pushed her falling locks back into place and smiled complacently. "It is good for you, you know!"

The earl thought, of a sudden, that she looked charming. He was just regarding the beverage with a curious mixture of horror and resignation when there was a small tussle in the hall way.

Clementine heard the lackey's expostulations, heard Curruthers's throat being cleared, she heard, in fact, the most bell-like accents demanding to be taken up to his lordship. All this she heard at the back of her mind, for her attention was taken up with her patient. He had paled again, and his hand had set the lemonade back on the silver salver with a tremor. Before Miss Deveraux could decipher this strange turn of events, the sturdy, oak door burst open.

A lady, not in her first bloom of youth, perhaps, but nevertheless elegant in a cherry-striped morning dress of finest silk, burst in on the tableau. Her wide, merry eyes took in the footmen, the valet, the earl, Miss Deveraux and the dinner in a single, sweeping glance. For an instant, her heart faltered. Had she been foolish? Was the young lady with the bright tumbling curls the earl's latest cher d'amour? Had she burst in on something singularly embarrassing and certainly not quite proper? She regarded Clementine closely. No, the lady was dressed modestly and demurely. She had been long enough about the world to know. The unknown lady smiled. All doubt was gone.

"My lord!"

"Maria?" The earl sounded incredulous, but there was no mistaking his joy.

"It is I, sir! And just in time, I see!"

"In time?"

"Well, you're not honestly going to eat that pap, are you? And as for the lemonade . . ." She gave a comical grimace of disfavour. "My lord!" Her hands rose to her face.

"Yes?"

"You are not in your dotage, are you?" For the first time ever, Clementine saw a smile creep into the earl's crusty, world-weary eyes.

"Not in my dotage, ma'am, but under this scurrilous, bossy, overbearing young woman's thumb! She demands I drink that . . . that—"

"Codswallop!"

Clementine started. "I beg your pardon. . . ."

The lady's eyes were shining with amusement. Lord Oscar settled back in his chair. He didn't know when he'd enjoyed himself so much in years.

"Codswallop, ma'am!" The lady repeated herself with satisfaction. "Lemonade for such a fine gentleman? Never! Curruthers!"

The door opened immediately and the lady winked.

"See to it that my lord has a fine bottle of chateau neuf uncorked." Her voice was authoritative and the butler found himself bowing.

"Oh and Curruthers . . ."

"Yes, ma'am?"

"If my lord still has those fine barrels of brandies laid down . . ."

The butler understood her meaning at once. "I'll attend to it straight away."

"I'm sure you will."

As the door shut behind him, Clementine could see her services would no longer be required. She tiptoed out of the sickroom, but she was certain that if she had trod like an elephant, she would not have been heard.

* * *

Lady Henrietta stared out of the long, curtainless window. She could see far over the flowerbeds, beyond the formal gardens with their central fountain and on to the hills. At the farthest corner of her eye she could catch a glimpse of the river, although not the exact point from which the highwayman had made his dramatic entrance. She was thoughtful now, more serene than she had been for quite some time.

The frightful scene enacted with Sir Andrew was over and done with. She knew with a positiveness that made her quite cheerful that he could threaten her no more. Grantham loved her and Grantham, after all, was all she cared about. Well, Miss Deveraux, too . . . It amazed her how close she felt to a woman she had so recently come to know and love. Her feminine perceptions were heightened by the personal experience of love and its heady sensations. She knew of a certainty that Miss Deveraux was a lady suffering similar pangs.

But with such a man! Lady Henrietta had not been so cosseted that she did not know of Randolph's reputation, nor of the disgrace that kept him in constant exile from Inglewood. That he was Randolph, Viscount Trent, was not in dispute. She knew as surely as if he had made a formal bow and introduced himself that day.

But Miss Deveraux? Henrietta was certain she did not know. Well, it was not her place to enlighten her. Randolph would no doubt do so in his own time. If he did not, he'd have the Lady Henrietta Stenning to deal with! A formidable thought.

It was some time later that the Viscount Trent received the astonishing missive. That is to say, the contents of the letter did not surprise him, for they stated in plain blue and white exactly what he had always known. What astonished him was the fact that the letter had been written at all and in such tones! Lord Oscar must have had a change of heart, indeed.

His eyes misted over as he read and reread the smart, frank

epistle. He could not have asked for or expected a more humble and self-effacing apology. Nor would he have demanded of the earl the sacrifice that he had taken upon himself. In short, the man had sent a notice in to the *Gazette,* raking up past history and exonerating Randolph entirely. A big gesture and one the brother, inclined of late to think ill of Oscar, could not help but recognise as brave.

He finished his repast of kippers, thinly sliced bread and fresh eggs. The ormolu clock showed it was just gone half eight, a most unfashionable hour for breakfast, but then, the viscount had ever been one to flout convention. He did not need to pull the bell pull twice. A footman, clad in the simple Trent livery of silver on royal blue was directly at hand.

"Have my chaise called round, Brewster! A trip into the country, I think. I'll take the greys. They are a well-matched team and could do with an outing. Have the stables see to it, if you will."

The lackey bowed. "Very good, sir!" He hesitated a moment. "The ostler will be wanting to know about Santana. Do we keep him stabled or—"

"Stabled, I think. Perhaps Anders can take him for a canter in Hyde Park before reining him in for a grooming. He will know what to do, never fear!"

"Yes, my lord." Not by a flicker of an eyelash did the footman reveal Anders's likely reaction to this sweeping presumption. He'd spent days speculating on Santana's sleek condition. The horse had been prodigiously well exercised and not by him. Some strange quirk had also led my lord to sell a gelding of similar temperament and looks. He shook his head. Properly harnessed, they could have made as high-stepping a team as ever the viscount could have wished for. Still, it was not his place to complain. Or not to his lordship at all events.

The lackey knew Anders's curiosity was fit to burst. He also knew, by the look in my lord's eye, that now was not the time for questions. He bowed and made his way below stairs, where he summoned a long suffering underling—the sixth footman to be exact—to make his way to the stables. He, Caldwell Brewster, did not consort with grooms.

"Two young persons to see you, my lord!" Curruthers's face was as disapproving as his tone. My lord was instantly apprised of the fact that his visitors were not ladies or gentlemen of quality. The butler's singular use of the term "persons" confirmed this fact.

"Send them away, my good man! I am not at home to visitors, nor yet to tradespeople." He smiled gently at Miss Lowenthal and inclined his head at Miss Deveraux. She took this to mean he considered her family and was well satisfied. It was dramatic how the man had mellowed in so short a space of time.

The butler cleared his throat. "I am aware, my lord. The persons, however, demand to see you. They say they will wait all day if that is what it requires."

My lord's eyes furrowed.

"Impertinence! And who might they be, I wonder?"

"I rather think they are runners, my lord." The butler uttered the words with distaste.

My lord's brow cleared. "The Bow Street set? Well, send them in, Curruthers! Send them in!"

The butler bowed, every vestige of his being displaying disapproval. There were a few words exchanged in the lobby. Clementine could hear the low monotone of the butler imparting, no doubt, little pearls of wisdom to the gentlemen he regarded as little more than insects. Finally, the long-suffering officers of the Bow Street court were ushered in.

"Yer honerable lor'ship, sir!"

Clementine wondered with faint amusement what excuses they were going to proffer for not having apprehended the highwayman. They must be suffering a severe blow to their pride. Had she not been so closely connected, she might have found it within herself to feel sorry for them.

Marlon Witherspoon effected the most startling bow the earl

had ever seen. He imagined that even the Prince Regent would not before have seen the like. The man's head was practically touching his toes, an unfortunate situation, since it sent his second in command headlong into the room.

Miss Lowenthal hid a smile beneath her long, slender fingers. The tableau looked to her like high comedy. Marlon would have something private to say to Jobbins Bingham, he would! Tripping in and over him in such a thoroughly ramshackle way! But to business.

The pair assumed portentous faces, and of a sudden their audience took note that these men were, after all, the famed runners of Bow Street.

"I assume you have something urgent to confide to me, gentlemen? You appear to have gone to extraordinary lengths to acquire this audience!"

Marlon nodded solemnly. "Indeed, your lordship, indeed! The butler is a rare curmudgeon, he is. A 'igh stickler, I'd say! Right 'igh!" He coughed. The earl felt the need to prompt him further.

"I assume you did not seek me out with a view to dissecting the character of my manservant?"

Even Marlon Witherspoon could detect irony when it stared him in the face. He reddened and took out his sheaf of notes. They looked, to the meticulous Maria, like a regular bumble bath. She vouchsafed not a word.

"Yer Lor'ship! Ye drew our honourable attentions to the fact of a 'ardened 'ighwayman roamin' and pillagin' 'ereabouts." He looked significantly at Jobbins, who took notes and nodded his head seriously.

"Well, I 'ave to say after extensive investigatin' and such like, we 'ave the criminal under arrest." His eyes were triumphant. Marlon Witherspoon, after all, always delivered the goods.

My lord was as startled as anyone. Miss Lowenthal looked benign and slightly blank, Miss Clementine Deveraux seemed about to swoon. Of course, she did not. That prosaic lady pulled herself together and started summoning her inner strength. If the highwayman was under arrest and awaiting trial, she would move heaven and earth in his defence.

She would beg—no *oblige*—Mr. Oldfield to divulge the secret of the extraordinary charity that had recently come the parish's way. The treasures would be identified and the whole of England appealed to in the man's defence. It would be a wonder, the beneficence of a man who called himself a highwayman yet divested himself of all his gains. She would fight and she would fight and she would fight—without end.

The runner continued. "Some time ago, little matters came to our attention. The gennelman we was seekin' was not in the common way, ye understand. No mention of 'im in any of the usual watering 'oles. No sign of 'im or 'is wares in any of the shifty coves we watch as a matter of course. We runners are watchers and waiters and listeners." He announced this proudly. "But do yer think we 'eard ought? No, not a thing! Not a thing, I tell yer, yer lor'ship!" His voice dropped to a whisper, and his eyes acquired a mysterious, secretive glaze. "Almost . . . almost as if such a man did not exist . . ."

"Impossible, I say! My sapphires—"

"Exactly so, yer lor'ship! I be comin' to that!"

"We noted that this 'ere 'ighwayman seemed mighty well aware of yer movements, ye ken, and we set to wonderin'. Why did 'e not 'old up the stage, which would be more profitable? Why 'ere of all places? 'E seemed to 'ave a good knowledge of 'ereabouts, where to position 'is 'orse, where to 'ide. Such like, ye ken?"

The earl nodded. He was singularly interested.

"My friend Jobbins, 'ere. 'E imagines 'e might 'ave a talk with some of the locals like. Some don't allus come forward with what they see, they don't. We wanted to know if anything was seed 'ereabouts. Anything suspicious like."

"And?"

"And it 'appens a farmer, a dairymaid and an ostler all catched sight of the man. A black 'orse, 'e 'ad. As black as night."

"So?"

Marlon licked his lips in satisfaction. This was the piéce de résistance he'd been waiting for.

"So the 'ighwayman was a gennelman, me lord!"

Clementine clasped her hands together convulsively. She had suspected as much when the highwayman had astonished her and the runners with his impeccable accents and haughty air of breeding. She felt the room sway, then righted herself.

"A gentleman?" The earl prompted Mr. Witherspoon. He found the man annoyingly tedious, but the words made sense. Only a gentleman would have returned something he recognised to be a family heirloom. The mystery of the necklace was in a fair way to solved.

Mr. Witherspoon surveyed the room to see the impact of his words.

"Get on with it, man!" The earl's tone was sharp.

"We 'ad our suspicions." He looked at Clementine intently. She flushed and dropped her lids.

"No proof, mind. No proof!"

"And so?"

"And so, we decided, beggin' yer lor'ship's pardon, to set watch 'ere on the estate. Strange comin's and goin's too, I might add."

The earl glared at him. It was lucky the Lady Henrietta was not present or she would most like have had a fit of apoplexy. It appeared the insouciant Mr. Davies's movements had been observed. The runner cleared his throat.

"'Owever! We waited to be sure of our man. We waited till we 'ad proof and then we acted! Us at Bow Street do be quick, yer ken! We do indeed!" He smiled his satisfaction. Instead of the rapt attention he expected, he found himself nigh on throttled. Mr. Jobbins Bingham took a nervous step backwards, too.

"*Tell* me, you wretch!"

"Ay! No need to 'andle an officer of the king's court so! Yer lor'ship, this day we appre'ended no other than Sir Andrew Busby Cunningham, heretofore residing at Upper Kensington Street, Lunnon, but latterly a guest in yer own 'ome!"

Clementine's hands stopped shaking and she unclasped them in sheer, bewildered relief. The earl's eyes looked fit to pop out of his head, but he, too, was silent. The runner, somewhat daunted by this reception of his news, cleared his throat and elaborated further.

"Sir Andrew's mount was our first inkling. Black as the night, she is!" He added this significantly. "When we catched sight of 'im climbing out of yer window in broad daylight we were puzzled, but not completely convinced." The earl nodded his head, amusement dawning. He knew well why Andrew escaped through the window, and it had nothing to do with highway robbery. Still, by the skin of his teeth the man was not a murderer. Certainly, he was a blackguard and a blackmailer to boot. He decided to listen to the runners without comment.

"There's no sayin' what the gentry morts be gettin' up to fer larks. Why, only t'other day we mistook this 'ere lady's bruver for a 'ighwayman simply for the way 'e chose to dash 'is 'orse right into the chaise." He smiled at her apologetically. "We took care not to make the same mistake twice. We followed 'im."

"You followed him?" The earl was astonished.

"We did. And do ye know what, yer lor'ship? He went straight to one of the pawnbrokers we watch in the city. Tipped us the double, they did! Caught 'im red 'anded with the goods. And a voucher for a channel crossing in 'is pocket!"

"You recovered the money? The promissory notes, the—"

The runner's face clouded. "Not them, yer lor'ship. Reckon we were too late for that. But this. We recovered this." He put his hand in his pocket. The only person in the room not surprised by what he withdrew was the earl. He had suspected as much halfway through the long and winding narration. When the man drew from his pocket the shimmering sapphire necklace, the earl stupefied everyone, even himself, by throwing back his head and laughing. It was the heartiest laugh of quite some time.

* * *

The Gainsborough was returned to its rightful place in the red salon promptly and without further alarms. As it happened, its return was something of an anticlimax, for Grantham happened to discover that his mother's abigail had an interesting attachment to the Inglewood fourth footman. It did not tax his brains overmuch to produce a passable tale of surprise, prank and friendly wager. A few coins passed scrupulously down the right hierarchy of under servants did the trick. The original for print switch was effected with ease

Mr. Davies had a number of good reasons for not repeating his by now tedious nightly vigil. Firstly, though every vestige of his being longed for Henrietta, protocol demanded he act the gentleman. He had never before been a one for protocol, but when it came to the reputation of his future wife, his actions did give him pause. A prank is one thing. To involve another, albeit willingly, in the madness, was ungallant. More than that. It was unthinkable, and he was a cad to have succumbed to temptation even once.

Which brought him to the second reason. Temptation . . . The thought of Henrietta in her night apparel was enough to overset any man's nerves. No, the best course was to transact the business with the servants and wait upon the earl in the morning. So thinking, he penned a delightful missive to his good friend Randolph, Viscount Trent. He enclosed the print and ordered it sent to his address. He was certain his lordship would appreciate the gesture.

Chapter Fifteen

"Compliments of the Viscount of Trent, sir!"

There was a faint hush in the room as Lady Henrietta looked to her guardian and Miss Lowenthal set down her needlework. Only Miss Deveraux seemed unconcerned as she closed the pianoforte she'd been playing and clasped her hands in a demure, governesslike fashion.

The events of the previous day had been enlivening, if a trifle tiring for the convalescent earl. He had himself accompanied the runners to have words with the Honourable Sir Nathan Mathews, magistrate. The contents of the discussion had not been revealed, but it seemed that the case against the highwayman was officially closed. Clementine could only close her eyes and give thanks to heaven.

She understood little of the exchange that had taken place between the gentlemen from Bow Street and my lord the earl. All she knew was that her highwayman, her own dear highwayman, was not now under threat of the hangman's noose. She cared not a whit what happened to the prisoner. As far as she was concerned, Cunningham had his just deserts. She could only pray the real highwayman would lie low and not decide to strike again. The thought afforded her some anxiety, but since she did not know the man's direction, nor yet his name, she was forced to simply wait and hope.

Lady Henrietta was looking at her strangely, and she vaguely wondered why. Not being acquainted with the viscount, she suffered none of the qualms of the others when his card was brought up for inspection. She noticed Maria move closer to the earl and smile with firmness—or was it reassurance? Perhaps, even a degree of pride. All these thoughts flashed through her head in an instant, for it was not long before the earl was ordering the lackey to usher the man in. If Clementine adjusted her skirts and eased out a ruffle on her sleeve, slightly, it was a curtsy she would have performed for any invited stranger.

She determined to make her curtsy to the gentleman, then usher both herself and Henrietta out. It was high time, after all, that she began earning her keep. Henrietta had the dancing master coming up and before that, quite a number of mathematical problems to decipher. Clementine was a firm believer in the value of a good scientific grounding. Any young lady destined to be mistress of a considerable establishment should be educated so. It was unfortunate that they were, in general, not.

She was determined Henrietta would not fall short, despite the risk of being labelled a "bluestocking." If her social graces were sufficient, after all, her mental agility need not be considered a concern. She shook her head at the ridiculous predicament in which the gentler sex found themselves. To be forced to hide one's intelligence seemed a shocking thing indeed, for without that valuable commodity, one became exactly like Lady Pringle, Mrs. Patience Ramstead and Lady Tiffany Marbridge. Pretty little dolls with not a thought to share between them. Still, it seemed gentlemen's preferences ran to the shallow, and she would be doing her charge a disservice to gainsay it. Well, then, an appointment with the milliner in the morning!

The Viscount of Trent was announced. He entered the salon to the sound of a light creaking of the floorboards and little else. The earl and Miss Lowenthal were struck dumb. So, it appears, was the Lady Henrietta. To Clementine, the silence seemed almost a tangible reality. Then the moment was broken.

"Welcome, my lord, to Inglewood." The earl's words were stiff, but Clementine could see tears in his eyes.

The gentleman did not execute the traditional bow. Instead, he walked across the room and took the earl's hand. This behaviour was exceptional, indeed, and Clementine found herself looking up. Looking up and into the strangest pair of eyes she'd ever seen. Into their very depths and beyond.

A wave of tremendous anticipation tingled through her. His smile was familiar and cherished, ice white in lips of burnished red. And yet . . . the hair was dark, making his angled jaw seem so much the younger. There was not a patch on his face, and she'd particularly remarked one on the upper lip. The hair was curly rather than powdered straight. It was a puzzle.

"Randolph . . ." The tone was anguished.

"Say no more, brother. Past is past and you have made amends."

Miss Lowenthal unclasped her gloves of pastel pink. The road, she knew, would not be easy, but Oscar was over the worst. For the first time in ten years, she felt proud. What *mattered* it that there still had been no talk of a marriage between them? She knew, with a sudden certainty, that her place was at the earl's side. For better or worse, as hostess or wife. She still could not bring herself to think the word "mistress." Old habits, it seemed, died hard.

Clementine's heart was pounding in her chest. She waited eagerly, breathlessly, for some sign of recognition. None came. Only the lazy, admiring, silently inquiring glance that flitted a trifle insolently over her person. She had to admit, however, that the insolence was tolerable when coupled with the wide, sensuous smile that seemed to warm the very corners of her mind. He turned now to her charge.

"Lady Henrietta! You have grown to a fine lady! I swear I would know you anywhere!" He was gracious as he bent to kiss the hand of the little tumbling hoyden he'd known so very long ago.

"And I you, my lord." Her voice was quiet, firm, slightly mischievous and pregnant with meaning. My lord took her hand and held it a trifle overlong. Clementine almost saw a wink pass between them, but the instant passed so quickly she was certain she'd been mistaken.

"May I introduce to you Miss Maria Lowenthal?" The earl stretched out his hand and touched her fingertips briefly. Randolph stopped an instant, looked from his brother to the lady, then bent over her hand. "My felicitations," he softly murmured in her ear. Since none of the others quite caught his words, they were surprised to see the lady flush quite so deeply. She gently extricated herself, however, and motioned to Clementine.

"Miss Deveraux, your lordship. Lady Henrietta's governess-companion. I hope also to say a good friend." She smiled, and Clementine saw, of a sudden, that she was quite beautiful. Her face was plain and pale, her carriage most correct, yet first impressions were misleading. When she smiled the warmth transformed her otherwise bland and gentle features.

"Delighted, Miss Deveraux." The gentleman executed a formal bow and she noted that his waistcoat was figure hugging, his breeches were immaculate and clearly not in need of padding. She coloured as she thought this immodest thought, but then, of late, confronted with eyes of deep, dark chestnut, she'd regrettably had thoughts less modest.

She supposed she must have performed the requisite curtsy, but for the life of her, she could not recall it. All she could recall was the man's eyes, boring into her being and undressing her as he spoke. Yet he was everything that was proper. He was solicitous and caring. He'd drawn Henrietta out and was even now making her smile. The easing of the tensions in the room was sensed by all. My lord seemed bent on pleasing, and please he did.

Clementine relaxed and watched as the curves of his mouth flickered in half amusement, as his hands, large and strong, cradled a malacca cane with careless grace. She watched and she wondered. Surely two men could not arouse such wanton stirrings within her breast?

The Viscount Trent and the highwayman must be one and the same. And yet, and yet . . . No sign, no hint, no moue of recognition. Admiration? Undoubtedly. Attraction? Possibly. She hoped so, though she knew it to be immodest in the extreme. Quite apart from being patently unsuitable, given her diminished social position. With a distinct sinking of the heart, Clementine realised that if the highwayman and the nobleman were one and the same, her chances of lasting happiness were doomed.

His family and title would demand more from him than marriage with a mere upper servant. With Quicksilver John, the choice of condescension would have been hers. She'd have taken it gladly, accorded the chance. The impeccable viscount was another matter. Condescension would all be on his part, and she doubted whether she could bear it. The thought rankled as no other had.

Why, she had been content enough not even to wonder at the highwayman's name! And why had he not acknowledged her? His eyes had not revealed the merry yearning she'd seen and hungered for in the past. He'd been impossibly correct! Maybe, after all, there were simply two people in the world very much alike? Altogether too endearing for her own comfort? Impossible! And yet . . . she hoped not. Her happiness hinged on there being two gentlemen of equal stature, equal attraction and equal nobility of face and bearing. She sighed. The time had come for her to take her leave.

"Lady Henrietta!" Her charge looked up inquiringly. She was throwing languishing glances at the viscount, glances Clementine knew to be not at all the thing. In fact, the minx was batting her eyelashes in such a teasing way that Miss Deveraux could detect the hint of a smile quivering on his lordship's mouth.

For an instant she felt she could not bear the pain. She was not jealous of Henrietta, who she knew simply to be playacting the coquette. She was merely envious of the melting glance the man cast her way. There was none of the aloofness in his demeanour with Henrietta that was in his polite attention to herself. She bit her lip, then lifted her head brightly.

"Time for your lessons, my dear. You will need to change, too, for Monsieur Rosseaux arrives in just under an hour."

It was at the tip of Henrietta's tongue to say, "Bother Monsieur Rosseaux!" She was having a fascinating time exactly where she was. She would have been intrigued to know the viscount was harbouring the same feeling exactly. While it was sweet torment to be in the same room as Clementine and not cling onto her skirts and bury his head in the deliciously warm, sweet-scented clefts that protruded demurely and ever so subtly from her square-cut bodice, he felt it would be all the more unbearable were she to take her leave.

She did and with firmness. One look at her governess and Henrietta's protest died upon her lips. With a meekness quite unusual to her mischievous self, she made a full society curtsy and allowed herself to be ushered out.

"It is settled, then?" The Earl of Inglewood looked hesitant. Maria thought he'd aged considerably, but then age had also tempered him with wisdom and humility. She liked him the better for it, though she knew it would be a hard road. Since the notice in the *Gazette,* not quite so many doors would be open to the lord as had been of yore.

Part of her was still shocked at the disclosures. The man she had loved—still loved—had committed an undeniable wrong. Still, he was now ready to pay the price and she was ready to pay it along with him. If he was a gentler person for the experience, she could not complain. The impulse that had made him throw over his pride like a discarded mantle was the same one that had led him back to her. She could not but be grateful. Happiness had eluded her for a long time. She would grasp it now and forge a reality that was not dependent on the good will of the *haut ton.* She was past all that. So, she felt, was the earl.

"It is settled." Lord Randolph extended his hand and the earl took it, though his own trembled. "You are perfectly certain you wish it this way? You are more than welcome to open the house in Chichester Street, if you will. The holland covers will need removing, but I believe all the staff—"

"No! I am resolved. I have presumed on you too much already. Lady Henrietta will be best sponsored by someone of untainted reputation and rank. Now that mine is somewhat murky . . ." The earl's voice trailed off in unlooked-for confusion.

"Think no more of it, Oscar! The tabbies will have a field day of it for a week, no doubt; then the next one-day wonder of society will arise to transplant the whole sorry scandal!" Randolph's voice changed.

"Believe me, they are not worth agonising over. I became quite used to the cut direct. It actually came to amuse me! Silly old toads! I wouldn't take it to heart."

"No. I won't. Not now that Miss Lowenthal has been restored to me." The earl looked across at the statuesque woman sitting just across from him, and he came closer to contentment than ever before in his stormy, rather brittle life. She lifted a brow, and he smiled.

"Lady Henrietta is best with you. You were always fond of her and I have a hunch you will be able to manage her quite tolerably well! She was a trial to me in her youth, but I believe I mishandled her. Sometimes spare the rod and spoil the child is not so true, after all."

"I find it never so, Oscar!"

The earl sighed. "She had a good taste of my whip on several occasions, but I swear she has never been so obedient as now, when she is indulged. Is not that strange?"

Randolph smiled. "Not strange at all, Oscar! What filly prefers a flogging to a gentle coaxing at the bit?"

"None, I suppose. I have bungled the thing, Randolph! And her father most particularly wished for her happiness. I am fearful she will fall into the hands of a fortune hunter. Sir Andrew was a narrow escape."

Lord Randolph did not need to say, "No thanks to you." The words hung in the air as clearly as if they had been spoken.

"I wish to make amends. She may draw on her allowance to the fullest extent. I will send a letter of credit to her banker.

"And Miss Deveraux?"

The earl looked blank for an instant. The viscount found his hands were strangely clenched. He dropped them to his sides and resumed his nonchalant air of easy breeding.

"Shall I dismiss her? Lady Henrietta will not need a governess now that she is to be introduced to society."

The viscount's heart missed a beat. "By no means! She is more in need of guidance now than ever. She requires a companion, and Miss Deveraux will suit most admirably."

"You believe so?" The earl sounded relieved.

"Certainly! She will, however, require funds. I would sponsor her myself, but it is not at all the thing."

"No indeed! I shall organise an advance on her salary."

"A handsome advance, if you please! By the time the ladies have done with their fripperies and parasols . . ."

"I understand you!" The earl's face lit up in a sudden, exasperated grin. "Don't I know it." The highflyers I have pandered to in my day . . ." he stopped, shocked at the stricken look upon Maria's face.

"Miss Lowenthal, I must beg your pardon! I do not know what came over me to speak so, with a lady present in the room."

Maria nodded, not trusting herself to speak. She was shocked. She had come to think Lord Oscar cared for her. Perhaps not yet sufficiently for marriage, but certainly with a renewed modicum of respect. If he did, though, surely he would not flaunt ladies of easy virtue in her face? True, he had apologised . . . .

His next words took her breath away.

"I would like the ladies to be dispatched to London directly, brother Randolph! There is another reason I shirk my responsibilities. The best I have yet to offer for so doing."

"And what is that?" Randolph asked, but his perceptive eyes could guess.

"I wish to travel abroad. Society is not as strict in Europe as it is here in England. The scandal will not long embarrass you, Randolph, if I am not here to eternally add fuel to the flames."

His lordship acknowledged the truth of this with a short nod. The earl turned to Maria, at his side.

"I wish it to be a grand tour! I never had the benefit of one, you know! Rome, Athens, Paris . . . all the great places of the world."

Miss Lowenthal's heart stopped. The earl was looking directly in her eyes, and she forgot the presence of the viscount and of the footman who was removing all traces of their repast.

"How perfectly splendid, my lord! I have read so much about these places. They seem wildly enchanting. Do you travel for long?"

His eyes remained upon her. "As long as you wish, my dear. It is, after all, to be *your* honeymoon trip."

She stood stock-still. Randolph could see from her sudden pallor that this turn of events was news to her. He wondered whether it was just the travel plans that were novel, or whether he was witnessing his brother's own inimitable way of offering a proposal of marriage. It appeared that it was the latter, for he was now removing his signet and giving it to a startled Maria for safekeeping. Well, let his brother woo his wife as he wanted, however strange.

He had other notions of the way to woo, and he was eager to set them into play. Eager indeed. The emerald queen was warm against his heart. In comparison to the real thing, however, she was cold. He longed to thread the wisps of Clementine's hair through his fingers, to gently caress her fingertips, her fluttering chest, her warm, enchanting mounds of softness. He longed to trace his fingers across her mouth . . . He would, by God. And soon, or he was not a man.

"Felicitations, brother!"

Maria's eyes were shining. He brought himself back to reality and bowed over her hand. "He is fortunate, it seems! Keep him well in hand, Countess."

Tears stung the backs of Maria's eyes. Though she had read the line many times, she now knew what it meant. Her cup truly spilled over.

It was with a faint inclination of the head that the viscount withdrew.

His exit was blissfully unnoticed.

Monsieur Rosseaux was even now mincing his way down the ballroom floor, adjuring Henrietta's correct and upright body to be a little more supple, to *melt* a little more freely. He emitted a few choice French oaths, then extended his arm once more. "Tempo, tempo!" He tapped time with his foot and made the sorry Lady Henrietta begin again. Normally, Clementine would have laughed and sympathised. Now, she felt badly in need of air. She decided to play truant. They could work on the steps without her contribution at the piano.

Monsieur Rosseaux was hardly a threat to Henrietta's virtue. Indeed, since he'd taken up a small Bordeaux tablecloth and wrapped it round his thin, gangling waist, he looked more ridiculous than ravisher. The man seemed bent on teaching her hoyden ward feminine charms. By Clementine's reckoning, they'd be at it till the dinner gong at least.

She excused herself, pleading a headache. Henrietta seemed suspicious, outraged at being left to her fate. Then she looked at Clementine and nodded.

"Best leave me to this beastly lesson, then!"

Monsieur Rosseaux seemed ready to protest, but she cast a sunny smile at him and the protest died instantly on his lips, though he looked a little uncomfortable.

Clementine made a mental note to teach her charge the delicate art of manners. Then she looked at Monsieur Rosseaux's tablecloth skirt and had to conceal a small chuckle. She closed the door, to the sound of the metronome relentlessly clicking on. Henrietta's sighs could be heard down the corridor.

A quick splash of cooling water upon her face was preceded by a change into a walking dress of russet merino. It was sprigged with green and did wonders for the healthful glow in her eyes, but she was not concerned with such matters at this particular point in her life.

She hardly had the energy to drag a comb through her hair before lacing her stout half boots of burnished kid. A bonnet was found, but its ribbons were tangled and its shade of olive green could hardly be considered a tolerable match. Still, Miss Deveraux made a very becoming picture as she set off across the fields.

Her mind was in a turmoil. It seemed that she had built up an image in her mind of a man who belonged exclusively to her. Perhaps that image was the type of schoolgirl fancy with which many young ladies are smitten, a fancy cast off when reality awakened them with a start. Calf love.

She believed it was called so and had heard that it was as prodigiously fast at leaving one as it was to impose itself upon one. She hoped so, for she had not slept for weeks on end and the nights had strange, unwholesome effects upon her normally compliant young body.

Unwholesome? No, perhaps that was the wrong word. Virtuous? Decidedly not. Clementine grinned. She had never been one for virtue. Perhaps that was why she and Henrietta understood each other so well. Still, none of this was to the point. And the point was, the handsome Viscount Trent and his tantalising, teasing, dazzling, yet unrecognising smile.

Was he set on tormenting her? Did he truly not remember their conversations, their unspoken communications, their electric touches and lightning glances? How was it possible not? And yet, so it seemed. Perhaps the man had a twin. A speculative look appeared in Clementine's eye. A twin was out of the question. But a brother?

One born to the manor house, another a little farther from it? She had always thought the highwayman to be a by-blow of a nobleman. Why not that of the late Earl of Trent? It would explain his education, his familiarity with the parts and his exact similarity with the current viscount. He was, after all, fairer, he had an intriguing patch above his lip that the viscount had not. . . . It was possible. It was just possible.

It would explain why only Inglewood chaises were stopped, why Inglewood lands were benefitted. . . . The man felt he had rights by blood if not by birth.

And who could blame him? It was not, after all, his fault that his parents had entered into an illicit union. It was common enough here-abouts. Clementine was not too missish to close her eyes to such facts, though Agatha would have scolded her outrageously. The idea appealed. The more she thought of it, the more she became convinced.

Inactivity was anathema to her. Now she decided to expend all her energy tracking down the elusive Quicksilver John. Quicksilver John! He could, at least, have presented her with a more believable name. She decided that her first tack must be the Vicar Oldfield. She half suspected he knew more than he was telling. If anyone knew anything about village life hereabouts, it would be the vicar. She changed direction and clung to her hat. She had no qualms.

When Mistress Clementine got a bee in her bonnet, the servants were well used to the outcome. They could lament, reproach, scold and even, at times, spank. Clemmy on a mission was unstoppable. Now was one of those times. At breakneck speed the very proper governess began to run.

Chapter Sixteen

"Stop the chaise!"

The groom responded to the authoritative tone and slowed the horses. Too late! The front right stallion reared slightly and the village miss that had been hurtling towards them at an impossible speed tumbled breathlessly into the ditch.

The viscount was not amused. His team was perfectly matched and even tempered, but a disturbance like this was unsettling. He was of a mind to let the wench struggle, but his chivalrous self emerged triumphant. He was not too noble, however, to deny himself a glimpse of the beguiling French lace that peeped out from the muddle of skirts, petticoats and halfslips. The maid must have a rich mistress!

His eyes darkened as he caught a glimpse of shining, unmistakeable gold. With a sigh he handed the reins to his groom and murmured that the chaise must be returned to Inglewood. No need for the man to ogle. Besides, if his trip was to be delayed, it could not be in a pleasanter manner.

"Mind your horses, sir!" Miss Deveraux was furious. It did not occur to her that she was at fault, for it seemed to her that running in a country meadow should not be encumbered by such hazards as oncoming traffic. True, there was a trace of a track where the grass did not grow so high, but that the man should choose such an offbeat path when there was a perfectly well-worn road just minutes away beat all that was rich.

She glared at him and felt the pulse nagging away at her chest. Her breathing was ragged and strangely quick. She could only ascribe it to the anger that she must now be experiencing. And that quizzical look! How *dare* the man? She was furious, furious! She put her hands to her cheeks and knew them to be uncommonly warm. There was only one explanation. Her anger did her credit.

The viscount watched the tumultuous thoughts cross her expressive face and was not displeased. A small smile flickered into view, then disappeared as swiftly as it had come.

"Apologies, Miss Deveraux! I had not thought to come upon you on this road."

"Apparently not!"

Even to Clementine's outraged ears, the words sounded rude. She felt she ought to apologise, but the heat was still in her cheeks and her chest and, indeed, strangely and not unpleasantly throughout her entire body. She stood still and looked at the man wonderingly. She did not apologise, for her very sensations told her that she was still angry.

It did not help when he sent the chaise back and chose to walk at a leisurely pace beside her. Her gown was muddied, but that was not the real cause of her confusion. The cause—and she had to admit it—was to the right of her side. His hand was dangling inches from her waist and she was very conscious of the fact. So conscious, in fact, that she neglected to notice that her deplorable bonnet was lying unmourned in the ditch and her hair was shockingly unpinned.

The viscount did not neglect to notice. Nor did he neglect to detect the considerable pique she must now be feeling. Almost he could catch glimmers of a pout. He smiled inwardly. If he had the power to so overset her nerves, he was well pleased.

For an instant the urge to reach out and envelop her in his

arms became an overwhelming, unmasterable force. His lips tightened as he sought to still his pulses and the urgent desires that coursed through his blood and drove him half-mad with unleashed energy. He stopped, and Clementine, sensing the change in his mood, stopped too.

His eyes were dark, and the heat from his body, close but yet not touching, was very apparent. Miss Deveraux misunderstood the gaze. She saw coldness and contempt. She felt the intimate heat of derision.

The reality of her situation suddenly struck her. If the highwayman was some unnamed sibling, then this gentleman— albeit beguiling in the extreme—was a stranger to her. He must think it odd indeed that she'd be roaming the countryside and leaving her charge unchaperoned in the hands of a French dance master. Worse, he must think her wanton. She stood before him, without benefit of bonnet or maid. Is it any wonder he was staring at her thus, bereft of words and coolly silent?

Her anger evaporated in a minute to be replaced by the more uncomfortable sensation of embarrassment. She bent to hide the flush on her smooth, high-boned cheeks. It was all the viscount could do not to pick her up and cosset her for all the world like a man besotted. And besotted he was; of this there could be no doubt. Still, he could not have her residing in his town house in the role of governess if his manner towards her showed the slightest degree of warmth.

Already, it was stretching the bounds of propriety, since she was undoubtedly beautiful, eligible by blood and by no means past her last prayers. Still, she was not in her first bloom of youth, and her servant status made the situation more conformable with public expectations. He must never, not by the flicker of an eyelash or the inappropriate tremor of a hand indicate he felt anything more towards her than as an employer, the surrogate guardian of young Henrietta. If he did, she would be ruined. Scandal, he knew, was no pleasant thing. He determined not to inflict it on her.

The alternative, one he had been toying with for many a day, was more satisfactory to his daydreams, his yearnings and his every waking fantasy. He could whisk her off out of hand and marry her. That would leave the tattle mongers in a tizz, but it would still not do. The season was just beginning and Lady Henrietta needed to be presented. When he married Clementine, he did not want her distracted with the necessity of organising balls, attending ridottos, overseeing Henrietta's apparel, chaperoning her from pillar to post. He would want her all, to himself.

When Henrietta was well settled and established, there would be time enough. Besides, the interlude in London promised well for further acquaintance. He knew his own feelings on the matter, but not Clementine's. It was no secret on the marriage mart that the delectable Miss Deveraux had turned down at least three offers for her hand. Title was obviously no consideration for the lady, for a viscount had numbered among the unhappy suitors.

My lord the Viscount of Trent had no wish for a similar rebuttal. His eyes blazed at the very thought. For the first time in several years, he actually felt unsure of himself. He had grown accustomed to his masterful ways, to the reverent appellation of a "nonpareil" wherever he presented himself.

He was quick witted and a master with the side sword, the duelling pistol and even his hands. Jackson's Boxing Saloon always held him up as an example to his less agile peers. His body was warm and lithe from years at sea, years in India. His mind was acute from the business acumen he had acquired during that time. He was not rich—mind blowingly, horribly, utterly over the top rich—for no reason. He had brains, wit and sense enough.

Lovers enough, too. And none of them, to his certain knowledge, had ever complained. He grinned a little. Some, in fact, were prone to be a little too addicted, a little too attached to his very handsome form. The farewell presents he'd been induced to part with to rid himself of some or other pretender to his attentions had not been inconsiderable.

And yet, here was the redoubtable Miss Deveraux, breathtaking beyond belief, and not seeming at all inclined to succumb to his many charms. Oh, a sigh here, a stolen glance or a flush there, but nothing to signify. My lord was not to guess at the inner turmoil of his lady love's mind and body. He did not know that his gaze was so stern or his thoughts so hooded. He did not know, in fact, that Miss Deveraux deemed him cold and contemptuous. He could only nod in tame consent when she retrieved her bonnet, placed it squarely on her head and suggested they return to Inglewood Manor.

It was a silent trip. Miss Deveraux thought it endless. She began to hate the eyes that she knew were boring into the very buttons on her back. She wished him to the devil! And yet, in her heart of hearts, she knew she wished him anywhere but that. It was so provoking! She felt indignant and cross. And strangely warm and very tingly . . . She held her head up and marched. My lord was forced to quicken his pace with a sigh. At times he wondered whether Miss Deveraux could be brought to be interested in him at all.

"Grantham!"

The Honourable Mr. Davies was puzzled. He could hear his name, but for the life of him, he could not see the caller. He considered matters carefully. If he proceeded, as he had intended, through the great portals of Inglewood Manor, he could be stuck there an eternity without the felicity of so much as a glimpse of his harum-scarum, shatterbrained and oh so adorable lady love. He feared this, for the voice he heard calling did not appear to be originating from within.

If, however, he retreated, he would be at just as much of a loss, for all that then would be gained would be an agitated groom, compelled to bring the horses round once more. On the other hand, standing with his well-polished boots immaculately rooted to the ground was also no great joy. Truth to tell, he felt a little foolish.

"Hen?" He whispered cautiously, loath for a footman to catch him rapt in conversation with himself.

"Here!" The words were uttered with scant regard for the servants.

"Where?" Mr. Davies must have been feeling particularly obtuse that day.

Some leaves shook above him. They were green and strong, not at all like the autumn leaves that drifted gracefully to the ground. As one particularly verdant leaf detached itself from a branch and landed with impudent ease upon his shoulder, he began to realise that nature was not entirely to blame.

He looked up to find his bosom bow grinning down disgracefully. Or delightfully, depending on the viewpoint you happened to choose. Mr. Davies seemed undecided on this point. Then he shrugged his shoulders, hitched up his inexpressibles and, with a graceful leap born of long years of practice, came to sit on the branch beside the miscreant.

"Still full of tricks, I see! Have they not made a lady of you yet, Lady adorable freckle-nose Stenning?"

Her indignation was great at this very unloverlike sally. "Grantham! For shame! And when I apply lemon juice every day three times a day forever! " Her voice was a wail. Then she relaxed as she thought a very consoling thought.

"You cannot hoax me, you know! There is not a freckle to be seen. I checked in the glass only today." She preened herself slightly, unaware how her expressive face lit up at the sight of the debonair Mr. Grantham. That gentleman took heart and was suddenly seized by the strangest notion to crush her in his arms and kiss her senseless. He proceeded with the first and was just proceeding with the second—much to Henrietta's satisfaction—when it occurred to them both that there was a good view of the tree from the second-floor windows of the manse. Mr. Davies released her, but with reluctance. He warned her he intended exacting his due in the none too distant future. She sank back into his arms and sighed with blissful satisfaction.

A very short time later—for Grantham was horribly correct when it came to her honour— Henrietta was induced to slide down from the tree, tidy her mangled dress and pin up her fallen locks. This done, she informed Grantham of the strange course of events she had witnessed within. She also disclosed a little matter that shocked her dear friend and gave him much food for earnest thought and triumph. It appeared the unthinkable had happened. The Viscount of Trent had met his match.

Henrietta was sadly scant on detail, but could only insist that this was the case. Grantham was sworn, on his honour as a gentleman, to facilitate the path of true romance. Rather to his bewilderment, it appeared that both parties were not yet fully apprised of their own feelings. Only the omniscient Lady Henrietta knew all. Grantham cast her a quick glance, and a withering reply died on his tongue. He decided to trust, after all, to women's intuition.

The Archbishop of Batten-on-Sea had nothing, it seemed, against issuing a special licence to the Earl of Inglewood. The man was a peer of the realm, well advanced in years—though not in his dotage—and the lady the same. While the marriage might have been somewhat unequal in rank, it was by no means a misalliance.

The licence was issued with alacrity, for with the signing of such an important document came the simultaneous advantage of a handsome fee.

The church roof was sadly in need of repair, and the simple matter of the suspension of matrimonial banns seemed a small price to pay. Thus it was that on a cold, wet and rather gloomy-looking day, his lordship the Earl of Inglewood finally married his Maria. None save the closest family was in attendance. For Miss Lowenthal's part, her only guest was an old lady well past her prime and bedecked in Indian silks and a crimson turban of startling effect. She declared, in her grizzled voice, that she was well satisfied.

Maria could do little more than hug her as tears fell readily from her eyes. The new countess was off on her marriage trip. Though she refused all the baubles the earl pressed on her, he was adamant on one point at least. The sapphire and diamond heirloom was to be hers. He placed the ornament round her long, slender neck with consummate care. For him, it was a turning point he would never forget.

Their departure from Inglewood was effected with surprising ease considering the number of minions involved in the stowing of linen, the organising of holland sheets, the preparation of portmanteaus and chests, the removal of furniture from the manse to London and even across to Europe. . . . The details were endless and need not here be discussed.

In these matters, Miss Deveraux proved, once again, her mettle. She endeavoured to keep angry creditors from bellowing in her ear, she soothed the ruffled feelings of the housekeeper who had not been apprised of certain changes, she admonished the land agent who appeared to be keeping two sets of books with respect to the Inglewood accounts—but no more! It was several weeks before the Lady Henrietta and Miss Deveraux could comfortably settle back in the luxurious barouche my lord the viscount had provided.

It might perhaps strike the reader as passing strange that Lady Henrietta was so quiescent in these new arrangements, or that Mr. Grantham Davies was happy to countenance the removal of his affianced for a season. The archbishop had been most specific that marriage to Henrietta required permission from her guardian. Had that permission been granted? And if so, why had a betrothal not immediately been announced?

If the truth were to be revealed, Lady Henrietta had mulled over these selfsame problems a great deal since news of her change of abode was explained to her. It had immediately seemed much more provident and fitting that she marry sooner rather than later. She was, after all, in the fortunate position of being beloved of a man she esteemed greatly and who, more importantly, was impatient to wed her.

It seemed ridiculous, indeed, for her to impose on Lord Randolph when she need only say the word and be mistress of her own establishment. In talking this through with Grantham, two inevitable conclusions were reached.

Upon her marriage, she would have no need of a governess. Miss Deveraux, she knew, would be too proud to accept the position of honoured house guest. Neither would she accept the role of paid companion when her presence must inevitably be a blight rather than a help to the honeymooning couple.

Further, more importantly, residence at my lord's London address would throw Clementine in constant contact with the said lord. Henrietta's eyes gleamed with the first glimmer of matchmaking mischief. She could think of no better match for her surrogate guardian and could think of none more advantageous to her former governess. If she could bring about such an event, she would be well satisfied.

Randolph's antics as a highwayman were still incomprehensible. It was clear, however, that he wanted this aspect of his activities kept a well-guarded secret. Well, she would keep it. She may have been a mere schoolroom miss, but the speaking glances she saw exchanged between the pair led her to believe her machinations would not entirely be in vain. London it was, then.

As for herself . . . Mr. Grantham Davies had been received very properly by the earl not two days hence. The topic of their conversation shall not be discussed, but suffice it to say it left both young people sighing in unspoken bliss. Miss Deveraux was apprised of nothing.

The carriage was extremely well sprung and the hot bricks provided for their comfort were warming, despite the chill of the day. How different from the accommodation coach! Whenever they stopped at inns, either for a rest or a change of horses, the innkeepers were passing civil, the landladies bowing and scraping in an excess of civility Clementine found amusing in the extreme.

Miss Deveraux would not have been human had she not exacted a great deal of satisfaction upon coming across Mistress Mudgely and her paltry rooms at the White Hart Inn. When that lady had seen the crested chaise and the four outriders, not to mention the groom, the party of housemaids and the baggage coaches that trailed behind, she had at once scurried forward with her most unctuously ingratiating smile.

The viscount himself had alighted from the horse he was

travelling on up front. He'd opened the door and kissed Miss Deveraux's hand as she descended. Mistress Mudgely had sunk into an even deeper curtsy before opening her eyes.

Her shock and horrified remorse was enough to give even Clementine satisfaction. Unfortunately, that lady could not deliver the crushing set-down she would have liked to give. She found her heart was racing and her tongue was too tied to be trusted. Besides, her creamy cheeks were flushed a rosy pink and her hand . . . well, her hand felt as though it had been touched by the gods. She was certain it would never feel the same again. And why had he done it? His eyes had been quizzical, slightly humorous. It was almost as though he knew . . . but that was impossible!

She had not time to adequately divine her own thoughts. To her immense satisfaction, she found that my lord was offering the set-down that she could not. The viscount could be extremely high in the instep at times and this, it seemed, was one of those. His bearing was so haughty and his contempt so palpable that the hapless landlady was rendered speechless.

She recovered quickly, however, and her manner was doubly fawning. Her quick, avaricious brain had not failed to assess the cut of my lord's jacket or the value of the signet that flashed emerald on his left hand. Nor had she failed to note the utter perfection of his six snowy horses—still fresh from the change—or the understated but impeccably fine livery of his servants.

My lord's condescension was deemed of the utmost importance to her establishment. If the plump, slightly sour-looking woman could have grovelled, she would have. Instead, she curtsied almost to the ground and in her shrill voice apprised the viscount of the many excellent services of the inn.

In a bored yet nonetheless devastating undertone, the woman was given to understand her services would not be required. Neither would they be solicited by several eminent young ladies and gentlemen of *ton*. The White Hart Inn now would have to aspire to a very different class of person.

She shuffled off, and the viscount, having ascertained that

Miss Deveraux and his ward had had sufficient time to stretch their legs, personally helped them back into the carriage.

His eyes were twinkling and Clementine had the sudden, awful sensation that it had been he in the taproom that day. Before she could open her lips to say something, he had doffed his hat and returned to the front.

Chapter Seventeen

London was bustling with new arrivals for the season. Brass knockers were being affixed to almost every respectable door in Curzon Street. Along the length of Mayfair, down the avenues of Cavendish and Grosvenor, an assortment of barouches, curricles and high-perch phaetons all converged elegantly, en route to morning calls, soirées and ridottos. The nightly excursions to Almack's, Watier's, White's, Boodle's and Brooks's were on the increase.

Mrs. Siddons was playing Ophelia. There was a recitation from *Childe Harold's Pilgrimage*. At the Globe, Mr. Kemble was in fine form with King Lear. The opera was at its grandiose, sparkling best. The gas lamps of London had been lit, giving it an elegant if somewhat eerie feel at night. The Regent's fireworks displays were about to commence. Weekly balloon ascensions in Hyde Park were an attraction, as were the waxworks, the daily concerts, the afternoon rides, the illuminations of Vauxhall Gardens.

To Henrietta, unused to the ways and wonders of the city, these pursuits were enchantment indeed. She was terrified she might miss out on some amusement or other and dragged poor

Clementine to every gallery, exhibition, ribbon bazaar and modiste within walking distance of the city centre.

She was tireless in her desire to see all, do everything. At times Clementine would smile. At others, her legs would grow weary and she would firmly call a halt to the day's extravagances. Keeping Henrietta out of scrapes was proving more troublesome than she had anticipated. Apart from the obvious pitfalls of nearly waltzing without permission, of accepting three dances from one paricularly dazzling cavalry captain— she would not have, of course, had Grantham been available— Lady Henrietta had to be coaxed not to ride her mare through Hyde Park in the morning, not to stroll up St. James Street out of idle curiosity, not to run when she ought to walk, not to slip out of the house without her maid—the list seemed endless. Clementine felt she had aged overnight. What was worse, she began to *feel* like a governess. The thought was morbidly depressing.

All was not compeletely bad, however. The balls were sparkling and Henrietta managed to wheedle Clementine to let down some of her hair. It rippled and flowed in inviting waves around her face, restricted only by a loose chignon at the back. She had been doubtful at first, but the viscount's blatant admiration when he'd taken her arm stilled all qualms.

That, it must be said, was all he stilled. For the most part, he set the demure Miss Deveraux's heart racing most unaccountably whenever he was near. If their hands brushed or she found her waist encircled as he solicitously lifted her into the carriage, her breathing deepened in the most extraordinary manner. Composure was most difficult to maintain. The only thing that helped her was the viscount's own calm.

He was so entirely correct in his treatment of her that Clementine found it lowering indeed. What was worse, she was amazed and ashamed at how fickle her heart could be. Had she not given it completely into the trust of an unknown highwayman? Though they had not pledged anything of the kind, she had seen it in his eyes and had acknowledged the truth— however unsuitable—deep within her.

How dared the viscount, then, make her heart flutter so? How dared he make his presence so keenly felt even when he was across a room and dancing obligingly with any of the hundreds of eminently suitable young ladies? Why did the simplest touch of his hand make her tremble and his wide, generous mouth make her yearn like a veritable wanton?

She felt as if she knew every aspect of his dark, slightly shadowed chin, of his firm jaw and masculine cheekbones, of his deep, infinitely subtle eyes, of his curling hair, pitch black as the night. His shoulders and muscular frame were etched into her mind daily. She could not stop herself gazing at his thighs and his . . . but no! She blushed crimson. Her thoughts did run on so.

At times, she caught an odd look in his eye and she would tremble. Inevitably, though, his gaze would be hooded and she would be left to decide whether the warm, passionate, distinctly earthy stare had been reality or merely her overactive imagination. Around the viscount she became clumsy and tongue-tied. Her poise escaped her whenever she needed it most. She was miserable, miserable!

And where was her highwayman? Where was her dear Quicksilver John with his sensuous smile and his admiring, bold and oh-so-stimulating humour? She did not know. Perhaps would never know. She broke a fan in her frustration. Henrietta looked at her very queerly indeed before dropping her copy of the scandalous Lord Byron and putting her arms around her friend and mentor. It was time she lent a hand.

"Please take it! The colour is so fetching! You were *made* for brilliance!" Clementine shook her head resolutely and pointed at a dull serge, elegant enough but drab in comparison to the luminescent, vivid material Henrietta fingered with such awe.

Henrietta stamped her foot crossly. Fortunately, there was no one besides Madame Fanchette, her servants and a very few curious young debutantes to witness her unladylike action.

"I swear, Clementine, if you could leave off your greys and your topaz and your boring blacks you could be quite beautiful!"

Miss Deveraux digested this oddly worded compliment with a small smile. She was too used to Henrietta's plain speaking to take offence or to misunderstand the good intentions behind the unmannerly words. She held out her hand for the serge. It had an understated spot imprint and would serve her purpose very well indeed. She depressed Henrietta's hopes kindly but firmly.

"You forget, Henrietta, that I am merely a paid companion. It is not my place to push myself forward and endeavour to stand out in a crowd. It is enough that I accompany you at all. Many would say a dowager would be more suitable. You can be thankful I am not in caps."

Henrietta shuddered at the thought. Then she laughed. Her friend was mesmerisingly beautiful. The thought of her as a dowager spinster could only be contemplated with the dismissal it deserved.

"Stuff and nonsense, Miss Deveraux! You are exquisite. Why should you not look it?"

Clementine flushed. She had never thought of herself as anything more than tolerable before. Her strange, doe-shaped eyes, emerald green and lashed in black did not seem, to her, very modish. Besides . . . that was beyond the point.

"Your ladyship!"

Henrietta knew she was in trouble. Clementine was only so formal when scolding.

"What?"

"Your language, my dear! Young ladies do not use cant or express themselves vulgarly."

A glimmer of mischief appeared in the Honourable Lady Henrietta Stenning's eyes.

"I swear it, Clementine, if you do not take that dress I shall say 'stuff' to Mrs. Drummond Barrel herself!"

Clementine was shocked. Mrs. Drummond Barrel was the most formidable of the hostesses at Almack's. A much lesser slip would see Henrietta barred forever. At a glance Clementine could see she meant what she said. Her charge was wearing her mulish expression, and Clementine did not set any misdemeanour above her in this scapegrace mood.

Besides, the deep green reflected her eyes exactly. The shade was magnificent. And the texture! The luxuriant feel was tempting her senses. Overwhelmingly so.

Madame Fanchette clucked over her soothingly. Before she knew what she was about, an army of helpers were pinning, taping, pricking and prodding. She was led to a change room without further demur.

The woman that looked out at her from the glass was breathtaking. Her hair floated over her shoulders like a halo. She was queenly in bearing and bold in beauty. In short, she was as unlike Miss Deveraux as she could be. And yet . . . And yet . . . There was a faint tugging at Clementine's conscience.

She shook her head firmly. "It is too low cut, I'm afraid." She looked into the glass again and blushed. Her creamy breasts were straining at the satin. If one were to apply a measuring tape, she was certain they would be found to be more out than in. It was indecent! Positively shocking!

Madame Fanchette seemed to see nothing amiss. In truth, she had cut gowns much lower than this in her time. The fashions were more revealing this season and that was a fact. Miss Deveraux could not be unaware of this phenomenon, for she attended all the best parties.

"It is zee prevailing fashion, my dear! You do not, I sink, weesh to present yourself as a dowd?"

Clementine had to admit that she did not. Still, that was no excuse for a gown like this. She knew she was not an antidote, but this made her look exceptional. And exceptional is what she had sworn not to be.

"Wrap it up!" In the end, the decision had not been hers. Lady Henrietta had been at her imperious best. Her eyes twinkled at Clementine. "No one of any consequence will even know who you are tonight. It is Lady Bartlett's masquerade, if you recall!"

She neglected to say that her handsome cousin would certainly know, and that was all to the best. The time had come, her ladyship judged, for the path of true love to be helped. Heaven knew, if it were left to Randolph and Clementine alone, they'd make the most dismal mull of it.

Her qualms somewhat mollified by Henrietta's declaration, Miss Deveraux resigned herself to her fate and watched with interest as the gown was carefully wrapped in a delicate pearl tissue. She could not help the frisson of excitement that flooded through her being at the thought of the viscount seeing her thus.

They left the salon in high spirits and decided to deviate only once from their planned itinerary, for a visit to the circulating library. There, Lady Henrietta indulged herself with a novel of romantic adventure while Miss Deveraux thought to sober herself with a good dose of Sir Francis Bacon's *Essays,* concentrating on the one on goodness. The short carriage trip home was uneventful, punctuated only by the lightest of conversation and the odd inclination of the head to new and old acquaintances alike.

A note from my lord the viscount sent the duo into a frenzy of irritation, annoyance, deep disappointment and bitter chagrin respectively. It appeared that the viscount would be unable to escort them to Lady Bartlett's that evening. He pleaded a most pressing appointment and consigned them into the care of his good friend Mr. Grantham Davies who was also escorting his beautiful sisters. This last considerably served to brighten Lady Henrietta's demeanour, but she nevertheless found herself extremely out of sorts that her well-laid plans had gone awry. Miss Deveraux had consented to the dress only because it had been a masquerade. There was no hope she would put it aside and wear it on another, more auspicious occasion. She bit her lip. Damnation and double damnation!

Clementine's disappointment was almost tangible, but not a flicker on her well-bred face showed as much. She thanked the kind footman who had delivered the salvo and repaired to her bedroom for a quiet rest. Somehow, Bacon's essays did not help her sagging spirits overmuch. She gave them up with a listless sigh. The night ahead would be more chore now than sparkling excitement. Still, it was not her place to be anything more than paid companion. If it was not quite to her taste, it would at least be good for her soul. On these lowering reflections, she fell into oblivious sleep.

The prison guard bowed obsequiously to the viscount and opened the heavy, metal gate. It grated as if unused to this exertion, then was clicked slowly back into place. The cell was dank and dark. The smell was not edifying, nor was the sight of a man sitting in a corner, his neck cloths all wrinkled and his customary sneer wiped entirely from his face. He stood up agitatedly as the men came in. The viscount's eyes met his, and he found them strangely compelling. He whispered something to the guard, and the minion bowed low once again. Then he coughed slightly and left.

"Newgate is uncommonly bad for the digestion, I hear."

The crisp words echoed eerily in the cell. The man had been unused to the sound of a refined, well-educated voice for some weeks. The diction was strangely soothing. He drew himself up and recalled a smidgen of his former bearing.

"Indeed it is, sir!"

"*Lord*, if you please! Lord Randolph De Lacey. The Viscount of Trent, in fact."

The man blanched. Those eyes . . . He should have known.

"Randolph!" He attempted a light-hearted, innocent banter. "It has been a long time. Several years, I think. I hear you did well for yourself. . . ." His voice trailed off.

"No thanks to you, Cunningham! You, it seems, were too busy trying to get your grubby hands on a few gold sovereigns to care to tell the truth of those forgeries! I might have been spared a great deal of pain and hardship had you come forward with what you knew ten years ago."

There was nothing to say to this. Cunningham deemed it prudent to maintain a stiff silence. All the while, his mind was hunting for clues as to why the viscount should suddenly interest himself in his case. Did he still need the proofs? His acute eyes took in the viscount's unwavering gaze assessingly. No, he thought not. What then?

"It is not pleasant to be punished for a crime one did not commit. I think you understand me?"

Hope flared in the baronet's eyes. Then Lord Randolph presumed him innocent? He would be the only one, but he was not without influence. . . .

"Indeed I do, my lord! I swear to you I am innocent of highway robbery. I swear it on my mother's grave!"

"As the Dowager Baroness Fawnstone is still enjoying excellent health, I presume you are being rhetorical, my friend?" The viscount's words were stinging.

Cunningham's heart sank. Why was Randolph here then? To taunt him? It seemed likely, on reflection. Were their roles reversed he would undoubtedly have done the same.

The viscount's next words took him by surprise. He almost missed them, for the man was gazing at his malacca cane, for all the world as if it were the dearest object in his possession.

"I, unlike you, can *not* let an innocent man suffer for crimes he did not commit."

So! The viscount knew him to be innocent. Hope soared yet again. Sir Andrew Cunningham despised Randolph for the power he held over him, yet he knew himself to be at his mercy. He became sycophantic and simpering. Randolph was sickened.

"Cut line, Andrew!"

Something in his visitor's tone made the baronet look up. He had heard it before, and not when they were mere striplings. The tone was firm but menacing. It brooked no nonsense. It was not unlike that of the highwayman who'd so boldly dressed him down that fateful day. Sir Andrew still smarted when he thought—briefly—on that humiliating encounter. And now . . . here was the voice, the tone, the very incarnation. . . . His eyes grew wide.

"You *devil!*"

Lord Randolph bowed. "Some may call me that. I prefer

angel of justice. But perhaps I grow whimsical." He smiled, but the smile held no warmth.

"What do you want?" Sir Andrew stared at him wearily.

He knew he would be shackled and sent off to Bedlam if he accused the suave Viscount Trent of the crime he was himself supposed to have committed. The terrible enormity of the whole situation suddenly was born in upon him. So, too, was the ever-present threat of the hangman's gibbet. Highway robbery was a capital offence. He need expect no mercy.

"I have come to save your life, Sir Andrew. Though you are undoubtedly a loathsome toad, I will not see you die for a crime you did not commit. I am not without influence in these parts. I will speak to the magistrate and have you released."

Sir Andrew sank back onto the hard chair that was at that time his only creature comfort. He rolled his eyes backward and thanked Randolph with slippery, rather distasteful fulsomeness. Already, his thoughts were galloping on ahead. If Randolph was amenable to his release, perhaps he'd be equally amenable to buying the proofs? It was obvious he'd burned his bridges with the old Earl of Inglewood.

When he slyly expressed as much, hinting with noisome bits of innuendo that his price would be more than equitable, Randolph clenched his fists and took three paces forward.

Sir Andrew was instantly apprised of his mistake. He found himself lifted by the scruff of his filthy shirt points and facing the viscount eye to eye. With a calmness of demeanour that belied his seething inner rage, the viscount informed him of the earl's belated efforts on his behalf.

Lord Oscar had confessed to the forgeries. Such stale news was it among the *ton*, that the scandal broth had long since been replaced by the latest *on dit* of Lady Caroline Lamb. Further, the earl had taken himself a most admirable countess and was now far beyond even Cunningham's machinations. As for the Lady Henrietta ... Well, she was enjoying a most successful season. It would not surprise the viscount if any number of eligible peers were shortly to sue for her hand.

Sir Andrew looked at the poised viscount with loathing. It

was difficult to express disdain when one's eyes were bulging from one's sockets and one's feet were not quite touching the floor, but he almost managed. He began to choke out a response. The viscount released him.

"Save your breath, Sir Andrew! There is little you can have to say that will interest me. Let me now outline what I intend to do on your behalf." Sir Andrew's mouth snapped shut, and his eyes acquired an interested gleam.

"I will swear you were in my company at the time the highway robbery was committed. I will depose this and sign it. I should imagine my alibi will be sufficient to secure your instant release from Newgate and from all danger of a hanging."

Sir Andrew moved forward.

"No! Do not, I beg you, sully my ears with your thanks! Truth to tell, a hanging is your just deserts, but I'll not have it on my conscience. You'll probably come by the same through your own endeavours shortly!" Sir Andrew made a choking sound at the back of his throat. Randolph could see his hands were clenched. Truth to tell, the viscount was beginning to enjoy himself. He continued.

"What interests me now is the matter of the sapphire and diamond necklace found in your possession. Not, I take it, a gift from Lord Oscar?"

The baronet was mute. He was beginning to feel as if he were the mouse in a cat-and-mouse game. Since he had always played the cat in such games, the feeling was both novel and nauseatingly unpleasant.

"So silent? I will take silence for guilt. There can be no other interpretation. Theft on that scale could also purchase you a hanging. The judges, I feel, will be merciful. They will reprieve you in light of the fact that you are a baronet of the realm. I should imagine you will be sentenced to no more than deportation to the colonies. New South Wales, most likely." Sir Andrew felt distinctly light headed. The room swayed.

"There *is* another option. Your only option, I feel."

His head cleared. "And that is. . . . ?"

"You will sign a confession of the theft. I will keep it. If I hear aught to your discredit—and believe me, my threshold is low—I will release the document into the hands of the authorities. If you maintain a low profile and never again speak to or *of* either Lady Henrietta Stenning or Miss Clementine Deveraux—''

Sir Andrew hissed. ''Her!''

The viscount's eyes grew dark, and he felt violence threatening yet again. ''Yes, her! If you so much as utter their names you are a doomed man. Do I make myself clear?'' Sir Andrew nodded.

''Good! Sign the document, then. I have had it drawn up by Messrs. Durham, Sallinger and Brett. I think you will find it most binding.''

He handed the paper to Sir Andrew, who took it up with bad grace. My lord called for some writing implements, and the transaction was soon completed. The viscount nodded the guard away once more.

''A few more minutes with the prisoner, I beg.''

The attendant bowed and retreated.

Randolph smiled. ''Your life is now no longer in danger. I am sure your release will be procured within hours.'' Perspiration poured from Sir Andrew's forehead.

''Are you well?'' For the first time, the viscount appeared solicitous. Sir Andrew nodded.

''Good! Then perhaps you will now roll up your sleeves and oblige me with a bout of fisticuffs. I have much to avenge.''

Sir Andrew looked amazed.

''Do it, man! At least I give you fair warning. Whatever the outcome, you will be released. Somehow, however, I expect I will be the victor.''

Sir Andrew did not move. The viscount sauntered up to him and slapped his face. The noise reverberated through the cell. ''Is that sufficient provocation, my dear sir?''

Sir Andrew rolled up his sleeves without a further word. He delivered a blow to the viscount's temple. The viscount ducked and the full impact was averted. He retaliated with a left hook that sent Sir Andrew staggering. Like a true gentleman, he waited for Sir Andrew to recover his balance and even deliver a firm blow of his own before closing in and punching the man with force.

The guard, when recalled, was surprised to see his prisoner sprawled clear across the floor. On the visitor's face there was a clear gleam of amused triumph. He shrugged. There was no telling with the gentry.

Chapter Eighteen

Clementine looked magnificent. She had allowed her hair to hang loose over her shoulders and down to her waist. The golden lights flickered and danced as long tendrils of curls framed her face and tantalisingly touched the creamy, forbidden mounds of flesh that she had been so conscious of earlier in the day. Truth to tell, the reason she had chosen such a hair style over the more severe forms to which she was inclined was just that. It lent, in her mind, a bit of modesty. She would have been amazed to know how this particular artifice had failed. She looked more delicious than ever. Several gentlemen—some, I regret to say, married—raised their quizzing glasses in her direction.

Her dance card was full to overflowing. The only notable omission was that of the Viscount of Trent. Mr. Grantham Davies gallantly led her out in the second dance. Miss Deveraux took the opportunity of this little interlude to admonish him on matters of propriety. Lady Henrietta was to dance no more than twice with him, no waltzes. Mr. Davies grinned at her impudently from behind his mask. It seemed he had already procured Lady Sally Jersey's good offices. Lady Henrietta was

to have the honour of waltzing. Clementine smiled upon him.
A man after her own heart! She knew Henrietta would be
straining at the bit to dance the rather fast new dance. Grantham
had effectively averted a calamity by using his influence in this
way. She opened her mouth to thank him.

He just laughed. It was a merry, throaty laugh, and Clementine was instantly charmed. Yes, her charge could have done
no better than to secure for herself this man. She had a feeling
he would be able to control Henrietta's wild impulses with
even wilder ones of his own. He would rule the roost, but so
subtly that even Lady Henrietta would be fooled. And if not
fooled, cajoled at least. Excellent!

His eyes twinkled. "Do not thank me, Miss Deveraux! My
efforts on your charge's behalf have been entirely selfish I can
assure you!"

"Then *I* can assure you I am well pleased!"

They smiled in mutual amity, and the dance concluded. Clementine found herself whisked off to the next set by an unknown
stranger. Unfortunately for her, he was none too adept and her
feet quite ached at the end of the dance. He, however, was
intoxicated both with her beauty and with the effects of too
large a portion of champagne on a decidedly empty stomach.
His efforts to urge her to a second dance were becoming embarrassing. Worse, her allotted partner seemed to have vanished
into thin air. She tried to scan the room for him, but the crush
of people made this an impossibility. Besides, her brilliant
emerald eyeshade obscured her view.

"Sir! I am promised to another! See here, on my dance
card!" She proffered the delicate card for the man's inspection.
He dismissed it with a wave.

"What is the good of some scribbling, dearest, if one does
not come forward to *claim* the promised dance? Come, another
with me cannot harm you! I insist. Absolutely I do!"

There was nothing for it but to resign herself to a second
dance with the irritating man. She deemed him to be a young
officer out for the first time. By the languishing glances he
persisted on throwing her way, she reckoned he judged himself

in the grip of some undying passion. Calf love. That was all she needed right now, to top her own trials. She was becoming a tragedy queen.

The music was just threatening to strike up. I use the word "threatening" for such was Miss Deveraux's disinclination to dance with the young incognito that she found any advancement towards that inevitability displeasing in the extreme. She had no wish to cause a scene, but she determined to blight the young man's pretensions quite firmly during the course of the next few minutes. He would have his dance, but possibly by the end of it he would wish he had not been so fortunate. She sighed and gave him her satin-gloved hand.

"Not so fast, sir! The dance is promised to me!" She turned. The voice was unmistakable. Her hand disengaged from the officer's. It remained suspended for a brief second before fluttering to her cheeks. They were flushed. Her heart had forgotten to beat, and her voice seemed utterly lost to her. The man was wearing a dark domino, encrusted with jewels and lined in red satin. His wig was fashionably high, the little patch above his mouth unmistakably attractive. There was only one thing Clementine knew for certain. This man was not the one who had signed her dance card earlier in the evening. Still, she was never one to quibble.

With an unaccountable lightness of heart that surged through her being and added a sparkle to her already jewel green eyes, she smiled decorously and curtsied.

"Is it not, my dear?"

"Indeed it is, sir! And I must scold you on being so tardy!" She could see the smile flit over his generous mouth in appreciation of her quickness of uptake. The officer stuttered a brief objection. He was quelled by a single look. The highwayman took up his quizzing glass, and the man paled to insignificance. Perhaps the effects of the champagne were just becoming clear to him. Whatever the cause, he found he had urgent business elsewhere. Clementine was never so pleased in her life.

"You have spared me a great deal of trouble, sir!"

"I have?" He was smiling at her so languidly that the whole room seemed to have stilled.

She swallowed. It would be hard to maintain an easy banter when her heart fluttered so. He was so strong, so male, so very, very attractive . . . devastatingly so. She wondered briefly how he had gained entrance to such a society event. Then she realised that the cover of the masquerade must have made entrée easier. She was grateful that he had thought to go to so much trouble on her account. On her account? She harboured a momentary doubt.

No, with the way he was looking at her, bold and warm and as shockingly sensuous as even she could wish, there could be no doubt. It *had* been on her account. She was glad. The smooth image of the Viscount of Trent flitted for an instant into her mind. Only he had the same powers of attraction as this man. It was to this man, however, that she had given her soul.

"Well?"

"Well what?" A small smile played at his mouth. She could sense that he had guessed the direction of her thoughts and blushed.

"Well, how have I spared you a great deal of trouble?"

"Oh!" Her eyes danced. "Let us just say my toes are extremely grateful to your timeous arrival! I fear they would otherwise have been subjected to the most horrendous fate. A minuet was bad enough. I shudder to reflect upon his performance of a waltz!"

The man smiled. "We've missed this one, I fear. The orchestra has struck up most inconsiderately without us. May I fetch you a lemonade instead? We may take it out to the balcony. I fear it is rather stuffy in here. You look as if you could do with some air."

"Do I? Fagged to death, you mean?"

"Now, Miss Deveraux, if it is compliments you are after, you need say no more! I will procure the lemonade and be back shortly to shower them upon you like rain. Fagged to death, indeed." His smile was heart-stopping in its intensity.

Clementine's throat constricted in wonder. He pressed the emerald satin briefly. "I won't be a moment, dearest."

The words, as spoken by him, had the most intimate of meanings. She flushed and found her eyes could not meet his. He laughed and put his finger under her chin.

"And don't you go disappearing while I am gone! I happen to know your charge is having the most engaging time in the hands of a certain Mr. Grantham Davies. She is well chaperoned, too, for the last I looked his sisters were clustered around her like a gaggle of beautiful geese. Shall I say a giggling gaggle?"

On this parting sally he was gone. Clementine had just time to press down her skirts and arrange some of her gleaming locks over her cleavage. She had not missed the odd glance he had passed in that direction. It had sent a shiver of delicious excitement right through her being. She was certain, however, that such delightful sentiments were not at all proper. She composed herself and waited for him with a heightened colour. On the exterior, at least, she appeared admirably aloof.

A searching glance through the crowd revealed that her highwayman had not been wrong. Lady Henrietta was smiling demurely up at Mr. Davies. Though his sisters appeared to be in the act of accepting the invitations of any number of suitors to dance, Clementine's mind was set at rest. With the decorous Mr. Davies she knew her charge to be safe.

"Here, sweet one!"

The highwayman had returned, and all thoughts beyond his most impressionable self vanished. She smiled and curtsied as he led her out into the cool, beautifully fresh air.

"Just what I needed!"

"And I!" His eyes were upon her and Clementine could almost feel them burning into her own.

"I did not mean . . ."

"Did you not? I am disappointed." His voice was silky smooth and sent shivers down Clementine's spine. The couples within danced on, oblivious to the tingling enchantment that was peculiarly hers.

''Shall I remove the mask?''

She nodded. His hands brushed hers as they moved up to her face. The moment was electric. He discarded the emerald eyeshade and moved a step closer. His hands reached out and touched a strand of her hair.

''You have no notion of how I have longed for this!'' His voice trembled with deep, heartfelt sincerity. Clementine forgot decorum and all that she had learnt about what civilised young ladies did and did not do. She stretched out her arms and removed the bandanna from his face. Then she was looking into eyes that were fathoms deep, brown and dark, yet gleaming with unspoken passion. They were the very twins of the viscount's . . . .

That was her last thought before she found herself engulfed in his arms and crushed in his embrace. His mouth was tender and fierce at one and the same time. She could feel the stubble on his chin and the warmth of his breath as he moved from her mouth to her neck and slowly down to her cleavage. Suddenly, all Madame Fanchette's assurances seemed to evaporate. She was indecent and she knew it. For that wondrous moment, she did not care. Not when he was showering her with kisses of such fiery abandon, such intimate, stirring, tantalising kisses that her heart trembled and her knees threatened to buckle at any moment. Not when her own lips touched his powdered wig, the back of his neck . . . his hands moved to her breasts. It seemed that he was in agreement with Madame Fanchette. More of her needed exposure. She felt him gently ease his way past the remaining flimsy material. She had not known that such wild, wanton feelings could possibly exist. She arched her neck in sheer, unadulterated pleasure. He stopped.

''We must not do this, my love!''

She straightened up in a daze. Her only thoughts was, ''Why ever not?'' Her eyes were glazed from the exquisite pangs of first awakening. The highwayman was sorely tempted to kiss her again. Then he recalled herself to reality.

Well, she was an abandoned woman. That was all there was to it! Half the world had probably witnessed their tryst. It was not as if her green gown was exactly inconspicuous. She flushed and looked up at the man she knew quite positively to be her one true love. He smiled reassuringly and lifted her hand to his lips.

"Come, we shall go inside, and I shall set those tattling tongues to rest."

"How?" Clementine did not pretend to misunderstand him. She knew she was ruined, but somehow the disgrace of it did not seem to affect her heady state and sense of dizzying happiness.

He looked at her, and his jaw set in grim lines.

"I shall find the busiest, nosiest gossipmonger among the dowagers. Not an easy task, for they are all equally so. However, I think Lady Thornton Prentice-Bird our most likely candidate. I shall tell her a piece of news—in utmost confidence—that should have her tongue wagging the rest of the evening and all the way through to morning."

"What will you say?" Clementine was mystified.

"Come, my child. Follow me and learn from a master!"

They entered the main ballroom yet again, and Miss Deveraux instantly felt the clammy heat that was generated from so many persons crushed into too small a space. Oh, the ballroom was large enough, but society was never satisfied unless there was a crush. Well, a crush there was. Clementine was amazed at how dexterously the highwayman threaded his way through the crowd. She noticed with both satisfaction and growing alarm that he never once released her hand.

He was headed for a dowager wearing an awe-inspiring turban of pale mauve. It was trimmed with a small veil and a peacock's plume several inches high. She was surrounded by a dragoon of similarly attired ladies. Their beady eyes were fixed on both him and his partner.

He did not stop until he was right before the redoubtable old tattle monger.

"Your ladyship! I trust you are well?"

"Indeed!" She looked affronted, but was evidently torn by her desire to converse with a handsome young gentleman and an urge to cut him for his rakish behaviour. She compromised. She affixed Clementine with her grimmest stare and simpered at the gentleman.

"My lord—"

"Hush, my dear! We are in fancy dress, after all! I daresay you should not recognise me, you know!"

"No, indeed." She sounded uncertain.

"I have something of a very particular nature to impart to you. You are, after all, the very *soul* of discretion, I know." She preened at the words and waved her fellow, tattling biddies away. Though they rose from their chairs and politely repositioned themselves some yards distant, Clementine could feel that the eyes behind their fans never once left them.

"May I present to you my affianced bride?" He brought the lady in shimmering green boldly forward.

"Affianced!" Lady Thornton Prentice-Bird became flustered, quite overset by this new intelligence. Miss Deveraux herself looked puzzled, but, nudged on by the highwayman, managed a suitable curtsy.

"Well, you've done well for yourself, miss. A viscountess, no less!" The voice was faintly disgruntled, but speculative.

Clementine looked bewildered, then enlightenment dawned. The dowager had perceived the likeness between the highwayman and the Viscount Trent. She had mistaken one for the other. Instantly, she was alarmed.

"Pray—"

She was silenced by a single glance from the highwayman.

"Viscountess? Now, now, your ladyship, you do not *know* I am Trent." The words were playful and the lady took up his meaning at once.

"Oh yes, my lord! I am truly at a loss to know who you may be!" Her voice was coyly mysterious. The highwayman allowed himself a satisfied nod. The news would be spread across the full extent of the Bartlett grounds and far beyond in no more than half an hour. Maybe less, if he judged it right.

All previous indiscretions would be forgotten in the light of this newest snippet. All the world knew Randolph De Lacey to be a confirmed bachelor. Well, now! The gossip would be tremendous. A minute well spent. He made an all-encompassing bow to the Thornton Prentice-Birds of the world and drew Clementine away. The crackle of fans snapping shut could be heard before ever he'd taken the first step.

"Why did you do that?" There was faint annoyance in Clementine's tone. She did not see why the Viscount of Trent needed to be dragged into the whole sorry story. She'd much rather lose her reputation than be thought by him to be a scheming hussy doing all within her power to entrap him. It was inconceivable that the rumour would not reach his ears. She was mortified!

The highwayman looked at her blandly.

"No one said a word about the Viscount of Trent! Indeed, I have been at considerable pains to disabuse the lady of that notion!"

"Knowing full well, nevertheless, that no such thing would happen!"

He bowed and his eyes gleamed.

"No one can say I am not cunning, my dear! Your reputation is now enhanced rather than shattered. I daresay you will receive any number of curious morning callers tomorrow!"

Clementine was indignant. Her eyes burned a deep, velvety green, but there were dangerous lights behind their smooth emerald surface,

"And what am I to say to them, my dear sir? That it was all a sad mistake and I am *not* engaged to be married to the most handsome and most debonair of all the peers of the realm? Not to mention the richest, the most—"

". . . Most what?"

"Nothing!" Clementine found herself stammering and then flushed to the golden roots of her shimmering hair.

"I insist you tell me." The highwayman's voice was stern. They had stopped in their tracks and were causing a minor obstacle on the way to the dance floor. Clementine began to faint. The highwayman's eyes were unwavering. In a flash of rebellion she shrugged her shoulders.

". . . Adorable! There, I've said it!''

The highwayman hid an inward chuckle. He was well pleased with her answer. He started moving again, and the crush of people flowed on behind him. He took Clementine's arm and led her to a quieter corner of the room. He handed her a glass of ratafia off the footman's salver. His voice was stern. "Is that what you think of the viscount? I see I will have to cut his heart out!''

Miss Deveraux looked alarmed. "You jest, sir!''

"Perhaps!'' His voice was mysterious. In her concern over the viscount's fate, Clementine forgot to scold him for his own shocking behaviour.

"It is nigh on midnight, my dear. Time for the unmasking. I will slip off now, I think.'' His tone grew gentle. He reached out and touched her chin. Clementine experienced that strange trembling again.

"Do not fret, my dear! This will have a happy outcome, I promise you.''

There was no time for doubts. Clementine closed her eyes and allowed herself to savour the gentle kiss that descended on her soft, rosy lips. When she opened her eyes, he had gone.

Chapter Nineteen

Lady Henrietta's eyes were suspiciously bright. If Clementine had not had her own deeply compelling concerns, she would have noticed it at once. As it was, she was wrapped up in her own thoughts, which hovered between beatific happiness at the highwayman's return and constant dread of imminent calamity.

The viscount would be perfectly within his rights to remove Henrietta from her chaperonage when rumours of the night's doings reached his ears. Worse, he would probably dismiss her without a character when he heard his own name coupled so freely with hers.

Tears welled up in Clementine's eyes. She pushed them away fiercely. At least she was secure in her highwayman's love. Quicksilver John! She must ask him what his true name was. It was inconceivable that she should be so intimate with a man and not even ascertain his rightful name. The world was probably correct. She was shameless.

Henrietta did not swallow a morsel of her food. She pushed the oats and warm milk round and round her plate until the porridge was quite thin and cold. Clementine did not notice,

and she was thankful. The last thing her ladyship needed on
her wedding day was dietary admonishments!

Her wedding day . . . A blissful sigh escaped Henrietta. She
would wear her pale muslin ribboned in satin and edged in the
most exquisite Bordeaux lace. Her maid had laid it out last
night, after her return from the ball. As Grantham had pointed
out, there was now no longer any need for matrimonial delay.
The relationship between the viscount and Miss Deveraux
seemed to be progressing very nicely indeed without their help,
thank you very much!

They were among the number who had accidentally witnessed that most interesting spectacle of the night before. Seeing
his good friend Randolph thus engaged had stirred the latent
lust within Grantham's own righteous person.

He, however, was more circumspect than his good friend. He
determined at once that the Lady Henrietta Stenning instantly
become the Honourable Mrs. Grantham Davies. How fortunate
that he'd had the immense good sense to return to the Archbishop of Batten-on-Sea!

Even now, the special license hugged his pocket snugly.
Once the good clergyman had sighted the Earl of Inglewood's
own seal of consent, there had been no further objection.
Besides, a brilliant panel of stained glass would complement
the church's new roof admirably. The transaction had been
completed without delay.

The only annoying impediment to Grantham's ardent wishes
had been Henrietta herself. She had refused to budge until her
dear Miss Deveraux was safely delivered into the hands of the
highwayman. Since Lady Henrietta was well aware that the
highwayman and the viscount were one and the same, she
harboured no qualms over disreputable connections. All she
desired was Miss Deveraux's happiness. Judging by the intriguing spectacle they had displayed to the world, she had
achieved just that.

Achieved? Oh, yes! Lady Henrietta remained happily convinced that it was Madame Fanchette's dress of emerald that

had done the trick. She could only be glad that she had remained firm on that point.

It struck her that for a lady in the passionate throes of romance, Miss Deveraux was looking remarkably pale and abstracted. Still, she thought, as she selected a small pastry from the basket and nibbled cautiously, love worked in strange ways. Different—though no less thrilling—for all.

How annoying of Grantham to be so secretive about the match! Heaven knew, she was only too glad to be wed that day, but it would have been pleasant to have Clementine's special brand of humour and common sense to support her. Henrietta glanced surreptitiously at Clementine, who stared listlessly at the ormolu clock on the mantelpiece while imagining a summons to the viscount's library and instant dismissal. Henrietta mused on telling her friend of her wedding.

Why had Grantham mysteriously forbidden her to mention it? Randolph was his best friend. Why should he not be there to support the couple? Why, why, why? When questioned, Mr. Davies had been as slippery as an eel. He'd ducked and dodged, deflecting all her questions with vague smiles and dexterous flummery. Too dexterous by far! She had not minded in the least. She smiled at the memory.

Still, the question niggled. She suspected strongly it had something to do with the wager between him and her cousin. It was that thought that made her hold her peace. Wagers between men were the strangest things. Even she knew not to interfere!

She rose from the table and excused herself. Clementine nodded absently and gave her a thin smile. Of an impulse, Henrietta walked round and dropped a cool kiss on her forehead. Miss Deveraux's face lighted up instantly.

"You are a wonderful girl, Henrietta! If I've made a dismal mull of all else in my life, you, at least, are my shining success!"

"You grow morbid, Clementine! Dismal mull, indeed! What is this? Morning indigestion? I can put these dismals down to nothing else."

"Perhaps you are right. I apologise for these doldrums and promise to do penance."

"Penance?"

"Yes! I am going to watch you try your petit point on that sofa cover. After that, you shall sing me an aria from the *Messiah. . .*"

A cushion was flung at her head. When Henrietta left the room, she was smiling.

It was perhaps no more than an hour later that Miss Deveraux was apprised of visitors below stairs. This in itself was not a surprising event, since the combined charms of the Lady Henrietta and her companion, Mistress Clementine, had not escaped the notice of certain eligible young gentlemen. Morning callers were to be expected, after all.

What was astonishing was that none of the cards presented by Masters belonged to men. They were all ladies—and ladies of extremely good *ton*. Clementine put her hands to her head. She knew what this was about! Especially as Mrs. Forbes-Davis and Lady Thornton Prentice-Bird featured prominently at the top of the list. She could not face them! No, indeed, she could not! What was more, she knew there was to be no more shilly-shallying. She must seek out the viscount and inform him of the calamity that had befallen her.

She schooled herself for the anger and mockery that must no doubt enter his eyes when he heard he was supposedly affianced. She just hoped there would be no contempt. If there was, she could not, in all honesty, blame him.

"Tell them I am not at home to visitors, Masters!" Her look was so pleading that the butler, who prided himself on his wooden features, was moved to pity. Truth to tell, he knew exactly what the tattling old gabsters had come for. Not much escaped the notice of the servants, and their quarters, were abuzz with the news. He only hoped there was some truth in the rumour. Miss Deveraux would make an uncommonly good wife for the viscount.

He could not have hoped for better and neither, he knew, could Pinkerton. Unfortunately, neither man had been apprised of the likely eventuality of wedded bliss in the household. My lord the viscount was closeted in the library with his accounts and was maintaining the most irritating poker-faced composure. His minions could get nothing out of him.

Masters bowed. "I will tell them at once, Miss Deveraux! I have already taken the liberty of intimating you are out."

Miss Deveraux shot him a shrewd glance.

"Not much escapes you, Masters!"

He bowed. "I hope not, ma'am. And now, if I might be so bold as to make a suggestion . . . my lord is in his library. If you use the west stairs I fancy you will not be seen."

Miss Deveraux's heart took a leap, then faltered. She swallowed hard.

"Thank you, Masters! You are an angel I swear." To Masters's professional chagrin, he actually smiled.

"Thank you, ma'am." He bowed and Clementine was left with the portraits of the late viscounts and viscountesses. They seemed to be telling her something, but she knew not what.

"Enter!"

Was it her imagination? The voice was stern and forbidding.

Clementine opened the door and curtsied. The viscount smiled at her and rose from his desk.

"Miss Deveraux!"

"Your lordship!"

"Sit down, please. I assume this is about the general commotion our names seem to have caused about town?"

His voice, contrary to expectation, had softened. He looked exceedingly handsome in his dark superfine. His cravat, as always, was perfectly tied. This morning, however, it was adorned with a single emerald of remarkable beauty. Clementine took all this in without moving from the door. She seemed petrified.

The viscount smiled.

"You might be more comfortable inside than out, Miss Deveraux!"

"Yes, you are right. Of course." She took a step in and shut the door. He indicated the chintz chair situated in front of his desk. She sank into it gracefully enough, but her rigid back did not go unnoticed by the viscount.

"Lemonade?" She politely declined. Where to start? There was an uncomfortable silence.

"My lord . . ."

"Yes?"

"I believe there is the most abhorrent rumour currently circulating. I can only apologise and hope that it has not yet reached your ears. Perhaps if you allow me to explain—"

"There is nothing to explain, Miss Deveraux."

"But there *is*." She waved her hands agitatedly. "Indeed it is hard to do so, and my tale will seem wild in the extreme, but—"

"Your tale will seem wild?" The viscount folded his arms.

"It will, but I will endeavour—"

"Hush, Miss Deveraux! If your tale is wild and improbable, why bother with it? Come here!"

"You do not understand, sir!"

"Indeed, I do. Someone has made free with my name. I woke up this morning to be apprised of the fact that I have overnight become your intended."

Clementine blushed to the roots of her hair. She knew the interview would be hard, but this!

"I am sorry, my lord. I can explain. Or rather. . ."—she looked around desperately—"I can try."

"As I said, Miss Deveraux, why put yourself to the trouble? I am told we are affianced. I can have no possible objection to this delightfully sudden occurrence, and so it remains only for me to slip *this* upon your finger." He opened a drawer and removed from the secret catchment a small, ruby red case. The mechanism fastening it was made of bronze and clicked open without difficulty. Clementine found herself gazing at the most magnificent emerald she had ever seen.

"My lord!"

"I am Randolph to my intimates."

"I am not your intimate!"

"No, but you *shall* be, my sweet!"

"You do not understand!"

"It is you who does not understand!"

"You are peeved. You find yourself in an awkward predicament and do the honourable thing. You cannot dismiss me, for fear of being branded a cad and a jilt. Oh, I understand perfectly!" Tears stung at the backs of her eyes. They were brilliant and shimmering, and it was all the viscount could do not to take her in his arms and kiss them away. He had just decided to commence with this interesting strategy when she pushed him away fiercely and slapped his face.

"You seem to think you can make fun of me, my lord! Well, you cannot! And I won't marry you simply that you may save face. I am sorry for the trouble I have caused. Indeed, I know you have been most grievously wronged in this, but I can only ask your pardon. Pray do not think I sought to entrap you with some horrid little scheme. I didn't."

"I don't think it."

"Then why are you punishing me with this nonsense? You want to teach me a lesson. Well, you have taught me. I am sorry, my lord, but I am leaving. My bags will be packed by the end of the day."

He gripped her arm and his mouth came dangerously close to hers.

"The only way you are leaving, my dear, is on our honeymoon trip!"

Clementine rolled her eyes in exasperation. "I thought I made my stance clear? I did not seek, mean or in any way desire to ensnare you. Were you the last man on earth, I would not marry you. If you must know—and may it be a blow, by the way, to your overarching ego—I am very much in love with someone else!"

"I suppose you love him with passion?" The viscount could not help baiting her.

"Indeed, yes! Passion and desire." Clementine drew breath defiantly. Once she'd started, she found herself unable to stop the outpouring. "Be shocked, if you will! I love him with all those forbidden feelings we ladies are not supposed even to dream, let alone speak of! So you can take your fine emerald, my lord. I desire nothing more than a base-born felon of the road. Does that shock you?"

My lord, far from shocked, was pleased beyond belief.

"And the base-born fellow? If he wished you to be a titled lady of wealth rather than an accessory to the fact?"

"He would not and how dare you?"

"This is how I dare." The viscount took a step forward and grabbed Miss Deveraux's arm. He clinched it behind her back so she was powerless to resist. Then he ruthlessly kissed her.

Miss Deveraux shut her lips firmly against this outrage. Then a warm glow stole through her and her lips took on a soft, sensuous life of their own. She did not feel responsible for the way her bodice was straining against his chest or the way her arm, once released, stole quite naturally around his back. His eyes had softened from the desire to dominate to the desire to overwhelm with gentleness. She saw the change, and though her mouth felt bruised and deliriously wanton, she knew she had to call a halt. She disentangled herself, and there was a strange, awed sense of wonder in her voice.

"You care about me!"

"Yes."

"You are not trying to taunt or punish me."

"No. Nor even"—his voice was wry—"trying to save face. I think my credit could stand a little gossip."

Clementine nodded. "You are right. I am sorry I lost my temper."

He grinned. "You can make it up to me, sweetheart."

The term of endearment was painful to Clementine. With sudden, awful clarity she knew she had done the unthinkable, the unforgivable. She was in love with two men.

Her hands rose to her face to cover her horror at the realisation.

"No!"

"No? You do not, I hope, deny there is an attraction?"

She put her hands down and thrust my head up high.

"To my shame, my lord, I fear I cannot. However, one before you has made prior claims to my love and devotion. He shall have them, for I fear he needs them more than you do."

The viscount looked at her strangely. His eyes flickered with a strange light. The world he had grown used to did not often nurture within its bosom a heart as unselfish as this.

"You might be mistress of all this . . . ." He waved his hands and indeed, the magnificence of the room was not lost to Clementine.

"My holdings in Trent are substantial. My wealth is famed. You will accede to all the honours as viscountess." He hesitated. "I fancy I am not displeasing of person. . . ."

Clementine chuckled in spite of herself. "Coxcomb! You know you are not!"

"Well then?"

She shook her head resolutely. "You cannot tempt me, my lord. My heart may be strangely fickle, but my mind remains resolute."

The viscount folded his arms. "In short, while all the tabbies are sitting in my various drawing rooms in hourly expectation of a felicitous announcement, you will have none of it?"

She nodded. "None of it."

He shrugged his shoulders. "Well then, I have done my best. The highwayman it shall have to be."

Clementine gasped. "You know of him?" He looked at her keenly. "Know of him? My dear, *dear* Miss Deveraux, I am most intimately acquainted with him!"

"I did not know. . . . I presumed . . . But then, he is so like you, is he not? Almost you could be twins."

"Almost, Miss Deveraux, but not quite."

She blushed. "No."

"I have a package for you."

"For me?"

"Yes. It is something that has not left my person since it was given to me."

"How extraordinary! What is it?" Curiosity could not be quelled.

The viscount smiled and placed his hand in a drawer. He withdrew a leather pouch and pulled from it something small and heavy and wrapped in tissue.

"Open it."

Clementine took the object from him. She found she was trembling like a leaf. She opened the wrapping clumsily. Inside, on a wisp of velvet, lay the emerald queen.

She looked at him wonderingly. "Can it be?"

"Come here, dearest! Quicksilver John has not yet been kissed this morning. I fear I grow impatient!"

"My lord!"

"Randolph, I think I said, to my intimates!"

She blushed. "Randolph! Can you really be my highwayman? I thought he must be a base-born brother."

"Base born? With such a regal bearing as mine? Come, come!"

"But the accent . . ."

"You could hardly have a felon speaking the King's English, now could you? I confess I nearly lost it at times."

"I did become suspicious. . . . At the ball you spoke impeccably, but then I thought you must have been educated at the manse."

"Well, I was!"

"Why have you been so cold to me? I could swear we were strangers to one another. I suspected, at first, but your manner has been so distant, so aloof. . . ."

"If it were not that it would have been the other. And *that,* my dear, would have been a scandal! Under my own roof I was compelled, do not you think, to act with propriety?"

She nodded in sudden understanding.

"I thought to see Henrietta safely settled. I was selfish. I did not wish to see her consigned to some paid chaperone's care.

I wanted her to have your care. For that, she needed to be under my roof. So, then, did you. And most unsettling it has been!''

"I would never have said so, my lord. You treated me coldly indeed.''

"Ice is akin to fire at times.'' His voice was seductive, like honey. Clementine moved towards him. It was quite some time before the urgent knocking awakened them to their senses.

"Come in, damn it, whoever you may be!''

Masters intruded apologetically. He bowed.

"My lord, not for the world would I interrupt. Indeed, unless I deemed it a matter of extreme urgency . . .''

"Yes, yes, Masters! I know your judgement to be unerring! What is it?''

"It is this, my lord.'' Masters handed a wafer over to Randolph.

"The third footman was given it this morning and forgot— *forgot,* mark you!—to deliver it into my keeping. It is a note from Mr. Grantham Davies, my lord. I perceive it to be about Lady Henrietta, since her chamber is empty, her abigail has taken sudden absence without leave and . . .'' His voice trailed off. The viscount had ripped the seal and scanned the single page at a glance. His lips quivered slightly. He looked up.

"Thank you, Masters. You have done well. Have the goodness to have my team of greys harnessed. I need a conveyance that will seat four at the least. My barouche, or perhaps the landaulet. Speak to the groom. He will best know. Also, arrange, if you will, the company of an abigail or chambermaid at the very least.''

Masters bowed. A trickle of perspiration sat wetly by upon his forehead. He had the strangest premonition that tragedy had been averted. He turned and stalked off. The third footman was not going to have a pleasant morning.

Chapter Twenty

"What does it say?" Clementine looked anxious. "I knew Henrietta had formed an attachment, but—"

"*Did* you?" The viscount looked amused. "By George, the young sprig did manage to put one over me. I am humbled."

Since he looked neither humbled nor perturbed, Clementine allowed herself to stop worrying.

"Here was I thinking he was courting her merely as a courtesy to myself. . ." The tone was mournful, but Miss Deveraux was not deceived. "Humbug! You knew what was in the wind, I'll wager!"

"Oh! The wagering type, are you?" The viscount glanced at her keenly.

"When it is a safe bet, my lord!"

He nodded. "Then read this."

Clementine took up the missive with undisguised interest.

My dear Randolph—regarding our wager.
    You will recall I mentioned I had yet a playing card up my sleeve? The Gainsborough fiasco I concede. How about this as a trump card?

*Lady Henrietta has this day agreed to become my wife.
I feel, in the interests of clarity, you should know that
my intentions are most honourable in this regard. I love
her to distraction and think, had I but known it, I always
have. However, to the business of the moment.*

*The Earl of Inglewood stands to lose forty thousand
pounds the day I am wed. This represents the compound
interest off her annuity, given the combined facts of her
age and likely time of otherwise wedding.*

*As executor to the trust, the earl loses substantially
the day the capital becomes my own. I need hardly assure
you the money is a trifling affair. I have sufficient income
of my own to make the matter a mere bagatelle, but I
believe, to Oscar, the sum is not inconsiderable. I pro-
pose, at all events, to make it over to the Inglewood
estates. A satisfactory conclusion to the whole affair, I
believe.*

And so, dear Randolph, the pinot noir is mine.

> *With much affection,*
> *Yours etcetera,*
> *Grantham*

*Post Scriptum—Should you wish to support me in the
happy event, I may be found at St. James's Cathedral,
Canterbury Square. Noon sharp.*

"Well!" Clementine was indignant. "I suppose the highway
robbery affair was also part of this strange and incomprehensible wager?" The viscount nodded.

"You have the gist of it, my dear! The money was to be
distributed among the tenants. Today is the deadline. Grantham
appears to think he has the advantage of me!"

"He has. I do not think the total you managed to rob was
worth forty thousand pounds!"

The viscount smiled mysteriously. "Maybe not, my dear.
Maybe not. I think, however, he has shown his hand too soon.
A trump card ought, after all, only be produced at the last."

"I should say this was the last!"

"Would you, my dear?" His eyes turned speculative. "You underestimate me."

Confused, Clementine tried a new tack. "You are not displeased with the match, then?"

"Not in the least! I think there could be no better matched pair of young pranksters in the whole of England!" He hesitated, then smiled. "Excepting, of course, ourselves! Their fortunes are well matched, too. No one could accuse Grantham of fortune hunting, and I am spared the painful business of screening all Henrietta's beau!"

"A rather selfish way of looking at it."

The viscount grinned. "Too right, my dear. My time, from now onwards, is going to be otherwise occupied." Clementine coloured, but, sorry to say, she was not overly displeased.

"You blush delightfully!"

"You flirt outrageously!"

The banter was still continuing when the carriage was announced. My lord took Clementine's arm. "Shall we?" She nodded. St. James's was at least a half hour away. The grand chestnut hall clock chimed the hour. Eleven o'clock and all was still well.

Lady Henrietta was a fetching sight in her white muslin, her hair adorned with simple cowslips. She also looked young, vulnerable and suddenly lonely. Clementine felt a pang for her as she entered the church.

She looked radiant, her hair golden in the streaming sunlight, her lemon morning dress sprigged in a crisp white lace of exquisite design. Of a sudden, the viscount dropped her arm and took a step outside. His sharp eyes had spotted sunflowers. He picked several and tucked one jauntily in Clementine's long, loose hair.

She, more sensible even at a time like this, ruffled through her hair for a pin. The flower's fate was now secure. The viscount smiled, and the couple at the altar exchanged glances.

It seemed that theirs was not the only romance flourishing that bright spring morning.

Grantham grinned. "Glad you could make it, Randolph! I was becoming concerned."

"Let that be a lesson to you, whippersnapper! Never leave an important message with a third footman!" He extended his hand.

"My felicitations, and may I see the special licence, please?"

"It is all right as a rig I assure you! Signed by the Archbishop of Batten-on-Sea himself. I had the earl's consent, you know."

The viscount nodded. "Glad you observed *some* of the proprieties, my friend! Now let me see the licence."

Grantham was puzzled, but he never questioned when Randolph used that particular tone.

"Here it is. See for yourself."

The viscount scanned the words. Then he nodded, as he casually slipped the authority into his pocket.

"I'll need that." Mr. Davies extended his hand. The viscount grinned impishly.

"No, you will not, my little stripling! The pinot noir is mine, you know. Revenue from the highway robbery proved most profitable."

"Never say you *did* it?" Grantham was incredulous.

"Of course I did. We had a wager, had we not? Miss Clementine will vouch for me."

Clementine stepped forward. She was suddenly as light-hearted as a spring day.

"Indeed I will! A most admirable highwayman he made. Shockingly daring, with a terrifying kerchief and a pistol as prime as they come. I was quite petrified, I assure you!"

"And I." Henrietta's laughing eyes met Clementine's. She was glad she had come.

"What? You, too? Treachery, I say!" Grantham looked stunned.

"Yes. We aided and abetted. That *is* the term, is it not?" The bride-to-be looked most cheerful.

Grantham was at a loss for words. He was just formulating a reply when the clergyman entered the church.

"Good morning ladies . . . and gentlemen!" He bowed and beamed seraphically. "Beautiful day for a wedding, is it not? I remember, when I was a wee lad. . . ." He was off. It was Randolph who gently recalled him to his duties.

"Ah, yes. Now which of you is the happy couple?"

Grantham stepped forwardly firmly with Henrietta. The viscount cleared his throat.

"I fear there has been some mistake, your reverence. We are the happy couple." He took Clementine's hand and stepped forward. There was a general gasp in the room. The clergyman had clearly not had to deal with complications of this kind before. Grantham stared daggers at his dearest friend. Said friend merely grinned unrepentantly and handed the bishop the special licence.

"All in order, as you see." The clergyman nodded.

"Well then, I see no other course than to proceed."

Clementine was still dazed when she stepped out of the church a viscountess. Henrietta had handed her the bouquet of spring flowers—sweet peas and snowdrops and daffodils. She kissed her governess. She could not have been more radiant had it truly been herself married that morning.

"You are not cross?" Clementine hesitated, somewhat diffident.

"Not in the least, Miss Deveraux—I beg pardon . . . my lady!"

Clementine blushed.

"There is time enough for Grantham and myself. Next week, perhaps, if he can ride fast enough to Batten-on-Sea."

Grantham groaned. "No doubt a new church wing will be needed! And to think the pinot noir was within my grasp . . ."

"It still is. Come and share it with us tonight. I would like you to have it before my wife and I . . ." The viscount stopped. His eyes feasted on Clementine and she flushed.

"Yes . . . well. I would like you to sample it. Come sooner

rather than later, I think.'' He grinned, then handed Clementine into the waiting chaise.

"Need a ride?''

Grantham looked at the very proper chambermaid seated inside. "No, I have my own team doing a turn about the place. I will hold you to that drink.''

"So you should! Come, Henrietta dear. You should not be out alone with single gentlemen. Step up into the chaise and we will see if we can preserve your respectability yet awhile.''

She smiled. "Indeed, my lord!'' She allowed herself to be helped up. She then afforded her intended a cheerful wave.

"Until tonight, my dear Mr. Davies!''

He bowed.

The last he saw of his intended bride as the carriage rolled off was an animated backward glance. She looked extremely fetching. Grantham sighed and signalled to his horses.

The cork was removed with admirable finesse. The viscount watched as the precious liquid was poured into four crystal glasses. He took up his own and sniffed appreciatively.

"Seventeen-eighty-four *was* a good year, Grantham!''

Mr. Davies nodded. He picked up his glass and twirled the stem like a connoisseur. Henrietta and Clementine exchanged amused glances.

"To our health!''

"May all wagers turn out to be as prosperous!''

The ladies lifted their glasses and delicately sipped. The Montagne de Reims pinot noir 1784 did not disapppoint. It was savoured to the last drop. When the bell pull was finally tugged, Masters emerged with an enormous wrapped gift.

"Open it Grantham . . . Henrietta. . .'' My lord bowed.

"You will excuse us, I know.'' He extended a hand and Clementine took it. Under the eyes of the benign, watchful and knowing staff, her ladyship the Viscountess of Trent was led up to her marital bed.

* * *

The viscount shut the door and smiled. He moved towards his new bride and sat at the end of the vast, luxurious tent bed. She opened her sparkling eyes wide and gave him something very like a saucy grin. His pulses quickened, but he stilled them.

"You are not sorry I stole a march on Henrietta?"

Her lashes fluttered entrancingly. "Sorry? It is exactly, my lord, what *I* should have done!"

He was encouraged to drop a kiss on the top of her nose. "Exactly?"

The delicious intimacy of the caress distracted her, but she would not be deterred.

"*If* I were as imperious, overbearing and sneaky . . ."

His hand moved to her laces, and she was most dangerously overset. When he kissed her again, first on her mouth and then with a trail of his lips down her neck that sent her reeling with abandon, she knew all was lost.

She gave up trying to scold and yielded to the delightful inevitable. What exactly transpired I am not at liberty to divulge. Suffice it to say that her ladyship was well pleased with her lord and master. My lord was similarly content in his choice of lady wife.

Below stairs, Grantham and Henrietta were enjoying an interesting little interlude of their own. Recalled, suddenly, to their not-so-virtuous senses, they decided to investigate the interesting, but faintly familiar-looking, package.

"Shall we?" Grantham fingered the wrapping.

Henrietta nodded. "I vow I am all curiosity! Open it at once!"

The paper was unceremoniously ripped and left scattered on the floor. Before them was the Gainsborough. The pair gasped in astonished amusement and pleasure. Then a sudden thought struck Grantham. It struck his lady love at one and the same moment.

"Print or original?" They studied it closely. There was simply no telling.

Above their heads, the ubiquitous portrait of Randolph, the Viscount of Trent looked down. To the fanciful, it might have seemed that he was grinning wickedly.

TALES OF LOVE FROM MEAGAN MCKINNEY

GENTLE FROM THE NIGHT*   (0-8217-5803-$5.99/$7.50)
In late nineteenth century England, destitute after her father's death, Alexandra Benjamin takes John Damien Newell up on his offer and becomes governess of his castle. She soon discovers she has entered a haunted house. Alexandra struggles to dispel the dark secrets of the castle and of the heart of her master.
*Also available in hardcover (1-577566-136-5, $21.95/$27.95)

A MAN TO SLAY DRAGONS   (0-8217-5345-2, $5.99/$6.99)
Manhattan attorney Claire Green goes to New Orleans bent on avenging her twin sister's death and to clear her name. FBI agent Liam Jameson enters Claire's world by duty, but is soon bound by desire. In the midst of the Mardi Gras festivities, they unravel dark and deadly secrets surrounding the horrifying truth.

MY WICKED ENCHANTRESS   (0-8217-5661-3, $5.99/$7.50)
Kayleigh Mhor lived happily with her sister at their Scottish estate, Mhor Castle, until her sister was murdered and Kayleigh had to run for her life. It is 1746, a year later, and she is re-established in New Orleans as Kestrel. When her path crosses the mysterious St. Bride Ferringer, she finds her salvation. Or is he really the enemy haunting her?

AND IN HARDCOVER . . .
THE FORTUNE HUNTER   (1-57566-262-0, $23.00/$29.00)
In 1881 New York spiritual séances were commonplace. The mysterious Countess Lovaenya was the favored spiritualist in Manhattan. When she agrees to enter the world of Edward Stuyvesant-French, she is lead into an obscure realm, where wicked spirits interfere with his life. Reminiscent of the painful past when she was an orphan named Lavinia Murphy, she sees a life filled with animosity that longs for acceptance and love. The bond that they share finally leads them to a life filled with happiness.

Available wherever paperbacks are sold, or order direct from the Publisher. Send cover price plus 50¢ per copy for mailing and handling to Kensington Publishing Corp., Consumer Orders, or call (toll free) 888-345-BOOK, to place your order using Mastercard or Visa. Residents of New York and Tennessee must include sales tax. DO NOT SEND CASH.

ROMANCE FROM HANNAH HOWELL

MY VALIANT KNIGHT   (0-8217-5595-1, $5.50/$7.00)
In 13th-century Scotland, a knight had to prove his loyalty to the King. Sir Gabel de Amalville sets out to crush the rebellious Mac-Nairn clan. To do so, he plans to seize Ainslee of Kengarvey, the daughter of Duggan MacNairn. It is not long before he realizes that she is more warrior than maid . . . and that he is passionately drawn to her sensual beauty.

ONLY FOR YOU   (0-8217-5943-4, $5.99/$7.50)
The Scottish beauty, Saxan Honey Todd, gallops across the English countryside after Botolf, Earl of Regenford, whom she believes killed her twin brother. But when an enemy stalks him, they both flee and Botolf takes her to his castle feigning as his bride. They fight side by side to face the danger surrounding them and to establish a true love.

UNCONQUERED   (0-8217-5417-3, $5.99/$7.50)
Eada of Pevensey gains possession of a mysterious box that leaves her with the gift of second sight. Now she can "see" the Norman invader coming to annex her lands. The reluctant soldier for William the Conqueror, Drogo de Toulon, is to seize the Pevensey lands, but is met with resistance by a woman who sets him afire. As war rages across England they find a bond that joins them body and soul.

WILD ROSES   (0-8217-5677-X, $5.99/$7.50)
Ella Carson is sought by her vile uncle to return to Philadelphia so that he may swindle her inheritance. Harrigan Mahoney is the hired help determined to drag her from Wyoming. To dissuade him from leading them to her grudging relatives, Ella's last resort is to seduce him. When her scheme affects her own emotions, wild passion erupts between the two.

A TASTE OF FIRE   (0-8217-5804-7, $5.99/$7.50)
A deathbed vow sends Antonie Ramirez to Texas searching for cattle rancher Royal Bancroft, to repay him for saving her family's life. Immediately, Royal saw that she had a wild, free spirit. He would have to let her ride with him and fight at his side for his land . . . as well as accept her as his flaming beloved.

Available wherever paperbacks are sold, or order direct from the Publisher. Send cover price plus 50¢ per copy for mailing and handling to Kensington Publishing Corp., Consumer Orders, or call (toll free) 888-345-BOOK, to place your order using Mastercard or Visa. Residents of New York and Tennessee must include sales tax. DO NOT SEND CASH.

ROMANCE FROM FERN MICHAELS

DEAR EMILY   (0-8217-4952-8, $5.99)

WISH LIST   (0-8217-5228-6, $6.99)

AND IN HARDCOVER:

VEGAS RICH   (1-57566-057-1, $25.00)